Dance of the Restless Soul

By Ren'e Fedyna

Cover design by Swift House Press

What they're saying about Dance of the Restless Soul ~

"I enjoyed how the main character developed from a spoiled child to a self-sufficient woman when necessary. Additionally, learning about the lifestyle of a dancer was a pleasure. Lastly, I found the different locations and styles of speech very entertaining!" – *Jennifer Cory*

"This book will entertain and also teach you a thing or two about the period in which it is set." – *Regina Potenza*

"This book was fun to like. It had some curious twists and turns to keep you guessing. It was fun exploring another place and time" - *Mary McNallen*

"I thoroughly enjoyed this fast-moving novel with the backdrop of one of the most romantic historical periods, the Belle Epoque. Lola may have been a restless soul but it cannot be said that she lacked focus or direction in her desire to be a great cabaret entertainer. A good read!" – *Sandy E.*

This book is dedicated to my husband George, who despite my whining and bouts of frustration, motivated me to fulfill my long-awaited dream to write. Thank you for your patience and support.

Prologue

The cabbie said, "This is the place, *Mademoiselle*. Are you getting out or is there someplace else you wish me to take you?"

Lola thought, *I wish there was somewhere else to go but my choices are few. I can either return to the convent or at sixteen be forced to marry a man I do not love.*

"*Mademoiselle?* If you please."

Lola looked out of the cab window into the bleak night. Before her were shabby buildings and poorly lit streets. She wrung her hands.

"*Mademoiselle*, I must leave. Please exit the coach immediately!"

She fumbled through her purse for money to pay the driver. When her nervous fingers found the coins, she paid him and opened the cab door. Seeing men engaged in a fistfight nearby made her shudder. Lola cautiously stepped from the cab and with regret, she watched as it disappeared into the mist.

Curses shouted from open windows pierced the darkness. The shatter of a broken window startled her. She ran to escape the shards of falling glass but gave wide berth to a man who lay on the ground before her, whether asleep or dead she could not tell. Now, Lola understood what Monsieur Salis meant about the danger.

She bolted towards the *L'antre Du Diable Cabaret*. At the entrance door, she encountered a surly man cleaning his fingernails with a knife. His hungry eyes looked her over as if she would be his next meal.

He whispered in her ear, "I've been waiting for you all of my life."

His creepy voice gave her shivers. Lola pushed him away and rushed inside hoping he would not follow. She slammed the door against his evil laugh. Leaning her back against the closed door, she surveyed the cabaret.

This room, it stinks of beer, sweat and cheap perfume. And these men, they look as coarse as the wooden tables at which they sit. The women wear too much make-up and look as hard as the men. Are they all pimps, whores, thieves and local toughs? Mon Dieu! What have I done?

Chapter 1

The horse-drawn carriage transporting Lola La Fontaine and her chaperone Teresa Cortes stopped outside the sprawling three-story Paris townhouse of Madame Morveaux. They arrived as scheduled for one of Madame's frequent afternoon parties.

Lola scowled. "Teresa, why must we attend Madame's party? I am bored already and we have not even entered."

"You ask this question every day." Teresa sighed. "You know it is required that everyone of your station attend these afternoon parties. Try to enjoy yourself, but for goodness sake, no more pranks!"

"But I love to watch the expression on Madame Morveaux's face when I embarrass her."

Teresa shook her head. "You will soon be sixteen years of age and no longer a child. It is time you acted responsibly. Your father is a government minister. You do not want to cause him embarrassment, do you?"

Her dimpled smile highlighted the mischief in Lola's sapphire eyes. *"Papá* does not have to know, does he?"

"Enough stalling! We must go inside. Just try to behave yourself!"

Together they stepped into the rotunda entrance hall that opened to reception rooms. Lola enjoyed the wary look on Madame Morveaux's face when she greeted her. She knew the Madame expected her to cause trouble and Lola planned not to disappoint her.

When Teresa left the salon to relieve herself, Lola sneaked into the kitchen and seated herself at the massive wooden table to smoke and joke with the servants.

Teresa marched into the kitchen with a frazzled expression. "What are you doing in here?"

Lola wasn't surprised to see her. She exhaled a puff of cigarette smoke and smiled. "Spending time with my friends."

"What did you say to Madame Morveaux? I saw her rush red-faced from this direction."

"Oh, Teresa, you are needlessly upset. We were just having fun with that nosey old woman. She followed me in here and watched me light a cigarette. When she said I should be ashamed of myself, hiding in here blowing smoke with the servants, I said, Madame, I am only blowing cigarette smoke. I hear you blow other things with your servants!" Lola glanced at the servants and giggled. "Then the old boar ran from the kitchen."

Teresa suppressed a smile and put out Lola's cigarette. "You cannot continue this behavior. It is not proper!"

Lola winked at the servants and allowed Teresa to lead her from the kitchen.

In the main salon, Teresa hastened to Madame Morveaux to apologize for Lola's behavior. Lola circled the room to display her low-cut *décolleté*, delighting in the attention of the young men who admired her bosom. Lola welcomed the venomous stares of jealous eyes in the arrogant faces of haughty women who whispered to each other behind their fans.

Teresa rushed to Lola. "You have had enough amusement. It is time to leave. You must practice and you do not want to keep your opera coach waiting."

"Why should I leave when I am having so much fun?"

"You promised to sing at your father's dinner party. You know he loves your beautiful voice. His chest swells with pride when you sing to his important friends."

Lola shrugged. "You are right. I am only too happy to escape from these pompous ninnies."

Bored with the familiar scenery on their return route along the Boulevard de Grenelle, Lola gazed out of the carriage window and yawned.

When she noticed a crowd she wondered, *What is going on there? Is he a...* She shouted, "*Stop! Stop!* I want to get out!"

Teresa began to object until she saw the crowd of onlookers surrounding a street entertainer.

Followed by Teresa, Lola jumped from the carriage and pushed her way to the front of the crowd.

"Look, Teresa! How wonderful he is."

"*Oui, ma chérie*, he is wonderful."

Lola watched with eager attention as he sang and danced. She tried to memorize the movements of his feet and how he gestured to his audience. She scrutinized the expressions on the faces in the crowd, striving to understand what caused them to give their best reactions. Lola loved to watch street performers and judged their abilities by the delight on the faces of their audience.

"Hurry, Teresa, I must get back and practice."

They returned to their two-story Neoclassical style townhouse in the fashionable Faubourg Saint-Germain district, where the oldest and most prestigious families resided.

Lola ran to her bedroom. Although her designated second-floor bedroom was larger, she loved this ground floor room with its French doors that opened onto a splendid garden replete with flowers, statues, fountains and symmetrically designed plant beds connected by paths.

Before Teresa could help her, Lola removed her hat and placed it on a side table next to pretty miniatures and small books in leather bindings. She tossed her cloak onto her Louis XV style bed and stood before the tall, finely carved, giltwood mirror. Lola fluffed the white embroidered ruffles at the square-cut neck of her dress, closed her eyes and imagined she was about to perform before a great audience.

Teresa hung the cloak in the closet among dozens of hand-sewn dresses and then seated herself on the raspberry damask chair near the French doors that looked out onto the garden.

Lola mimicked the street performer repeatedly until she thought her performance resembled his routine, then added gestures she recounted from other entertainers she had seen. She turned to Teresa. "What do you think? Am I ready for the stage?"

Teresa's dark eyes sparkled with mirth. She applauded and said, "Oh yes, *ma petite*, you are a fabulous entertainer. But now you must practice with your opera coach."

Lola dismissed this comment with a wave of her hand. "It is not opera lessons I want. I want to perform on the great stages of Europe and America, like the singer Lillian Russell and the dancer Lola Montez."

Teresa frowned. "*Ma chérie*, you know I want that for you too, but it is impossible."

"Why is it impossible? You say I have the talent."

"*Ma petite*, your father would never allow you to become an entertainer. You are the daughter of the Finance Minister of France. You must maintain the dignity of your position."

"Is it my position to be bored to death? To go to mindless parties?"

"I thought you enjoyed parties and balls. You always seem so delighted."

"I love to dress and go to parties and balls and to hear the whispered gossip of scandals and love affairs. But these people are so shallow. We are all expected to act in the same boring way. And the social calls we must make every day are the worst. We see the same people and talk about the same things." In a snotty tone, Lola mimicked them. "*I gave my best ball gowns to the pauper's charity. Oh, but I sent tons of food scraps to the poor orphans. Did you see madame's new hat? It is so ugly!*

These pompous women do nothing but devote their time to frivolous chatter. No one tries to do or say anything unique because they fear they will be scandalized. Why should I care what they think of me? That is if they can think at all!"

The faint lines in Teresa's face etched deeper as she tried to restrain her exasperation. Lola had seen that look often and knew she was about to get a lecture.

"Lola, you must care what people think of you. Your father would be humiliated should his daughter not be accepted in society. You love him and would not want to hurt him."

"Why should these people care what I do? It is none of their business! What is wrong with performing before an audience? I perform for *Papá* and his colleagues—"

"Performing for your father is a private affair," Teresa said. "You are performing in a dignified setting amongst your peers. It is a different thing than performing in a music hall."

"What is the difference?"

"You belong to the top hierarchy of society, which means you have many privileges, but you are also required to conform to the required code of behavior. To do anything else would upset the balance of society. You would be an outcast, someone only to be scoffed at, whispered about and ridiculed."

Lola stomped her foot and shouted, "Why should I care about the arrogant imbeciles who think I must be just like them? Those women, they are *empty* inside, they have no *soul*. I have a *fire* inside me, a fire that drives me. I want to be an *entertainer*!"

"You know that is impossible! You are betrothed to the Marquis and, when the time is right, you will be his wife."

"Betrothed! Am I chattel to be sold to the highest bidder? This is 1880, not the Middle Ages! *I do not want to be his wife!* I am only fifteen—it will be years before I must marry."

"Lola, it is wonderful to have a dream but you must also understand reality. To do anything but obey your father's wishes would cause him great pain. He loves you as he loves life itself, as you love him. You do not wish to hurt him, so forget this foolishness and save yourself heartache. Now, your opera coach is waiting. You must get ready for him."

Lola cursed under her breath. She stormed from her bedroom to meet her opera coach. She never liked Professor Umberto Bellini. He had no sense of humor and he sniffed as if he were smelling something bad. She had little interest in opera, but her singing gave her father great pleasure and so she pursued it. But Lola was bored with her lessons. To alleviate her boredom, she would invent ways of frustrating her professor by repeatedly interjecting phrases of popular music into her warm-up exercises or by purposely singing off-key. However, her performance this evening was important to her father, so she was the perfect student.

Relieved when her lesson had ended, Lola couldn't wait to bathe and dress for the concert. She perused her closet and disregarded the handsome brocades, lush satins, velvets and soft woolens. Lola selected a new white accordion-pleated chiffon gown custom made by her favorite Rue de la Paix fashion house. She chose it because it emphasized her lustrous black hair, alabaster complexion and narrow waist.

When Lola stepped into the dome-ceilinged dining hall, her father, Émile, and his guests rose from their silk-embroidered dining chairs. Lola received their lavish compliments with a charismatic smile, but thought, *These men, they are such hypocrites. If I sang at the Folies Bergère they would spurn me and treat me like a pauper!*

Lola offered a genuine smile to Émile when, with an elegant flair, he took her hand and escorted her to the seat next to his.

Before them, a sumptuous table had been set with lovely gilt-edged silver plates, Venetian goblets and fine crystal. An attentive staff catered to them as they enjoyed the finest wines and dined on an elaborate array of vegetables, roasted meats, grilled fish, fabulous desserts and aperitifs to accompany the extravagant dinner.

After dinner, they withdrew to the music room where chairs were set around the piano. Lola stood by the finely crafted piano designed by the acclaimed artist Sir Lawrence Alma-Tadema, adorned with mother-of-pearl inlay and with an exquisitely hand-carved case, top lid and legs.

Seated at the piano, Professor Bellini awaited Lola's nod to begin.

Lola thought, *If it would not embarrass Papá, I would sing a bawdy song just to see the reaction on the faces of these oafs!*

Her father sat near her, smartly dressed as always, gallant and distinguished with his close-cropped beard and wavy, brown hair. She smiled at him and he returned her smile. His soft brown eyes were filled with pride and love and made her feel as if she could accomplish anything.

Lola began by singing Rosina's cavatina, "*Una voce poca fa*" ("A voice a little while ago"), from her favorite opera *Figaro*. She identified with Rosina, the young ward of the grumpy, elderly Bartolo, who allowed her little freedom and planned to marry her once she came of age and thus appropriate her dowry. The opera ends happily with a marriage between Rosina and the man she loves.

She had been complimented often for her voice. Her father's friends called it angelic and rich with a warm timbre. Lola loved how all eyes focused on her as she sang and watched for their pleased reaction when she tilted her head in a particular way or flexed her arms at a certain point in the aria. Lola knew that despite her father's objections, one day she would be a famous performer.

Chapter 2

Each night before bed, Lola sat at her tortoise shell vanity table and enjoyed the way Teresa brushed her long hair with loving care. Above the table hung an oval mirror made of matching finishes. On the table sat perfume bottles of varying shapes and sizes and a sterling silver hand mirror with raised decorations.

Lola regarded Teresa's image in the mirror. "You always look so serene when you brush my hair."

"That is because I remember brushing your mother's hair when we lived in Spain. You look exactly like her, and sometimes I forget you are Lola and not Doña Dolores."

Lola turned to Teresa. "Tell me about my mother."

"Come sit with me." Teresa took Lola's hand and brought her to the raspberry velvet banquette near the French window framed by the delicate curtains of Leavers gold lace.

A smile, both tender and sad, appeared on Teresa's aging face. Lola could sense Teresa missed her early life. "Just like you, your mother was beautiful. She had the same lustrous black hair and sapphire blue eyes. And, of course, the same dimples when she smiled. She was vivacious, with a quick wit and charming personality. When she walked into a room, everyone wanted to be near her. When I look at you, I see your mother's face."

Lola asked, "So, you have attended my mother as you have always attended me?"

"Yes, it had been my pleasure then, and it is my pleasure now."

"Was *Mamá* happy?"

"Oh yes! She had an easy, melodious laugh and a gentle nature. Even though the marriage between your parents had been arranged, they fell in love from the moment your father arrived in

14

Spain. Their wedding was performed at the Cathedral of Saint Mary of the Sea in Seville, one of the most beautiful cathedrals in the world. Your mother was exquisite in her wedding gown."

"How did they come to live in Paris rather than in Spain?"

"As a Frenchman, your father's life was here. He brought her to Paris where they enjoyed a wonderful life but were unable to have children for many years. When you came along, I was delighted that your mother arranged for me to care for you.

You were named Dolores after your mother, but since the day you were born, your father called you by the nickname, Lola. Even though he loved you, he said there could be only one Dolores to fill his heart.

Lola felt tears well in her eyes. "I miss my mother. Do you think it would it be possible to meet my Spanish family?"

"No, *ma chérie*. They blamed your father for taking your mother from her loved ones. They said she died of a broken heart. Of course, that was not true. When they insisted that you that live with them, your father refused, and so, they disowned him."

Teresa dried Lola's tears with a handkerchief and kissed her forehead. "Now it is time for you to go to sleep and dream wonderful dreams."

Lola awoke and rubbed her eyes to see Teresa engrossed in the newspaper. She sat on the banquette they had shared the previous evening.

"*Bonjour,* Teresa, have you been there all night?"

"*Bonjour, ma chérie.* I entered your room this morning, expecting you would be wide awake and ready for breakfast. Did you have a good sleep?"

Lola sat up. "I had a fabulous dream! I performed on stage in a beautiful gown that sparkled in the light. All eyes were upon me, enjoying my performance. In the end, everyone stood, applauded and shouted, Lola! Lola! Lola!"

Teresa clapped her hands. "Ah, such a wonderful dream. Now it is time for you to make a performance at the breakfast table. Monsieur Marchand will be here soon to give you your scholastic lessons."

Lola announced, "I have decided it is time for me to go to a cabaret."

Teresa laughed. "Very funny. It is time for your breakfast."

"I want to go to a cabaret!"

Teresa lowered the newspaper and removed her spectacles, "*Ma petite*, why on earth would you want to go to a cabaret?"

"I want to learn more than what I learn from street entertainers. It is time for me to learn from professional stage performers."

Teresa narrowed her eyes. "*¡Madre de Dios!* Surely, you are joking!"

When she exclaimed frustration in her native Spanish, Lola knew that she had upset Teresa. But Lola continued. "What makes you think I am joking?"

"You are much too young to enter a cabaret."

"Why do you say that?"

"There are some things a young girl should not see."

"Teresa, you yourself said I am almost an adult, so is it not time for me to learn about adult things?"

"A lady does not need to learn about such things!"

"Oh, but you are wrong! There is much for me to see and learn."

"Maybe so, but not at a cabaret!"

"Why not? What is so terrible about a cabaret? Is there really anything more scandalous than the stories I hear at these so-called proper parties at the home of Madame Morveaux, or the parties of those other ridiculous old biddies?"

Teresa drew in a breath. "There is no need to be disrespectful! Besides, you know your father would never allow it."

Lola batted her long black eyelashes and said, "But *Papá* does not have to know. It can be our little secret."

"Please, Lola, let us discuss this when you are older."

"I want to go to the Folies Bergère. I have heard so much about the delights of this famous and fascinating place. I want to see it with my own eyes, and I want to go *now!*"

Teresa's jaw tightened. "*Ay, ¡Caramba!* Folies Bergère. Oh no, no, no. That is not a place for you!"

Lola folded her arms across her chest. "Teresa, I insist you take me to the Folies Bergère!"

"Dearest Lola, I cannot take you there. If your *Papá* should find out, he would never forgive me and might even release me."

Lola left her bed and sat by Teresa. She put her arm around Teresa's shoulders and said, "*Ma chère mère*, besides *Papá*, I love you more than anyone in the world! For most of my life, you have been my mother, my nurse, my teacher, and my dearest friend. I would never let anyone…even *Papá*…cause you to be unhappy. You need not have fear of my father. He will not find out, but if by some stroke of bad luck he does, I will tell him I forced you to take me and all the blame will fall upon me." Lola wrapped her arms around Teresa's neck and hugged her close. She whispered in her ear, "Please, please, take me to the Folies Bergère, please!"

Teresa sighed. "I love you, and no matter how hard I try, I am powerless to resist you. *Oui, chèrie*, even though I should not, I will take you."

Lola hugged Teresa and gave her little girl kisses. "Thank you! Thank you so much!"

On a day when Émile was away for a conference, the conspirators snuck off to the Folies Bergère. When she entered and surveyed the theatre, Lola's eyes widened. The Folies Bergère had a plush interior under an ochre and gold ceiling of ruffled and tasseled fabric. Seated on rattan divans, they watched a trapeze duo, ballet dancers, a snake charmer, wrestlers (both male, and female), a kangaroo boxing with a man, and an array of other spectacles.

Everywhere Lola turned, her ears filled with a variety of wonderful music blaring over the cries of program hawkers, audience chatter and applause. The air was laden with perfume scents, cigar smoke and beer—and the entertainment was not just confined to the stage.

From the entrance hall, magnificent staircases led to a balcony with private boxes and stalls, behind which was the gallery-lounge known as the *promenoir*, and its elegant bar. Teresa forbade her to go upstairs, causing Lola to be all the more curious. So up she ran. Teresa called after her, to no avail.

Lola snickered when she saw the *mondaines*, the prostitutes, who wore too much makeup, too much perfume, and too little clothing, as they strolled the *promenoir* to attract clients. She thought, *Why would anyone want to make a living this way?*

Short of breath, Teresa arrived at the top of the stairs. Lola hooked her arm and propelled her to an empty private box. Lola's body swayed to the musical rhythms of the bawdy songs floating up from the stage. Her eager eyes were wide with delight as she watched the performers dancing around the stage. *Oh, how beautiful the ladies are! How wonderful it must be to perform in front of a crowd in a theatre like this! This is the type of performer I was born to be!*

Fascinated by this cabaret life, Lola insisted Teresa take her to other café-concerts like the Bal Mabille and Le Chat Noir. Despite Teresa's strong objections, they went to the working-class Le Mirliton, which soon became Lola's favorite. She savored the genuine working-class humor of Aristide Bruant. In his sensational one-man show Bruant stared rudely at the middle and upper-class patrons and called them filthy pigs and *salauds,* bastards. The more he insulted them, the better the audience liked him.

Lola felt quite pleased that her father had not become aware of her little deceits and continued attending the cabarets.

Chapter 3

Lola loved to accompany her father horseback riding in the Bois de Boulogne. Where, in a daily display of high fashion, elegant carriages and horseback riders paraded around the lakes for one or two hours, then returned to their Parisian residences via the prestigious Avenue de l'Impératrice.

She admired the curtains of foliage that draped from thousands of trees, the aroma of countless clusters of flowers, the picturesque lakes and waterfalls, and she delighted in watching children play in the recreation park custom-designed for them. On occasion, her father brought her to enjoy the races at the Hippodrome de Longchamp, the park's horse race track.

Lola also delighted in the attention of the young men who halted their horses to greet her. With a seductive smile and a twinkle in her eye, her flirting became more deliberate with each passing month.

On this day, when they stopped to let their horses graze, Lola asked, "Why the frown, *Papá*? Do you have something on your mind?"

Émile straightened his back and said proudly, "Yes, I do have something on my mind. I have been waiting for the right time to tell you of my surprise and now is the time. I have good news for you, *ma belle.* I have obtained permission for you to marry in the Church Madeleine, the most fashionable in Paris. Not only will *le tout Paris* attend, but President Grèvy, the most important man in France, has indicated his intentions to attend. You will have the most magnificent wedding, my pussycat."

Lola rolled her eyes and said, "Oh *Papá*, do not bother me with such things now. We have plenty of time to talk about marriage."

"That is not so. It saddens me to lose you, *ma chérie*, but it is time for you to become a wife."

"*Papá*, do not joke about such things! After all, I am only fifteen. I shall not be married for many years yet."

"Lola, you will soon be sixteen. I married your dear *Mamá* when she was your age. You are a beautiful young woman, and soon life's temptations will be too much to resist. You know that you are betrothed to Marquis Bernard Bournazel and have been so since your birth. Now you shall be his wife."

"How can you expect me to marry that ugly, pimple-faced boy? Do you realize he picks his nose all the time? Every time I see him, his finger is up his nose. You would think he has a treasure buried up there!"

Émile chuckled. "Ah, my dear, try not to be so hard on him. You will grow to love him when he becomes a man. He is only seventeen now, an awkward age for a boy. Marriage will mature him. When he marries you, he will realize he is the most fortunate of men. He will adore you and lay the world at your feet. After all, he will be quite rich and will inherit all of his father's properties and—"

"I do not care about such things. I do not care if he is the richest man in the world! I will not marry him. I will not marry anyone now. I do not wish to be married, and that is final!"

"Enough!" Émile shouted, "You have no choice in the matter. We will return home and I will not hear another word from you!" Émile slapped Lola's horse on the rump and they galloped towards the stables.

This had been the first time in Lola's life her father had raised his voice to her. It would not be the last.

Chapter 4

Émile barged into the house and stomped through the main salon. Lola chased him and pleaded, *"Papá, please wait!"* When he entered his study and slammed the door shut, Lola's body recoiled at the loud reverberation of wood striking hard against wood. Lola felt like he slammed the door to her heart.

Astonished by the commotion, the ubiquitous house staff disappeared.

Pained and confused, Lola wished her mother was there to comfort her. Through resplendent doors adorned with gold paneling, Lola entered the large salon, the room her mother decorated with such care. She stood in the center of the room and took notice of every detail. She had been told her mother loved this room. This room meant more to her today than ever before.

It was a beautiful room. Lola inhaled the scent of flowers and lush plants invigorated by the sun that poured through the tall windows. Tapestries and paintings by old masters hung above the fine furniture. The Renaissance mirror reflected an elaborate rock-crystal chandelier. Striped champagne-yellow silk-covered walls lead to a vaulted ceiling.

Lola walked across the 18th century Versailles parquet floors to the white Venetian silk-draped French windows and ran her hand over a panel. *Imagine if Mamá's hand held this drape where I am holding it now. It would be as if we were holding hands.*

An immense portrait of her mother hung above the exquisitely-sculpted marble chimneypiece. Lola gazed upon the portrait with saddened eyes. Seated atop a magnificent white stallion, her mother looked dashing in her refined black riding outfit. Her blue eyes were bright and confident, her bearing regal, her smile impish.

Lola thought, *Mamá, they say I am much like you in appearance and temperament. Papá tells me I look exactly as you did when you were my age. You were fortunate to marry Papá. To marry a man you had loved so much. Would you have been so quick to marry him if you hated him? It is not that I hate the Marquis, I barely know him. It is the idea of marriage I hate. Did you ever feel like me? Did you ever want to do something else with your life? How would you advise me if you were here by my side? Mamá, I do not know what to do, I only know I cannot live the life Papá wants me to.* Tears brimmed her eyes.

She didn't hear Teresa approach but felt the light touch of her arm guide her to the bedroom.

They sat together on the settee. Lola asked, "Why is *Papá* so angry with me?"

Teresa took Lola's hand. "Your father loves you but he sees that you will soon mature into a beautiful woman. Many men will desire you. Your father fears you will be enticed by young men who may not have your best interests at heart. Your father is a proud man and he has given his word that you will marry the Marquis. His honor is at stake so he must keep his word. In addition, he has invited the President of France to your wedding. He would not be able to tell the President the wedding will not take place. It would embarrass your father beyond endurance."

Lola jumped from the settee. "I hate this!" She paced the room and pounded her fist into her hand. "I hate this so much!"

Teresa patted the settee. "*Ma chère fille*, please sit and let us talk."

"What is the good of talking? It will change nothing. Whatever *Papá* wants me to do, I must do. I have no choice! He says he loves me. How can he love me when he wants me to marry so young? Just because he and *Mamá* married when she was sixteen, does that mean I should have to? And why did he have to invite the President?"

"You have no idea how privileged you are. Any other girl would be beside herself with happiness to marry in the Church

Madeleine. To have the President attend the wedding is a fabulous honor. You will be the envy of all Paris."

Lola covered her eyes. She pleaded, "Why does no one understand *me*? Why is it that no one understands that *I do not wish to marry?*"

"Your father only wants the best for you?"

"How can this be best for me? I will be expected to sit and be quiet. The demure well-behaved little lady at my husband's beck and call. I will be expected to spew out one little spoiled babe after another until I am a haggard old woman. However, *Monsieur Le Pimple Face* will do as he damn well pleases. He can hunt and fish and ride and enjoy Paris nightlife, drinking and gambling—and mistresses! He will have scores of mistresses, while I am not allowed to enjoy sex!"

Teresa's mouth dropped. "Hush!" She craned her neck to see if anyone was within earshot of the open door, then she shut it. "Lola, you cannot say such things. It is unbecoming! If your father should hear you speak like that—"

"You are such a prude. Madame Pouffard told me all about it. She said husbands and wives often sleep in separate bedrooms. Madame Pouffard told me her husband has never even seen her in her undergarments, and they have five children! Can you imagine? She said she would not be having any more children. To keep her husband away from her, she hired a pretty chambermaid to keep him busy. If he tires of her, she will get another, and another one after that. No!" Lola stamped her foot. "That is not a life for me, I will not marry that stupid lout and I will not be the obedient little fool!"

"Please," Teresa implored, "You must understand your place."

Lola stared at the ceiling. Shaking her fists at the heavens, she wailed, "My place! Do you know how much I *hate* those words? All anyone ever talks about is *my place!*"

"Please calm down. I know you are frustrated but you are not thinking. You have no choice but to obey your father. To do anything else is to cause him pain."

Lola screamed, "What about *my* pain? I am the one who must marry the ugly bastard!"

Red-faced, Teresa shouted. "Stop this! "Marry him and bear his children. Try to win him over and stay in his good graces. If he is a good man, he will allow you to enjoy your life within reason."

Lola forced back her tears. "Do you hear what you are saying? He will allow me. *Allow me!* What am I, an obedient dog? Why do men have so much power over women? Why is it I cannot make decisions about my life?"

Teresa took Lola into her arms. She kissed Lola's forehead and stroked her hair. "*Ma chérie,* I hope things will change for you in the future. Nevertheless, for now, you must accept your life as it is. You do not know how fortunate you are because you have no knowledge of the real world, where pain and suffering is an everyday occurrence. I hope you never find out. Go to sleep now, *ma petite*, and dream of your wedding day."

Chapter 5

Lola slept little that night. When she awoke, her thoughts were as rumpled as her bedclothes. She asked herself, *How can I find a way to prevent the wedding without dishonoring Papá?*

She needed fresh air to clear her head. She rose, put on her cloak, opened the French Doors, and stepped from her room into the garden. The stars faded into the light-gray sky. Chittering birds, sounding as if they were gossiping over breakfast, greeted her. Early morning dew moistened her skin. Her hair tickled her face as she inhaled a fragrant breeze. With closed eyes, Lola raised her arms and began to dance. Her cloak sailed behind her as she spun in a circle. Her bare feet tingled in the damp grass carpet. She twirled until she felt dizzy and collapsed onto a wooden bench.

Her *Papá* had played games with her in this garden when she was a child. Sometimes it was Hide and Seek, sometimes he would hide little gifts for her to find. Memories of those happy times turned yesterday's anger into today's sadness.

She devised many plans, but each plan resulted in her father's humiliation. A thought flickered in her mind. She had been looking at this all wrong. *Rather than Papá cancel the wedding, what if the father of the Marquis canceled the wedding? Papá would not be dishonored. It would not be his fault if the Marquis changed his mind. How can I make this happen?*

Lola smiled as the perfect idea came to light. But, for now, she must apologize to *Papá*, and convince him to postpone the wedding.

Lola needed to catch *Papá* before he left for work. She dressed and rushed to breakfast. Pleased to see he still sat at the table, she hoped he would give her his normal cheery greeting. But the newspaper he read covered his face. He made no indication that he noticed her.

"*Bonjour, Papá*. Did you sleep well?" He gave no response. Lola approached him and placed her hand on his. "*Papá*, I want to apologize for my behavior yesterday. You took me by surprise and I over-reacted. Please forgive me."

Émile put down the newspaper and looked at his daughter. His facial features were tense. He spent a moment looking into her eyes before his lips eased into a soft smile. "My dearest, I am glad you have come to your senses. Perhaps I should have handled it differently. I thought you would be delighted with the magnificence of it. Now I realize marriage is a big step for you, and you will need time to get used to the idea."

Lola's face brightened. She thought, *Yes, he's willing to wait until I am older.*

Émile continued, "The wedding will not occur for three months yet, so that should give you plenty of time to adjust."

Lola groaned inwardly. "*Papá*, are you sure you want it to be so soon? There is so much preparation to be done. I think three months is not nearly enough time."

"Do not worry, *ma petite*. I will see to it that you have plenty of help."

She racked her brain and tried again. "But *Papá*, I must tell you the real reason it is too soon for me to marry."

Émile's face tensed once more. "The real reason? What do you mean?"

"I am embarrassed to say."

"Embarrassed? What troubles you, my child?"

Lola put her head down. She even managed to blush as she whispered to her *Papá* in her little girl voice, "I feel I am not old enough to be someone's wife. I do not know how to be a wife. I am not much more than a young girl. I am frightened to marry."

Her father thought for a moment, put his arm around her shoulder and brought her close to him. He said, "My poor sweet Lola, I understand how this might be of concern to you. You have no mother to teach you the things you must know to be a good wife. Now I understand why you reacted as you did. But have no fear, the mother of the Marquis will tell you all you need to know."

Lola tensed with anger. She closed her eyes and tried to remember she would soon be free. "Oh, thank you, *Papá*, I knew you would have the solution to my concerns."

She fumed when her father said, "I am so happy we have resolved this. Now we can prepare for your wonderful day. I must be off now." His eyes smiled when he kissed her cheek and left the room.

She was determined to prevent the wedding. Lola knew that in order to keep her father from suspecting her plan, she must continue her customary routine. She decided it was best not to tell Teresa her plan. If Teresa knew, she would do her best to dissuade her or might tell *Papá*. If Teresa kept it a secret from *Papá*, he would be extremely angry with her.

As the weeks passed, Lola continued her life as before. She walked the magnificent and spacious boulevards with her friends: The Avenue de l'Opera, the Capucines, the Italiens and the elegant Boulevard de la Madeleine, where the most fashionable cafes were situated. She went to parties and behaved properly. She attended the opera and dined lavishly with her father at the fabulous Grand Vefour in the arcades of Palais-Royal, Laperouse by the Seine, or Ledoyen on the Champs-Elysees. Her opera lessons continued and she met with the many proprietors, secretaries, caterers, florists, and all others responsible for developing the extravagant wedding plans. Lola endured several formal dinners with the family of the Marquis.

Lola loved her *Papá* but nothing made her happy. Every smile, every exuberance, every appearance of delight was a sham. Her life hadn't changed, but life seemed more meaningless than before.

With her father out of town at one of his frequent conferences and Teresa on her regular night off, Lola knew the time had come to implement her plan.

Lola told her maid *Marguerite* to bring the dress she had specially designed for this evening's performance. Made of blue silk, with short sleeves and a white satin de Lyon skirt that draped into a long train, it was perfect. She ran her hand over the fine fabric and imagined how it would be to appear in front of an audience of strangers. She heard the music in her head and saw herself performing as the audience cheered her on.

Tonight, she would set the course for the rest of her life!

Chapter 6

That evening, Lola held her dress against her body and admired herself in the mirror.

"*Mademoiselle*, your bath is ready."

"Thank you, Marguerite."

Marguerite accompanied Lola to her private bathroom. The luxurious room contained elaborately painted cabinets with ornately carved, raised-panel doors. A gilded wash basin sat atop a long black, marble-topped vanity. The over-sized gilded tub rested against a wall of mirrors. As a child, Lola would use her fingers to draw faces on the steam-covered mirrors as she bathed.

"*Mademoiselle*, your dress is so beautiful. Are you going somewhere special this evening?" Marguerite asked as she helped Lola into the tub.

Lola smiled. "Yes, Marguerite, I am going someplace special and I will be with a most charming man."

"A man? Is he your fiancé?"

"Oh no. This man is handsome, intelligent and talented. I never met anyone like him. He is a real man with strong shoulders and beautiful red hair and beard. You must not tell anyone, not anyone at all, not even Teresa. Do you understand?"

Marguerite smiled conspiratorially, "Of course, *Mademoiselle*, do not fear, your secret is safe with me. Is there anything else I can do for you before I leave you to your bath?"

"No, thank you." Lola lay back in the tub and enjoyed the warmth of the water. She thought of Louis Rodolphe Salis, the owner of Le Chat Noir, "The Black Cat." She had been thrilled to learn that every Friday he hosted afternoon luncheons to review the acts of performers and she had insisted Teresa take her to his club.

She remembered her first meeting with Monsieur Salis. She had been tickled by his look of surprise. Not expecting a young girl to enter a cabaret in the middle of the day, he greeted them graciously. She smiled and recalled their conversation.

"Bonjour, *Mademoiselles*, how may I help you?"

Lola inquired, "Are you Monsieur Salis?"

He smiled. "Why yes, my dear, and to who do I have the pleasure of meeting?"

"I am Lola and this is my chaper—my good friend Teresa. We have heard so much about you. We just had to meet you."

"Ah, really, and what have you heard?"

"So many things, I am not sure where to start."

"Let us have some coffee and you can tell me all about what you've heard."

They sat at a small table. Lola hoped Monsieur Salis would be impressed by the information she gathered about him. "I learned of your fondness for processions and how you have used them. As when you first opened Le Chat Noir. You led a torch-lit parade across the Seine to make patrons aware you were open for their entertainment pleasure. And, you once greeted your patrons at the door with the announcement of your own death. Then went you on to lead your funeral procession through the streets of Montmartre to drum up publicity."

Salis laughed. "My dear, it seems you do know a great deal about me. So, what do you think of me?"

"You are the most unusual man I have ever met."

"I am happy to be considered unusual. Well then, would you like to see my creation, Le Chat Noir?"

"Oh, yes, please!"

Salis showed her a poster entitled *La tournée du Chat Noir de Rodolphe Salis* where a black cat sat against a yellow and red background. I named my cabaret Le Chat Noir when one evening I came to this abandoned building with an interest in purchasing it. I had been greeted by the meowing of a poor skinny, black cat perched on a nearby lamppost. I decided to keep the cat and thought The Black Cat is the perfect name for my club. I commissioned the artist Théophile Steinlen to produce the poster.

Lola recognized the poster and was delighted by the story. She admired the flamboyantly decorated interior was with its mish-mash of heavy antique furniture, lamps and paintings. He showed her a breathtaking fireplace with Byzantine columns. Lola asked about the skull that sat atop the fireplace. He jokingly said it belonged to Louis XIII as a child. He chuckled when he told her a splendidly bedecked Swiss guard covered with gold from head to foot greeted guests at the door. The guard had been instructed to allow painters and poets to enter the club, but to disallow infamous priests and the military. He boasted Le Chat Noir was the most extraordinary cabaret in the world and a fashionable late-night club for all Paris society, where anyone could rub shoulders with the most famous men of Paris.

Lola fell in love with Le Chat Noir. The atmosphere was so different from any place she had ever seen. So informal and yet crackling with excitement! She had been told Le Chat Noir was the best place for an emerging artist because Monsieur is always looking for new talent. She decided this must be where she would make her debut.

The following Friday, she had returned alone to Le Chat Noir and asked Monsieur if she could perform there. He had been reluctant, but when she provided sheet music to the pianist and sang for him, Salis had been pleased and agreed she could perform.

Lola thought Monsieur Salis was—except for her *Papá*—the most wonderful man in the world.

She couldn't wait to dress and prepare herself. After her bath Lola sat at her vanity table and told Marguerite that rather than wear her hair down in her usual youthful style, she wanted her hair pinned in a more adult fashion. Lola licked her fingers to curl some loose strands that fell forward onto her forehead. She and Marguerite spent a great deal of time making her up to look alluring and seductive. Lola wanted the world to see her as a professional performer, rather than just a young girl who likes to sing. When she decided she had done everything possible, she smiled at herself in the mirror, winked and said, "Lola, here is what you have been waiting for. It is time for you to show the world who you really are."

Not to be seen by the house staff, Lola left her bedroom through the French doors. She met the Hansom cab she had ordered earlier in the day. On her way to Le Chat Noir, Lola reviewed her plan. *It is well-known that the father of the Marquis attends Le Chat Noir. Surely, he will recognize me. I am looking forward to seeing his shocked face when I appear on stage. Of course, he will be incensed to see the future wife of his son performing like a common trollop. He will notify Papá that the marital agreement is void. Papá will be furious. However, after begging his forgiveness, and having done everything to appease him, he will eventually relent, and once again, we can be happy together.*

Lola smiled. *How clever I am to come up with this foolproof plan.*

Lola arrived at Le Chat Noir and thought the evening candlelight, with its glittering light and shadows, made the objects d'art décor more enchanting. Monsieur Salis stood joking with friends. She approached and said, "*Pardonnez-moi,* Monsieur Salis, I am Lola. You said I can perform tonight."

"*You* are Lola? Surely, you are not the little girl who was here last week. You are her older sister perhaps?"

Lola laughed. "No, I am the same person who was here last week."

"You look ravishing, my dear. I hope you are prepared. You are next to perform."

Pleased with herself for accomplishing the look she desired, Lola felt confident her performance would be spectacular. She chose a song from the new comic operetta by Offenbach entitled *The Drum-Major's Daughter*. The operetta was about Stella, the daughter of Duke Della Volta. Stella, a young heiress in love with Robert but had been betrothed to a feeble-minded old marquis, Bambini. When she received the news that in reality, she was the daughter, not of the duke, but of a French drum major and was now free to marry Robert, she sings of how happy she is to no longer be a noble surrounded by luxury.

When the curtains opened Lola's self-assurance vanished. The expectant faces of the audience brought butterflies to her stomach. She feared she would forget the words of her song. Lola's frigid fingers wrung her handkerchief. She forced her legs to drag her to the stage. She felt meek and tentative. When she began to sing her voice sounded shaky and off-key.

Lola scanned the audience searching for the father of her betrothed. She saw no sign of him. She should have been disappointed but instead felt relieved. Her confidence returned and she began to sing with poise. Never had she experienced the thrill of performing to this degree.

Now more self-assured, she teased and joked with the audience. Before she knew it, her performance ended. Lola held her breath until she heard the audience break into applause. Flushed with excitement, she raced from the stage and searched for Salis. She discovered him in a booth accompanied by patrons. With exuberance, she asked, "Was I good? Do you think the audience liked me? Do you like me?"

Salis looked around and saw the pleased faces of the customers. "You were good, my young friend. It seems the audience likes you."

Overwhelmed with joy, Lola forgot about her plan and wanted to start her career at once. She looked at Salis. "Does this mean I can work here? Please say, yes!"

Salis laughed. "Yes, all right, you can work here." Salis introduced her to the men he sat with, poet Paul Verlaine, composer Erik Satie, playwright August Strindberg and several other famous Parisians. They complimented Lola's performance and offered her a seat at their table. The group chatted and watched other entertainers for hours.

When the evening ended Lola felt giddy with excitement. She had no idea a world so different from her own existed. All the way home in the carriage she reflected on her evening. She loved the relaxed atmosphere of the cabaret, her opportunity to meet so many remarkable people and how much she had enjoyed herself.

When Lola approached the French doors to her bedroom, she remembered the Marquis' father hadn't attended. She realized she would have to return again and again until he appeared. This was a prospect that gave her great pleasure— providing he showed up before the wedding.

Lola sneaked into her unlit bedroom and closed the French doors. She thought she smelled her father's tobacco—impossible since he was out of town.

The words she heard struck terror in her heart.

"Where have you been?"

Chapter 7

Papá could not be here! Surely, I have imagined his voice. She heard his voice again, louder and harsher.

"Where have you been?"

In the shadows, she couldn't see his face but she could feel his presence. The full moon's light shined through her bedroom window like a beacon and washed her with its cold, white glare. Her heart pounded. In her sweetest little girl voice, she said, "*Papá*, you frightened me!"

"Answer me," he demanded, "Where have you been?" His rasping voice was like coarse sandpaper dragged against her skin.

"*Papá*, I did nothing wrong. Oh, *Papá*, please do not be angry with me." Lola's first thought was to go to him and hug him and play the little girl making up some silly excuse for coming home so late. But she feared he would push her away and she couldn't bear that. She hung her head and said nothing.

"So, you are too ashamed to admit what you have been doing. You disgrace me in front of the entire world! Have you no decency? You show yourself as a cheap dance hall girl. Have I raised you to have no self-respect?"

Lola felt sick to hear her *Papá* speak about her with such disgust. Holding back tears, she asked, "But how did you know?"

He shouted, "Do you think I am an idiot? Do you think I know nothing? You prance like a *demimondaine* in front of some of the most important people in Paris, and you think I will not hear of it?"

"But *Papá*, I was not trying to hurt you. I did it because I love to sing and dance. If you only knew how much the audience loved my performance, you would not be so angry."

He stepped out of the shadows. His face convulsed in anger, Lola could see droplets of spittle escape past his lips as he screamed, *"This will stop immediately!* Do you hear? Immediately! Tomorrow you go to a convent!" He marched from her room and slammed the door, rattling the windows.

Lola threw herself onto her bed. She cradled her head in her arms. Tears flooded her face. She had been impetuous and felt crushed by the weight of the consequences. *Why did I not realize Papá's colleagues might be in the audience? His so-called friends delight in the misery of others. Of course, they had been only too happy to rush the humiliating news to him.*

How stupid of me! Now I am worse off than before. I will be miserable for the rest of my life. There is no choice. I will have to marry the Marquis to appease Papá. I cannot return to Le Chat Noir.

It was impossible to fall asleep. She pounded her pillow in frustration. Then rose from her bed and paced the floor. She couldn't stop worrying.

He was not serious about the convent. He just said that in anger. He loves me too much to send me to one of those horrible places. Besides, there is still much to do before the wedding. He will cool off by morning. I will beg for his forgiveness. Once I become Madame Pimpleface, he will forgive me.

Lola was unable to sleep until just before dawn. Realizing she had slept late, she ran to her father's bedroom. It was empty. She searched his study and other rooms where he might have been, but she couldn't find him. Disheartened, she returned to her room thinking she would dress and see him at his offices. But when she returned to her room Teresa and Damien, one of the footmen, waited outside her bedroom with a packed bag. Lola could see by the drawn expression on Teresa's face, that she was about to receive awful news.

Teresa said, "I am sorry *ma petite*, but we must leave at once. I have packed only your essentials and I will send you the rest of your things soon."

"Leave? What are you talking about?"

Damien announced, "I have orders to take you to Convent Grandchamp immediately."

Lola never liked Damien, bald as a knee, short and barrel-chested with great tufts of hair growing from his big ears. He always seemed to stand a little too close when he spoke to her, and his breath smelled of old garlic.

Lola brushed her hand. "Bring me to a convent? That is ridiculous! You must have misunderstood. *Papá* was just upset. He did not mean for me to go to a convent."

"There is no mistake, *Mademoiselle*. I have strict orders. I must take you to Convent Grandchamp at once."

"Absolutely not! I demand you take me to see *Papá*!"

"I am sorry, *Mademoiselle*, but we must leave at once for Convent Grandchamp. I will take you by force if necessary." Lola could see by the intent in his eyes that Damien meant what he said. He looked a little too eager to get his hands on her. Talking to him is useless.

She turned to Teresa and pleaded, "Please, do not do this!"

With tearful eyes, Teresa uttered, "Dear Lola, you know I would help you if I could. I begged your *Papá* to reconsider, but I have never seen him in such a temper. My pleas only angered him further. You must go. Give him time to cool down. I am sure he will forgive you, but for now, you must go."

"All right, at least allow me to get dressed." Teresa followed Lola into her bedroom. Once inside Lola whispered, "Help me sneak out."

Teresa shook her head, "It will do no good. Your father anticipated you might try to run away. Look out of your window and you will see the garden is filled with servants waiting to catch you."

Lola hurried to the window and saw three servants standing around smoking, talking and laughing amongst themselves. *This is intolerable!* Her breathing became audible through her gritted teeth. She shouted, "This is outrageous! I cannot believe *Papá* would treat me like a prisoner!"

Teresa's expression changed from sadness to irritation. "If you told me what you were planning, I would have saved you from your recklessness. Instead, you chose to deceive me and your *Papá*. You have brought this upon yourself!"

"But, Teresa, I did not tell you because I feared you would get in trouble for helping me."

"Nonsense! You did not tell me because you knew I would stop you. I told you many times that because you are born to privilege it is required that you obey the conventions of your station. You got away with being the rebel at tea parties so you became bolder and thought you could get away with anything. Now you have gone too far. You have made a mockery of everything your father has taught you to respect. Now you will have to suffer the consequences."

"I never wanted to hurt you or *Papá*. I just want to sing and dance."

"*Madre de Dios!* Sing and dance, hah! Your father suffers humiliation and disgrace. He fears the scandal may cause dismissal from his position. He is certain that once the Marquis hears of this, he will not allow you to marry his son. You have dishonored your father. I hope after you have spent some time in the convent, the Marquis will be reassured that you are a good girl, and worthy of his son. Do not cause your father any more distress. For once, do what you are told!"

"But Teresa, I want to tell *Papá* how sorry I am for the trouble I caused him. I implore you, please let me speak with *Papá* before we leave."

"No, Lola. He refuses to speak with you. He believes you must pay for your impudence. Now hurry and get dressed. You do not want Damien to take you by force."

"All right, Teresa, I will do what you ask." While Teresa helped her to dress, Lola tried to make sense of her father's behavior. *How could he send me to a convent? Why will he not see me and let me apologize? He is not the same man who told me funny stories and held my hand as we walked through the park. He is not my sweet Papá who sang lullabies and kissed my forehead every night. Where is the wonderful Papá who granted me my every wish? How could he change so abruptly? How could he be so cruel to order a footman to take me by force?*

An idea came to her about how, with Damien's help, she might escape. Without Teresa's knowledge, Lola hid her purse in a drawer.

Lola accompanied Damien and Teresa to the awaiting carriage. Seated inside she said, "Teresa, I have forgotten my purse, can you get it for me, please?"

Teresa hurried off. As soon as she was out of sight, Lola leaped from the carriage and ran to Damien, who was about to climb to the driver's seat. Lola tugged at his coat and whispered, "I have a great deal of money. Take me away right now. Take me to Le Chat Noir or anywhere but the convent, and you can name your price." Damien looked at her and said nothing. Lola's voice became louder, firmer, and smug, "Do you hear me? I will give you anything you want, anything, just take me away from here now!"

Damien leaned his face close to Lola and put his fat, hairy hand over hers. "It is not your money I want." His salacious grin made it clear what he wanted. He moved even closer as if he was going to kiss her. Suddenly he yelled, "Ow!" He put his hand to his head. Teresa had given him a hard knock with her umbrella.

To Lola, she said, "You! Back in the carriage, now!" Turning to Damien, "You! Get going or I will hit you again!"

Lola returned to the carriage. She watched as the home she loved disappeared from view. She knew her life had changed forever. She and *Papá* could never have the same relationship. *How will I survive in a convent? Impossible! I hate Papá and I will not spend one night in a convent!*

Chapter 8

Lola and Teresa stepped from the carriage and entered Convent Grandchamp. Damien followed. He carried a small case containing Lola's essential belongings. A large plaque mounted on the wall of the building entrance stated the school's prospectus:

To form our students by inspiring them to a solid, enlightened piety.
To develop their intelligence and good judgment.
To embellish their minds with all useful knowledge.
To contribute as much as possible, toward making their company agreeable and their virtues sweet.

Lola read the plaque and thought she would vomit. She felt hopeless when she looked at the huge, heavy front doors that separated her from freedom. She inhaled and blew air from her puffed cheeks. She could think of nothing but escape.

Sister Adele greeted them with a pleasant smile. She explained that the Convent Grandchamp was an Augustine convent school, founded in 1768 under the patronage of Louis XV's consort, Queen Marie Leszczyńska, for daughters of the nobility and run by the Sisters. The Sister explained that Grandchamp offered its students handsome, commodious, well-ventilated classrooms and dormitories, large gardens, three wooded parks, an infirmary, a chapel for daily religious services, and rooms for weekly baths. After a few pleasantries, she suggested Teresa and Damien leave.

Teresa reached out to hug Lola, but she remained stoic. *Why had Teresa not tried harder to convince Papá to allow me to stay home?*

With tears, Teresa said, "I will miss you."

Lola watched Teresa leave. "Wait!" She ran to Teresa and hugged her. She pleaded, "I love you so much Teresa, please take me with you! I will do anything you want. I will do as I am told and be your most trusted companion. Please help me."

With a gentle movement, Teresa released herself from Lola's embrace and stepped back. She looked into Lola's eyes and said, "Listen to me. You cannot keep disobeying your father. He insists you stay here until he knows he can trust you. He is angry. Do not anger him further. You will not like the consequences. You must stay here until your *Papá* believes you will submit to his wishes. Only then will you regain his trust. Please be a good girl, obey the convent rules and, maybe, one day you will return home. I am sorry it has to be this way." Teresa gave Lola a hug.

Lola watched as Teresa left the convent. Her cheek was still moist from the sad, teary kiss Teresa had given her. Lola felt deserted. She felt as if she would never smile again. No matter what Teresa said, she would not stay.

When the sister showed her around the convent, Lola paid close attention. She needed to learn any escape route and asked questions that might help her.

After dinner, she was brought to her dormitory, meager by the standards she was accustomed to, but Lola didn't care. She wouldn't be staying long. She shared the room with Bernadette Broussard, who talked about herself nonstop.

Bernadette lived at the convent since she was a small child and knew the routine well. Lola asked her many questions. "What time do the sisters go to sleep? Do they check the beds? Is there a guard watching?" Lola had the information she needed and would flee that night.

Later that evening Sister Adele entered Lola's room. She sat next to Lola on her bed and held her hand. Sister Adele smiled and said, "My dear, I have heard about your unruly nature and want you to believe that no matter what it takes, we will do all we can to help you find your way. Just know you will find happiness and comfort in God's love. In time, you understand that goodness and virtue conquer evil. Through sacrifice and prayer, you will be purged of the devil's temptations." She kissed Lola's forehead and then kissed Bernadette's forehead. "It is time for sleep now, children. Say your prayers and sleep well knowing God is watching over you."

Lola whispered under her breath, "The devil with this!" She had been eager to leave before the sister entered her room, but now she realized how miserable she would be if she had to stay imprisoned in this cloister.

When Bernadette closed eyes to say her prayers, Lola pretended to change into her nightgown, but slipped it over her clothes. She jumped beneath the covers. Lola hoped Bernadette would soon fall asleep. When a sister peeked into the room, Lola was thankful to hear her say, "No more talking, children. Go to sleep now." Bernadette told Lola what she waited to hear. "That is our only bed check. Goodnight, Lola."

Lola waited in the dark for Bernadette to fall asleep. It seemed like hours. When she could wait no longer, she pulled back the covers and rose. The closed drapes blocked the moonlight. In the dark she removed her nightgown and felt for her kit. Finding it, she tiptoed to the door. Her fingers found the doorknob and twisted it.

"Ah-ha! I knew it!" shouted Bernadette. "You thought I was stupid. All those questions you asked, I knew you would escape."

"Sssh, escape? Of course not. It is just that I cannot sleep. and I wanted to walk a little. I was afraid to wake you."

Bernadette's whiny high-pitched voice grew louder, "You cannot fool me, I will call—*mmmph.*"

Lola put her hand over Bernadette's mouth. Lola's whisper came hard, fast and breathless, "Quiet, you little fool, you will wake everyone." Bernadette bit Lola's hand and ran for the door. Lola grabbed Bernadette and threw her onto her bed. Her panicked hands searched the darkness for a weapon. Bernadette jumped from the bed and rushed towards the door once more.

Lola discovered a hefty book and walloped Bernadette on the back of her head. She heard Bernadette groan as she slumped to the ground.

Merde! Did I kill her?

Seeking a sign of life, Lola touched Bernadette's limp body. She prayed Bernadette was still alive. At last, she felt Bernadette's beating heart. *Dieu merci, she has a thick skull!* Lola pulled the sheet from her bed and tied Bernadette as best she could in the darkness. She gagged her with a pillowcase. Then shoved Bernadette under her bed and rumpled the covers and pillows of each bed to make it look as if they were sleeping.

With a clammy hand, Lola turned the doorknob and peeked out, checking in both directions. She scrutinized the darkness and saw no one. The striking of her heels against the stone floor would echo in the cavernous room so she tiptoed down the hall. She used the railing as her guide and made her way downstairs to the main hall.

Her feet cramped from tiptoeing. *I should have practiced my ballet lessons with more diligence!*

When she reached the main entry doors, Lola searched in the darkness for the door handles. She pulled the latch but it wouldn't budge. A groan escaped her throat. *To come this far and fail? No, I will not fail!* Lola yanked and pushed but the heavy doors held fast. *Idiot! They must be barred!*

Her fingers explored the door until she felt the wooden beam held there by metal braces. A splinter from the wooden beam pricked her finger.

"Ouch!" she cried. She froze for fear someone may have heard her and waited.

With unladylike sweats and grunts, she summoned her strength and lifted the heavy beam it off its hinges. The weight of it caused her to lose her balance. She dropped the beam and fell on her haunches. The loud boom resounded throughout the hall. Dormitory doors flew open. The Sisters scurried about, holding lighted lamps, with worried looks on their faces. Lola searched for a place to hide when she realized no one was looking at her, everyone scurried toward Bernadette's room. She heard yelling from that direction and determined that Bernadette must have come to and was screaming for help.

In the confusion she pulled open the heavy door and escaped into the black night. Uncertain which way to go, she scrambled and pumped her legs towards a light in the distance. She didn't care how far she had to run. Ignoring the pain in her lungs, she wouldn't stop, until at last, she saw a Hansom cab and hailed it. Lola shouted to the cabbie, "Take me to Le Chat Noir!"

Ren'e Fedyna

Chapter 9

Lola jumped from the cab and ran towards the entrance of Le Chat Noir. The Swiss guard, in all his regalia, stood at his post. She smiled and said, "You do not understand how happy I am to see you!" He returned her smile and saluted her.

Inside the cabaret the music blared with full swing entertainment. Lola's heart fluttered with excitement. She searched for Salis and spotted him in conversation with a patron. Lola rushed to him, hugged and kissed him on each cheek. She blurted, "*Bonsoir*, Monsieur Salis, I am sorry to be late. It was most unavoidable."

Salis looked surprised. "Lola, are you all right? What happened? Have you been in a fight!"

Lola fussed with her hair. "Oh, Monsieur, you have no idea. But that is not important. I'm here now. Is it too late for me to sing tonight? I know I am not dressed for it but—"

"Lola, what are you doing here?"

"Why do you ask such a question? You told me I could work here."

"No, dear heart, things have changed. You cannot work here."

"What are you talking about? I know I was late tonight and I look a fright, but I had no choice. I assure you it will never happen again."

"Being late is not the problem."

"Monsieur Salis, please, are you firing me? What did I do? I thought you liked me."

"My dear, of course, I like you. However, the Prefect de Police has given me strict orders. If I let you perform here, they will close me down. Can you believe that? They will put me out of business! What have you done? You must have been naughty."

"Monsieur Salis, there must be some mistake! It must be someone else to whom they were referring. Did they say my name specifically, Lola La Fontaine?"

"Oh yes, they were very clear. I think you have made some important person angry. If fact, I had been told that if you ever showed your face here again, I should give you this." He removed an envelope from his coat pocket and handed it to Lola. "As you can see it says, Lola La Fontaine."

Lola ripped open the envelope. It was from her father. Her eyes read the words her mind refused to believe.

Lola,

If you are reading this letter, it means you have disobeyed me once again and for the last time. I demand you return to the convent immediately. If you do not, I will consider you to no longer be a member of my family. You will be disinherited and will have no dowry. The pain and shame you have brought upon my name is unforgivable. Return to the convent or you will never be welcome in my home again. This is your final warning.

Should you disobey me, as I expect you will, for the sake of your dear mother change your name. Bring no more shame to a family that has given you only love, honor and happiness.

Émile La Fontaine
Minister of Finance

With legs too weak to hold her, she crumpled into the nearest chair. Lola's throat soured with bile. Tears stung her eyes.

How can Papá be capable of such cruelty? Writing these callous words on an official government document rather than on personal stationery. Am I a stranger who means nothing to him? She rested her forehead in her hand and stared at the letter. Through incredulous eyes, she kept reading those cold-blooded words. Tears slid down her cheeks.

How could my life have changed so much in just twenty-four hours?

Her first instinct was to run to Papá and beg his forgiveness, to do anything to ease her pain. But she soon felt the heat of anger build within her.

Papá claims to love me, but am I just a beautiful object d'art for him to show off to his friends? If he loves me, how can he treat me like a dirty rag to be tossed away when I am no longer of use? What kind of man would care more about other people's expectations than the needs of his own flesh and blood?

Lola stood. Adrenalin flushed her cheeks. Aloud she said, "To hell with him then! It shall be Lola who refuses to see him, not the other way around!" Salis stood nearby. "I need to work," Lola demanded. "You must let me work here."

Salis looked at Lola with sad eyes. "I have no idea what is going on in your life. I am sure things must be difficult for you. But you cannot work here—it is impossible!"

"Mon Dieu! I am penniless and have no place to turn. I cannot go home. I refuse to return to the restrictions of the convent. Teresa rebuffed me. My hypocritical friends will laugh at me, or worse, pity me.

"Impossible?" She pleaded, "Please, Monsieur Salis do not turn me away. I have no money and nowhere to go! You must help me!"

"My dear Lola, I would like to help you but I cannot let you work here."

"If I cannot work here, I must work somewhere else. Can you give me a reference to another cabaret?"

"I would be happy to give you a reference, but it will do you no good. When the police were here, they said every decent cabaret in Paris has had the same warning."

Lola panicked. "Oh no! What will I do? Must I beg for coins in the street?"

Salis placed his hand under her chin. His eyes were soft. "Dearest Lola, there is someplace you can go, but I do not recommend it. It is obvious you come from a wealthy family. You are used to a life of safety and privilege and do not understand what life will be like without these protections. Many people will want to take advantage of you and may wish you harm. Go home, no matter how bad it is. You will be better off. Otherwise, you may regret the decision you make this day."

Lola thought for a moment before she answered. "I appreciate your advice Monsieur Salis, but I cannot take it. I have no choice. If you know a place where I can work please tell me."

"If you insist. I will write you an introduction to a friend of mine, Jacques Moreau, who owns *L'antre Du Diable,* The Devil's Lair. You must be careful. It is a dangerous place."

Lola thanked Salis. She exited *Le Chat Noir,* hailed a cab gave and gave the driver the address of *L'antre Du Diable.*

The cabbie said, "This is the place, Mademoiselle. Are you getting out or is there someplace else you wish me to take you?"

Lola thought, *I wish there was someplace else to go but my choices are few. I can either return to the convent or at sixteen be forced to marry a man I do not love.*

"Mademoiselle? If you please."

Lola looked out of the cab window into the bleak night. Before her were shabby buildings and poorly lit streets. She wrung her hands.

"Mademoiselle, I must leave. Please exit the coach immediately!"

She fumbled through her purse for money to pay the driver. When her nervous fingers found the coins, she paid him and opened the cab door. Seeing men engaged in a fistfight nearby made her shudder. Lola cautiously stepped from the cab and with regret, she watched as it disappeared into the mist.

Curses shouted from open windows pierced the darkness. The shatter of a broken window startled her. She ran to escape the shards of falling glass but gave wide berth to a man who lay on the ground before her, whether asleep or dead she could not tell. Now, Lola understood what Monsieur Salis meant about the danger.

She bolted towards the *L'antre Du Diable Cabaret*. At the entrance door, she encountered a surly man cleaning his fingernails with a knife. His hungry eyes looked her over as if she would be his next meal.

He whispered in her ear, "I've been waiting for you all of my life."

His creepy voice gave her shivers. Lola pushed him away and rushed inside hoping he would not follow. She slammed the door against his evil laugh. Leaning her back against the closed door, she surveyed the cabaret.

This room, it stinks of beer, sweat and cheap perfume. And these men, they look as coarse as the wooden tables at which they sit. The women wear too much make-up and look as hard as the men. Are they all pimps, whores, thieves and local toughs? Mon Dieu! What have I done?

Ren'e Fedyna

Chapter 10

Lola chewed her fingernail as she examined the habitués. Her pulse raced. *What should I do? Return to the convent with the hope that one-day Papá will accept me and allow me to be his puppet? Or do I try to get a job in this miserable place and get my throat cut? To hell with Papá! I will see this through!*

She braced herself and made her way to the bartender. His back was to her. Her voice was soft. "*Pardon, monsieur*, I am looking for the manager." It appeared he hadn't heard her so she shouted, "*S'il vous plait, monsieur!* I am looking for the manager, Monsieur Jacques Moreau." When he whipped around to see who was speaking, his milky eye and scarred face startled her.

He appeared confused at seeing her, but smiled and spoke in a gentle, concerned voice. "*Mademoiselle*, are you sure you are in the right place? You are young and beautiful and should not be in a place like this. Perhaps you are looking for a different Jacques Moreau?"

His soft tone was not what she expected and it made her feel less frightened. "Thank you, but this is the right place. Please point him out."

"It is better for you to wait here. I will get him."

She watched the bartender disappear into a back room. She thought about her father's letter and her anger flared. *It is his fault I am in this awful place. If he disowned me, why not let me live my life as I choose? He wants me to change my name, so why will he not let me stay at Le Chat Noir under a different name? I suppose he knows his friends will recognize me, which would cause him embarrassment. Not that I care. In fact, I would enjoy that. It serves him right. For now, he wins. Since I cannot perform in better place, I will work here. I hope it will not be long until I can seek employment elsewhere.*

Papá is right about one thing, I do not want to be known as the daughter of Émile La Fontaine any longer. But what name do I choose?

She thought hard. The only name that came to mind was Amantine Lucile Aurore Dupin, the novelist. Much like Lola, she was born of an aristocratic father, spent time in a convent in Paris and lived an unconventional life. She was so brave she wore men's clothes, making it the mark of her rebellion against a priggish society. Lola had read many of the novels she wrote under the name of George Sand. *Yes, she thought, from now on I am Lola Dupin!*

The bartender returned along with a portly man, better dressed than his patrons. "I am Jacques Moreau, how can I help you, *Mademoiselle*—?"

"Monsieur Moreau, my name is Lola Dupin and I am here to sing and dance in your cabaret."

The owner's eyes twinkled with amusement. "You want to work here? Are you serious?"

"Yes, I am serious. I have a letter of referral from my friend and former employer, Monsieur Rudolphe Salis. Here is his letter of recommendation."

"Salis? Salis employed you? Remarkable!" Moreau read the letter with widened eyes. He looked Lola over as if inspecting a counterfeit five-franc bill. "*Mademoiselle*, if you do not mind me saying, I can tell by your clothes and your demeanor you are from a rich family. This is not Le Chat Noir. The clientele here is rough and crude. The people who work here have had difficult lives. They differ greatly from those you are accustomed to. These people know hardship and understand what it is like to work hard for little reward. What makes you want to work here?"

"To be honest, Monsieur Moreau, I do not want to work here but circumstances cause me to have no choice. Do not be concerned about my willingness to work hard. I promise you that will not be a problem."

"Well, if Salis recommends you, you must have some talent. But even though you may think you are ready to work here, I am sure you will find you are not."

What can I do to make him hire me? She raised her chin and boasted, "Monsieur Moreau, I am Mademoiselle Lola Dupin. I am an excellent singer and dancer and you will be happy for me to work here. It would be a mistake for you not to hire me!"

Moreau chuckled. "So, my little Goody Goody, you think you are hot stuff, eh? Well, I suppose you can bring some class to this place. You say you can sing and dance, but can you do *le chahut*?"

"*Le chahut?* What is that?

"Ah, so you do not know everything. To work here, you must perform *le chahut*. It appears you will need some training. Let us see how well you do tonight, if you please the audience, I will see to it you are taught a proper *chahut*."

"Have no fear Monsieur, the audience will be pleased."

Moreau showed her to a seat. "Sit and watch the other performers. I will let you know when it is time for you to go on."

Lola watched the performers intently and saw they were bawdy and uncouth. She thought hard to put her routine together. When he pointed at her to go on, she was ready. *I am no longer Lola La Fontaine, the little girl singer. I am Lola Dupin, the professional entertainer extraordinaire and my performance will prove it!*

Lola sang and moved provocatively. She teased and pleased the audience with her hip-swaying and sensual facial expressions. Lola used her voice to bring the audience along for a ride, changing from high-pitched and sweet to a low animal growl, and all in time with her seductive dancing.

After her performance, Moreau came to her and said, "*Très bon*, my little firecracker. You have done better than I expected. Come with me. It is time for you to meet someone." He brought her to a table where a short, wiry, older woman with haggard features and sharp eyes sat. She smoked a thin cigar and sipped a glass of absinthe. "I wish to introduce you to Nini. She will teach you what you need to know. I will leave you two to get to know each other."

It had been quite a day and Lola fell into the chair next to the woman.

Nini cackled. "So, you think you are a dancer, eh?" Lola started to speak but Nini ignored her. "Do you know why they call me, Nini-Foot-in-the-Air?"

Lola laughed. "Nini-Foot-in-the-Air! Why do you have such a silly name?"

"Because that is how I dance and no one can do it better than me."

Lola smirked. "That is a strange way to dance."

The old woman leaned forward, resting her hand on her chin, she looked into Lola's eyes, "You think so? So, you do not know *le chahut*, eh?" Nini leaned closer to Lola and began to feel her shoulders and legs.

Lola pushed Nini's hand away. "Stop that! What do you think you are doing?"

"Ha! So foolish one, you think I am touching you for pleasure? Moreau calls you little Goody Goody, I can see why. You think you are too good for this place, *oui?*"

Lola didn't like this crazy woman. "I have no idea what you are talking about and I do not wish to be mauled by you or anyone else."

"So, I am mauling you, eh? I think you are too sensitive, too gentle to become a dancer of *le chahut*. I think you should stay with your little girl dancing. You can go now." Nini waved her hand to dismiss Lola and went back to her absinthe.

This crazy woman has the nerve to insult me? Nonsense! I will show her.

Although drained from such an emotional day, Lola would not pass up a challenge. Lola stared at Nini with fire in her eyes. She shouted, "So, you think I am too sensitive and too gentle! Let me assure you, I can do anything I set my mind to! There is no dance I cannot do, even your stupid *chahut* that you make so much of, Madame Ass in the Air!" Getting no response from Nini, Lola pounded the table with her fist. "Do you hear me, old woman?" She screeched, "I will be the best dancer you have ever seen."

Nini turned her head with a devious look. "So, you do have some fire in your veins after all. I think maybe I will give you a chance if only to watch you break your silly little neck. But if you decide to do this, you will work hard. I have no time for crybabies. You will live with the other girls. Room and board will be provided, but you must do exactly as I tell you and practice, practice, practice until you think you will die from overwork. If you can survive and you are good enough, maybe then you can work here."

The orchestra began to play a frothy Offenbach tune. Women in scandalous costumes raced through the audience yelling, clapping and twirling like tops. At the center of the dance floor, they lifted their legs and swirled their skirts. They bent over and threw their skirts over their backs, presenting their bottoms to the audience and exposing their grubby petticoats. Some turned cartwheels while others stood on the toes of one foot, holding the other foot straight into the air with one hand and spun round and round. The raucousness ended with each dancer doing a split in turn, sitting on the floor with legs stretched in a horizontal position. It was a noisy, stomping dance, earthy and animal, performed for a boorish but appreciative crowd.

Lola gasped at the raw vulgarity. "This is what you want me to do? Is this *le chahut*?"

Nini chuckled. "Ah, Mademoiselle Goody Goody is offended. So, you are too fancy to do this dance. Nini looked at Lola with disgust. "Go away. I have no time to waste on such a prissy ass." Nini turned her back to Lola and moved to another table to talk with a patron.

Lola sat stunned. Her entire life changed in a flash. It was all happening too fast. *What will I do now? I want to be an entertainer but these girls are more like streetwalkers than dancers.* She closed her eyes. *I am much too tired to think about this. I will decide in the morning.* Lola stood and was about to leave when she thought. *Where can I go? I have no money for a hotel. Where will I sleep?* She sighed. *It seems my decision has been made for me* "Did you say you provide lodging?"

Lola could see by Nini's expression she was about to be rejected again. Lola felt defeated and hopeless. Nini's face softened. She took a piece of paper from her purse, scribbled a note and handed it to Lola. "Here is the address, give this note to the concierge. Get a good rest. You will need all your strength for the training."

Chapter 11

Lola took the note and headed to the door. She reached for the door handle but drew back her hand. The man with the knife could be waiting outside for her. She turned back to see who might help her. She caught the eye of the bartender. He poured drinks for two men sitting at the bar when he looked her way. Then he approached her. "Are you leaving now, *Mademoiselle*? It is too dangerous for you to go outside by yourself. I will fetch you a carriage. Have a seat and wait for me."

"You are very considerate, *Monsieur*...."

"My name is Bertrand. I have two daughters close to your age and I would not want them to be alone in such a dangerous place. Please sit. I will return soon." Bertrand returned and said, "Your carriage is here. I will walk with you."

Lola reached into her purse to give him a tip but her hand came out with only two *centimes*. Not enough for a tip and not enough for the carriage. She looked up at the bartender, tears of frustration and embarrassment rimmed her eyes.

"Do not be upset, I have already given the address to the driver and paid him."

She hugged him. "I cannot thank you enough. You are very kind, *Monsieur* Bertrand."

The streets were dark and deserted when Lola arrived at the address given to her by Nini, but at least there were no drunks sleeping in the gutter.

She rang the doorbell. An elderly, stern-faced lady dressed in black, answered. "Can I help you?"

Lola handed her Nini's note. The concierge asked her to come in. She brought the note to the lamp to read. With a disapproving look, she picked up the lamp and said, "Follow me." Lola trudged behind her, eyelids weighted with fatigue. The concierge brought her into a dormitory with many beds. She pointed to one and told her it would be hers and left. Lola dropped onto the bed in her clothes and fell asleep.

It seemed as if she had just shut her eyes when she heard loud laughter. She blinked her eyes open. Lola must have slept for several hours because the sunlight was shining through dingy windows. She rubbed her eyes and saw several girls around her bed tittering and pointing at her.

A tall, skinny girl with a long beak-like nose and with hair and eyes black as a crow said, "Look who's here, it is Mademoiselle Goody Goody! Shall we have a look at her fancy clothes?" She pulled the cover from Lola with a quick snap and grabbed her skirt. She cackled. "You wear fancy bedclothes Mademoiselle Goody Goody. Did your maid dress you this morning?"

Lola shook her groggy head. For a moment, she'd forgotten where she was. The girls sat on her bed. They groped at her clothes and made disparaging comments. Lola was too stunned to react. Suddenly she heard Nini's voice shout, "Girls, have you nothing better to do? Maybe instead of breakfast, we should start practice right now?"

The girls scurried from the room. Lola tried to blink the sleep from her eyes as she heard Nini say, "I suggest you have your breakfast now because practice begins immediately after."

She asked, "Nini, I only have the clothing I am wearing. I do not think they are appropriate for dance practice. What shall I wear?"

Nini smirked and left the room. Over her shoulder, she said, "No problem, just strip down to your underwear."

Lola shouted after her, "You cannot serious?" Unsure what to do, she glanced around. The room was small for the ten crudely built beds with their threadbare sheets and thin scratchy covers. It appeared each girl had a footlocker for belongings. She hoped she might find an appropriate outfit in hers, but it was empty. The windows were on one side of the room. They were small and high. She could only see the shoes of people passing by. She didn't remember descending any stairs but realized the room must be in a cellar of some sort, which felt chilly and damp. A washbasin sat atop a small table. A cracked mirror hung above. Lola thought of her bedroom at home and shook her head. *Is this a room for entertainers or prisoners?*

Lola walked to the basin to wash her face. She searched for a clothes closet but found none. She shrugged her shoulders and removed her clothes down to her underwear. This was the first time she had ever undressed without the help of her maid.

Hearing voices and laughter through the open door, she followed the sound to the upstairs dining room. Many girls sat around a large table chatting. She felt less awkward when she saw the other girls sitting in their underwear. Even underclothes separated the poor from the rich. The girls wore plain, utilitarian white cotton while Lola's underwear had luxuriously embroidered cream-colored silk and lace.

A girl said, "Sit here next to me." Lola liked her smile and took the seat. "My name is Giselle. You must be Lola." Giselle had a round face with heart-shaped red lips, sparkly blue eyes and ringlets of golden hair that spilled onto her shoulders. "I am new, also. I have been here for only one month."

Lola stared at the meager *petite dejeuner* of bread, jam and coffee placed on the table, so different from the extravagant offerings had been accustomed to. She turned to Giselle and asked, "What is done about clothes? I have only the one dress I came with, and I cannot wear the same one every day. When are we to be paid? I will take the money and have someone make new clothes for me."

Giselle tittered. "Paid? Do you not know? We are not paid. We receive room and board and dance lessons. The only way to make money is to go out with the men who come to Nini's salon."

"Nini's salon? Where is that?"

"There is a separate entrance to this place, referred to as The Salon. That is where the gentlemen call on us every evening.

They take us to dinner and cabaret, and we reciprocate them for their generosity."

"Reciprocate? You mean they pay you to be with them?" Lola's mouth dropped open. "You mean you are—?"

Giselle gave her a knowing smile. "A *demimondaine*? Yes, of course. Why are you surprised?"

"I suspected some of you might be, but you as well?"

"We cannot always choose the life we want. Sometimes our lives are chosen for us, even before we are born."

"Although, for different reasons, I can understand what you mean."

"But you must tell us, why you are here? Everyone is curious. They say you are rich and you have come here just to see what it is like to be with poor girls like us. They say you are doing this for fun."

Lola couldn't believe what she heard. She exclaimed, "Fun! How could anyone think this is fun?"

The girl who pulled the cover from Lola stood and shouted, "Why else would you be here? Either you stole your clothes or you are crazy. No rich person would come here. You just want to make fun of us." Another cried, "Yes, you want to make fun of us!" The black-haired girl grabbed several pieces of bread and threw them at Lola. The other girls followed suit.

Lola put her hands up to bat away the bread. She stood and shouted, "You think you are the only ones with problems? Yes, I come from a wealthy family but that does not mean I am happy. Do not envy me. My father has disowned me, I have no money and no place else to go, so I live here with you. Does that make me crazy? Maybe so. If I cannot live here, I will have to live on the streets. I have no choice."

A ringing bell interrupted her. Everyone raced off. She felt Giselle grab her hand and pull her along. They ran past the concierge who was ringing a large bell. Giselle brought her into a spacious room where Nini waited, holding a long, gnarled wooden cane. The girls stood in a straight chorus line. Giselle ran over and took her place in line. Lola awaited directions from Nini, who appraised her height and said, "Line up next to Hortense. Hortense, raise your hand."

Lola groaned when she saw Hortense. The girl who removed her cover that morning. She took a deep breath and walked to her place next to Hortense at the end of the row.

Nini rapped the cane on the floor. "Let us begin with the *rond de jambe*. Lift your right knee high and point your toes."

She followed Nini's instructions and waited for the next command. It didn't come. Nini left the room. Everyone held their position. Lola wobbled in an effort to keep her balance. Hortense leaned into Lola and made her tip over, knocking over every other girl in line. They shouted at her, cursed and called her names. Lola turned to Hortense and was about to push her when Nini returned.

She admonished them. "You call yourself dancers? You cannot hold your leg up for a few minutes? How do you expect to have the balance you need?"

The girls complained that it was Lola's fault, that she could not hold the position and made them fall. Nini shouted at them, "You think this is an excuse? What will happen when you are dancing? Do you think the audience will listen to your excuses? Now, lift your knee and do not move until I tell you to."

Lola did as she was told, but gave Hortense a dirty look. When she saw the wicked grin Hortense wore, Lola knew her problems had just begun.

Chapter 12

Sweaty and breathless after hours of dance practice, Lola felt exhausted.

Giselle walked to her and said, "Are you all right? You look like you might faint."

Before Lola could answer, Nini approached. Her eyes bored into Lola. She shouted, "So, there is no dance you cannot do, eh? You will be the best dancer I have ever seen, *oui?* I think not. If you want to be a dancer you must learn to control your breath, you must learn balance and timing. You must continue to practice and prove to me you are worth my time. Otherwise, leave now before I kick you out! But if you choose to stay you must change your undergarments. You cannot wear any color but white. It is a strict tradition, so get rid of your fancy underwear." Nini marched from the room.

Lola's face burned with anger and chagrin. *To go through all of this and not be good enough? Could it be I am not the great dancer I believe myself to be? This dance is much more difficult than I imagined, but do I give up? No! I will have to work harder. Nini will see I am a great dancer, but first I must find underwear!*

Giselle gave her a sad smile. "Do not be discouraged, we have all heard the same lecture. She does that to get the best out of you. This dance is very hard and takes a lot of practice. We are all trying our best but there is much to learn. Come. Let's clean ourselves. We must prepare for the gentlemen who will be waiting for us in Nini's salon."

"No, no. I cannot meet those men. I must continue to practice. Besides, I have nothing to wear. What am I to do? I have only the undergarments I am wearing and no money to buy anything. Am I to be dismissed because of my underwear?"

"Do not worry. I will loan you clothes."

"Giselle, you are so sweet. I cannot tell how much I appreciate your help. But my clothes need to be laundered, who do I give them to?"

"Give them to Madame Joseph, the concierge. She can have them washed for you but you must pay her."

"Pay her! I have no money."

Giselle grinned. "You can earn money tonight or wash them yourself."

"Wash them myself? *Mon Dieu!* I do not know how. I have never washed clothes." She shook her head. *I hate being poor!*

The *demoiselles* were busy changing and fussing with their hair and makeup in the dormitory. Hortense saw them arrive and laughed at Lola. "So, Mademoiselle Goody Goody cannot wear her fancy underwear? Give them to me? I will look better in them than you."

Reaching into her footlocker, Giselle said, "Ignore her." She pulled out underwear and a dress. "Take these, keep them for as long as you like. You should come with me and meet the fellows. Some of them are nice."

Lola shook her head, "Not tonight. I think I will need to learn how to wash my clothes." A bell sounded. "What is the bell for?"

"That's dinner," Giselle said. "If you come with us tonight, I guarantee the dinner at the cafés will be better."

Lola realized how hungry she was. "Not tonight. I will eat here even if it is not as good as what you will have. Thank you so much for the clothes. Have a wonderful evening." She put the clothes in her locker and made her way to the dining room.

Lola entered the dining room just in time to see the steaming stew ladled into bowls. It smelled delicious. She looked for a place to sit. Except for one other *demoiselle*, the dining room was empty. She assumed the others were getting ready for their evening out. Lola selected a stew bowl and walked over to the young lady, "Do you mind if I sit here?"

The young woman looked towards the voice and offered a weak smile. "No, have a seat. My name is Martha, and of course, you are Lola. You have caused quite a stir. The others are jealous of you, especially Hortense."

"I know that one will be trouble for me. You are not going out tonight?"

"No, I hurt my leg and I can barely walk, so I must stay and rest it. If I cannot dance, I will have to leave."

"Did you hurt it dancing?"

Martha frowned and nodded her head.

Lola looked at Martha. "Nini is a cruel taskmistress. I think she is too hard on us."

"It is true, Nini puts up with no-nonsense and works us like slaves. But once you prove yourself, she is the first to help if you need money or a shoulder to cry on. It is not Nini's fault that I keep hurting myself. Nini is afraid the same thing will happen to me that happened to Jeanne Faès. She died of severe internal injuries from performing jump splits."

Lola was shocked to hear someone could die from dancing. Now that she knew how hard the dance was, she had to make sure she would not end up like Jeanne.

Although Lola wanted to continue their conversation, she felt exhausted and could see Martha was no longer in the mood to talk. They sat together in silence until they finished their meal. Lola said, "I wanted to practice dancing and wash my clothes but now I feel tired. I am going to bed. Can I help you to your bed?"

"No thank you. I want to rest a little longer. Sleep well."

"It was nice to meet you. I hope you feel better tomorrow. *Bonsoir*, Martha."

Lola dropped into bed and pulled the cover over. She felt something squishy and smelled a horrific odor. Tossing back the cover she realized she had just laid in excrement. Lola jumped from the bed and screamed, "Hortense did this!"

Lola ran to Madame Joseph. "Madame Joseph, look at me! That *putain* Hortense put shit in my bed! Please help me!"

Madame Joseph's eyebrows shot up. *"Mon Dieu!* What is going on? You shit in your bed?"

"No! Hortense put it there. She must have done it when I was eating dinner. Please help me. I must have these clothes washed and take a bath."

"Yes, of course. It will cost you two francs."

"Oh please, Madame Joseph. I have no money. This is an emergency. Please help me this one time."

Madame Joseph frowned and thought for a moment. "Well, all right. I will loan you the money but you must repay me three francs when you have it."

"Yes, anything. Just please have it cleaned. Also, my sheet and blanket. No, wait. I have an idea."

Lola bathed and put on the underwear she had borrowed from Giselle, went to bed and fell asleep. Several hours later a loud shriek awakened her.

Lamps illuminated the dormitory. She burst into laughter when Hortense ran from the room screaming, "There is shit in my bed! Lola, you whore, you'll be sorry!"

Chapter 13

The dancers practiced for hours every day except Sunday. Over and over they went through the positions: *battement*—the high kick, the *rond de jambe*—quick rotary movements of the lower leg with knee raised and skirt held up, the *port d'armes*—turning on one leg while grasping the other leg, the *grand ècart*—the jump splits, and the cartwheel.

Nini pounded into their heads, "You dance like elephants! When will you learn? To do this dance you must develop balance, rhythm and stamina. Are you doing the best you can? You must take pride in what you do!"

Nini would show them again and again how to do a proper *chahut*, explaining why she did it better than they. She was lithe for someone her age. Lola began to respect the talent she possessed.

Lola practiced constantly, determined to dance better than anyone else. She had no interest in going out with the male callers. She used her free time to learn how to wash her clothes and asked the dancers to teach her how to sew. It surprised her to find she enjoyed sewing. Impressed by Lola's skills, the dancers paid her to repair their clothes and asked her to design clothing for them.

Most of the dancers had grown up on the streets of Paris with little opportunity to learn social graces. They realized Lola's knowledge of fashion and etiquette could be useful and asked her advice on how they could refine their appearance. Happy to demonstrate, she showed them how to use less makeup and restyle their clothes to give them an air of refinement. She taught them to eat using the proper utensils and to present themselves in a cultured manner. The dancers, thrilled to learn these sophistications, said they felt certain it would help them snare rich lovers and husbands.

Except for Hortense, the dancers appreciated how hard Lola worked and accepted her as one of them. Hortense continued to harass her at every opportunity. At first, Lola paid no attention to her constant belittling, but when Hortense tried to trip her, Hortense got her foot stomped for her effort.

Hortense's disparaging remarks increased in intensity and became more difficult for Lola to ignore. One day, Lola walked into the dormitory to see Hortense bent over her footlocker about to steal her clothes. Lola sneaked behind Hortense and kicked her so hard that she fell inside the locker.

Hortense screamed.

Despite her attempts at self-defense, Lola got Hortense's body inside the footlocker. She closed the lid and sat on it. She could feel Hortense pounding on the lid. "Let me out, you bitch! I will rip your eyes out!" The locker muffled the intensity of her voice, reducing it from threatening to comical.

Hearing the commotion, several of the *demoiselles* came into the dormitory. When they realized what was happening, they broke into hearty laughter. "Leave her in there," they yelled. "That's the best place for her!"

Lola shouted to Hortense, "I will let you out only if you promise to leave me alone. You must swear not to bother me or steal from me or anger me."

She heard Hortense mutter, "Shut up you cow and let me out!"

"If you do not swear, I will lock you in and you will stay there until you rot!"

Hortense said nothing.

"All right, if that is what you want." Lola looked at Giselle, "The key is in my purse. Please give it to me."

Giselle was laughing so hard tears poured down her face. "I will be happy to."

Hortense shouted, *"Non! Non!* All right! I will not bother you, just let me out!"

"I did not hear you, what did you say?"

"I will not bother you anymore. Now let me out, damn you!"

"No, I think you do not mean it. I am locking you in now."

"No! Lola please, I swear I will never bother you again. Just please let me out, please!"

"Are you sure?"

"Oh yes, I swear on my life!"

Lola stood and put her finger to her lips. She waved to the dancers to follow her and tiptoed from the room.

"Hello? Are you still there?"

The group peeked in from outside the doorway and waited for Hortense to realize she was free to go. In a moment the lid opened. Hortense peeked out, her beady black eyes moved from side to side. She shoved back the lid and jumped out. Rubbing her behind where Lola kicked her, Hortense sheepishly scurried past the laughing dancers.

Chapter 14

The dancers continued their strenuous practice routine. Days blended into weeks and weeks into months. But this morning the breakfast chatter was more animated than usual. There was a rumor Nini would make an announcement.

The dancers rushed to line up in excited anticipation of the news. They expected a dancer would be selected to perform at L'antre Du Diable. This meant they would be paid for their dancing and have exposure as performers, and for someone, it might be the start of a dancing career.

Nini stood before them and announced, "You may have heard Martha Darceau has injured her leg once again and can no longer perform. I am sorry to say we must replace her. You have all worked hard and deserve a chance to perform, but right now I have room for only one and that dancer is…."

With her crooked finger, Nini drew a line through the air passing each dancer. They waited expectantly as if her finger was a roulette ball about to land on their number. "Giselle, you have proven your abilities. You are an excellent dancer and you are ready to dance a proper *chahut*. You begin tonight."

The dancers were about to gather around her to congratulate her when Giselle stepped forward and said, "Thank you so much, Nini. I am grateful you selected me. But I planned to tell you after practice today that I am to be married soon, and I will be leaving." The dancers jumped and squealed with surprised delight, shouting congratulations to Giselle.

Nini smiled. "*Félicitations!* We are happy for you and wish you a wonderful life. I hope he is a good man and will treat you well. Now girls, get back in line." The dancers were happy to have another chance and rushed back into place. Nini scanned the dancers and stopped. "Lola, it took you a while, but you have worked hard and proven yourself. Tonight, you will dance *le chahut* at *L'antre Du Diable.*"

Except for Hortense, the girls gathered around Lola and congratulated her. She was thrilled Nini had finally pronounced her ready to perform at L'antre Du Diable. Lola laughed at herself for feeling so honored to do a dance she once thought so vulgar. But it was a difficult dance that required talent and perseverance. She was proud of herself. After all of her hard work, Nini knew she was good enough to do *le chahut.* However, her excitement was mixed with sadness. She would miss her friend Giselle.

After practice, Lola said to her, "I am so happy for you, but you never mentioned you were to be married."

Giselle smiled. "I am surprised myself. Last night Robert LaForge, a businessman who I have been with many times, said he had to leave for Egypt and insisted I come with him. He has talked of marriage before, but I did not believe him. I have heard those words from others who never meant it. But Robert says he loves me and cannot live without me! Soon we are leaving for Egypt where we will be married. Can you imagine? I am off to marry a rich, handsome man who loves me and will whisk me away to an exotic land. Romantic, *non*? Maybe in Egypt I will learn how to belly dance!"

They hugged and wished each other a good life. Wiping tears from their eyes, they parted.

That night, surrounded by the *demoiselles* who gathered around her, Lola prepared for her performance at L'antre Du Diable. Excited for her, they helped her dress. She slipped her long, shapely legs into thigh-high black stockings. Over the stockings, she wore white cotton culottes from knee to waist, with lace and ribbons at the knee. Above the culottes, she worked herself into a tightly bound corset, a frilly petticoat and a sleeveless lilac dress with a fitted bodice and full skirt. She slipped her feet into black low-heeled shoes.

Lola walked over to the cracked mirror hanging on the dormitory wall to do her hair and makeup. She gazed into the mirror and remembered the night she performed at Le Chat Noir without her father's knowledge. Although only six months had passed, it seemed like a lifetime ago. She thought about the life of privilege she had left behind and laughed at the small cracked mirror she used now. So different from the Louis XV style giltwood mirror in her bedroom where she once preened, admiring her magnificent blue dress.

How my life has changed! If I knew in advance I would escape from a convent, be disowned by my father and become a dancer of le chahut, would I have done it anyway? Or, would I have stayed and married Monsieur Pimpleface and lived the life of tedious melancholy, following mindless restrictions on my life?

She arrived with Nini at the L'antre Du Diable and met the other dancers who greeted her politely, but with little enthusiasm. Everyone was milling around doing their final preparations for the dance: adjusting their costumes, fixing their makeup or practicing loosening-up exercises. The time to perform arrived and the ladies lined up ready to begin. Lola's belly fluttered with nervous excitement.

Nini took her hand. She said, "Have no fear. You are an excellent dancer and you will do well tonight. I am proud of you."

It surprised Lola to hear such praise from Nini. With her confidence bolstered, she felt eager to perform.

The music began and the dancers ran out into the crowd. They scattered among the audience heading in different directions, shouting, clapping and twirling. Lola looked into the faces of the people she once had scorned and now hungered for their approval. She danced near them to observe their expressions and was delighted to hear the onlookers shout, "Beautiful woman, tell me your name!" or "Come dance closer to me, be my wife tonight!" Encouraged by the lusty delight of the audience, she threw herself into the performance with more gusto.

Jacques Moreau told Lola he could see she had the makings of a popular entertainer and asked her to create a solo routine for the next evening. Overjoyed, Lola worked hard and was ready to perform.

She began her routine with the *gavotte*, a French dance that had been around for centuries. With delicate turns mostly on tiptoes, slight bows and measured steps, her dance performance was light and dainty. At the finish of the dance, it was the custom to kiss your partner, so she blew a kiss to the audience. The crowd laughed and returned the kiss. She sang the part of Bettina, the mezzo-soprano, from the popular comic opera "La Mascotte" about a virginal maiden supposed to bring good luck to whoever possessed her. Lola followed with a bawdy ballad, teasing the audience with winks and pouting lips.

After the song, she danced again. At first, her movements remained slow as she swayed her neck and weaved her arms in the air with the grace of a ballerina. At the same time, her torso undulated in a suggestive manner. Her dance steps quickened. She danced steps from *le chahut* and ended in the jump-split. The audience cheered with enthusiasm.

Thrilled that the audience attendance grew with each performance, Lola knew it would soon be time to leave L'antre Du Diable.

Chapter 15

At Nini's place, the *demoiselles* sat together enjoying their usual late Sunday breakfast. Lola asked, "My friends, I long to enjoy Paris nightlife, but of course, I must be accompanied by a male companion for an evening out. Can anyone suggest a well-bred gentleman?"

Lola heard the scape of their chairs against the worn wooden floor, when, as a group, they rose and with dirty stares, they marched to the dormitory. Lola ran after them. "What is wrong? What did I say to upset you?"

They shouted in turn, "It is time for you to leave! It is bad enough you steal our place as a dancer of *le chuhut*, now you want to steal our customers, too! Go find somewhere else to live! We do not want here you! Get out!"

"Ladies, please, I am not trying to take anything from you. I will only accept invitations from men who agree to my terms. I have no interest in a romantic or sexual relationship and I will not accept money."

Some dancers laughed in her face, while others pranced around like aristocrats with their noses in the air.

Hortense could see the tide had turned against Lola. "Oh, Mademoiselle Goody Goody, you are too virtuous to live our lifestyle. You are so prim and proper. I bet you have never had a man!"

Lola blushed.

"So, it is true," Hortense snarled. "You are an innocent flower. With these men, you will not be one for very long!"

Two girls began imitating the way their customers treated them, feeling each other's bodies and pretending to kiss, making smooching sounds.

"But you do not understand," Lola protested. "I only want a *companion*. Someone willing to take me to the cabarets, but that is all! I have no desire for anything else!"

Raucous laughter ensued. Hortense shouted, "If you only want a companion, you should get a dog!"

This place is intolerable! I cannot bear it any longer! Tonight, I must find a gentleman to take me to Le Chat Noir. I will convince Monsieur Salis to hire me.

Lola had no appropriate dress to wear for her evening out so she designed one using scraps from the repairs she made to the dancers' clothes. It was of blue and yellow striped silk with blue satin double-puffed sleeves and a ribbon sash trim. Although simple, she took pride in its construction.

Before she entered Nini's Salon, Lola peeked into the room. She saw the grouchy face of the concierge, Madame Joseph, who greeted guests and took their outerwear.

Through hazy smoke from cigars and cigarettes, Lola could see the walls hung with paintings of women in various stages of undress. The customers were of every age, size and shape, dressed in evening wear with starched shirts and collars.

Mon Dieu! These are not like the boys I teased when I was young. They are wolves ready to pounce on their prey. If I am not careful, tonight I will be in danger!

Lola swallowed hard and hesitated to enter. The dancers cursed and pushed her out of their way as they rushed into the room.

Holding her head high, Lola glided into the room with a false air of confidence. Her heart pounded when all eyes turned to stare at her. Men raced towards her. Lola gasped when they swarmed her, each pushing to be the first to offer her an invitation for the evening. Overwhelmed and frightened by their intensity, she pushed her way through the throng.

When she emerged, she noticed an elegantly dressed young man standing apart from the crowd. He was tall, with thick black hair and mysterious dark eyes. He watched the crowd of clients with a raised eyebrow as if he thought their unbecoming behavior ludicrous.

Lola hastened to him.

He watched her approach. His crooked smile gave him a rather confident but mischievous look. She offered her hand. "My name is Lola Dupin. May I have the pleasure of knowing your name?"

"I am most delighted to meet you, Mademoiselle Dupin, I am Baron Phillipe Martin and I look forward to our evening together." He kissed her hand.

Lola beamed with delight. "A baron! *Splendide!* I assume you are a man of principle and know how to treat a lady of high moral character?"

Phillipe's eyes twinkled. "High moral character? Oh yes, I will treat you with the respect you deserve, Mademoiselle Dupin."

Lola believed Phillipe was a true gentleman and would treat her with deference. She regained her poise and responded, "*Excellent!* May we leave now? I wish to go to Le Chat Noir."

"*Le Chat Noir?* Really? Why go there when there are so many other places that offer more entertaining amusements?"

"It is important for me to go there. I need to meet with Monsieur Salis. I would like to perform there."

"Why? I understand you are quite popular at L'antre Du Diable, are you not?"

"I may be popular there but I would rather be popular in a cabaret with a better reputation."

Phillipe offered a roguish smile. "I see. All right then, to Le Chat Noir we will go." He offered his arm and brought her to his waiting coach.

After they were seated at a table in Le Chat Noir, Lola rose and said to Phillipe, "Please excuse me. I must see Monsieur Salis. I

79

will return soon." Before he could respond, Lola hurried off. She did not see the angry expression on Phillipe's face.

When she spotted Monsieur Salis, she sauntered over and tapped his shoulder. He turned and said, "How may I help you, *mademoiselle*?"

Lola offered a radiant smile. "Monsieur Salis, do you not remember me?"

Because of the loud music, Salis asked her to repeat what she said and brought his ear closer.

She spoke into his ear, "Do you not remember me?"

He looked at her face. With eyebrows raised, he exclaimed, "Lola? Are you Lola La Fontaine?"

She laughed and raised her voice over the music. "Yes and no. I was Lola La Fontaine but now I am Lola Dupin and I am working at L'antre Du Diable. I can dance *le chahut* and I also have my own routine."

Salis smiled and took her hand. "*Trés bon!* It is noisy here, come to my office where we can talk."

In his office, they sat together on his divan. "So, you now work at L'antre Du Diable?" he said. "I never thought you would work there and hoped you would take one look and run back home. I am amazed and happy it has worked out for you."

"Yes, thank you. But now I am ready to move on and I would like to work here."

"Here? At Le Chat Noir? No, that is impossible. I would like nothing better, but you remember they will close me down if you were found working here."

Downturned lips showed her disappointment. "But now I have a different name and even you did not recognize me."

"Yes, that is true. But it has been only a short time. Perhaps in a year, things will have died down and then you will be most welcome."

"Monsieur Salis, I have become quite popular at L'antre Du Diable. I think if you would allow me to perform for you, you would want to hire me. It is unlikely anyone I know would recognize me now. I am no longer that fifteen-year-old child. I have learned much about performing. At least let me show you what I can do."

"I am sorry but I cannot take that chance." Salis thought for a moment. Then his face brightened. "Ah, but I have an idea. Have you heard of the Bal du Moulin Rouge?"

Lola tilted her head in thought. "No, I cannot say that I have."

"It is new. My friends Monsieurs Zidler and Oller founded it. I think it would be a perfect match for you. Especially now that you can do *le chahut*, or as they call it, the 'can-can.' If you like, meet me here tomorrow afternoon at three and I will take you to meet them."

Lola's sapphire blue eyes sparkled. "Oh, Monsieur Salis, I cannot thank you enough! I am so thrilled!" She hugged Salis and thanked him again. When she returned to her seat she was flushed with excitement. She told Philippe she will work at a new cabaret called Bal du Moulin Rouge. Lola expected Phillipe would be happy for her. She didn't understand the scornful look in his eyes.

"You were gone for quite some time and you look flushed. What were you doing with Salis? Did you provide him with favors to get your new position?"

"Favors? What do you mean?"

"Do not act coy with me. I do not expect you to play the coquette with another man when I am spending my time and money on you!"

"What are you saying? You think I am—?" Lola narrowed her eyes. "You insult me *Monsieur*! I think it is time we leave."

"You are right—it is time!" Philippe threw money on the table and gripped Lola's arm. He marched out of Le Chat Noir dragging her behind him.

His driver opened the carriage door to help Lola inside. When she leaned forward Philippe pushed her from behind. She fell forward onto the seat. Philippe sprinted into the cab and pounced on top of her. She tried to scream, but he covered her mouth with one hand and pounded the top of the cab with the other. The driver took off.

Philippe's strong hands roamed her body, squeezing and prodding her, while his smarmy lips slavered her face. Lola squirmed. She tried to push him away, but he was too heavy. She screamed for help but he shouted back at her "Shut up you slut. I will make you sorry you were ever born!" He grabbed her chin in a vise-like grip and thrust his long tongue into her mouth. She gagged but bit his slimy tongue. Philippe punched her in her stomach, grasped her bodice and ripped it from her.

Winded from the blow, for a moment she ceased to fight him. When she dug her fingernails into the back of his hands, he slapped her face. She felt his hand slide under her skirts and move above her thigh. Lola ripped his face with her nails. Philippe yelled in pain. He sat upright, his hand to his face. In the faint light of the street lamps, Lola could see blood oozing from his wound. With his hair in disarray and his sneering wild-eyed expression, he looked like a madman. She sat upright and struggled to open the cab door but he caught her. By her hair he yanked her towards him. She slammed her knee into his groin. He grabbed his injury with both hands and howled like a beaten dog. Lola opened the carriage door and jumped from the moving cab.

Lola fell hard onto the street. Stunned, she lifted her head to see Philippe's cab continue onward. A man's fearful shouts and the terrifying sound of horse hooves against the cobblestones caught her by surprise. The whinnying of a panicked horse with reared hooves horrified her. When Lola watched the treacherous hooves about to crush her, she rolled out of the way. The hooves crashed, missing her head. The carriage driver worked hard to control and calm the horses. He alighted and rushed to Lola, who had made her way on to the sidewalk.

The driver helped her to sit upright. He asked in a shaky voice, "*Mademoiselle*, are you hurt? I am so sorry but you were lying in the gutter and the horse…he did not expect you. When I saw you, I tried to stop him, but he was so startled. Can I get you anything? Do you need a doctor?"

"No thank you. I am all right. I need a moment to catch my breath. Please, help me stand."

"I will take you home." The driver lifted her to her feet. "Where do you live?"

Chapter 16

Relieved that the other dancers were already asleep when she arrived back at Nini's place, Lola removed her clothes and jumped into bed. Burying her head in her pillow, she wept silent tears of anger and humiliation. *How could I have been so stupid? So naïve? What made me think honorable gentlemen would come to this place? I am an imbecile! This place is filled with prostitutes. Why would any man come here for anything else? Stupid! Stupid! Stupid!*

Lola had no sleep that night. She wished she could have been someone else. Someone with no feelings. Even to be a stone or a piece of wood would be welcome. Better to feel nothing than such excruciating anguish.

When the morning breakfast bell rang, Lola remained face down in her bed feigning sleep. She couldn't deal with the dancers' taunts and ignored their giggles but Hortense would not pass her without saying something nasty. "You must have had a rough night. Your dress is torn and dirty. So, *Mademoiselle* is a Goody Goody no more! I hope you had fun. You slut!" Hortense broke into a wicked cackle.

Drained, nauseated and disgusted, Lola dragged herself out of bed. She caught sight of the dress she threw off the night before. Her impulse was to burn it. To purge it from her memory. But she remembered her scheduled meeting with Salis at the Moulin Rouge this afternoon. This opportunity could be her escape from this horrible place.

Lola inspected the dress. It was torn at the bodice where Phillipe had ripped it free and soiled with mud from the street. The little money she earned at L'antre Du Diable was not enough for her to purchase a decent dress and she had nothing else suitable to wear, so she would just have to mend it. She spent her day repairing her dress, improving her routine and making sure her makeup covered her scrapes and bruises. Nothing would stop her. She will leave this place today!

Lola arrived at the appointed time and found Salis waiting for her. Salis enlightened her with the history of the Moulin Rouge. He told her the creators of the cabaret, Joseph Oller and his manager Charles Zidler, are wise businessmen who took a gamble in buying the old White Queen Dance Hall with its crumbling, peeling façade and seedy reputation. They rebuilt it into the Moulin Rouge, an elegant music hall to attract all economic classes and to appeal to the sensibilities of its upper-class clientele, who wished to 'slum' in a less than fashionable district. While the lower classes enjoyed many of the performers and spectacles like the comic clowns, Foottit and Chocolat, and Le Pétomane, the professional farter.

Salis explained that they offered festive champagne evenings where people danced and were entertained by amusing acts that changed often. There were the popular can-can dancers and many famous dancers like la Goulue and Jane Avril, also known as "the unruly girls."

Thrilled by the mystique of the Moulin Rouge, Lola could barely wait to arrive. Before she knew it, they stood at the foot of Butte Montmartre on La Place Blanche. Lola's face brightened to see the building's façade with a huge red windmill and a fabulous stone castle at the front, decorated with glittering electric lights,

Salis smiled at her and said, "I think you will like this place."

Lola felt like a child with a shiny new toy. The stylishness and sophistication of the ambiance dazzled her. The extravagant atmosphere had a huge dance floor, crystal chandeliers and mirrors throughout. He took her to the outdoor garden known as the 'Jardin de Paris'. Lola's mouth dropped open when she saw a giant fake elephant next to an outdoor stage. She tilted her head back to take in the mammoth structure. She heard braying and turned to Salis. "What is that sound?" Salis took her hand and brought her to the other side of the elephant where several donkeys were honking or munching on grass. Lola approached a donkey and stroked his nose. "What are the donkeys for?"

"Donkey rides have been provided as a special treat for the ladies' pleasure."

Lola beamed, "This place is amazing! A wonderland!"

"Come with me. There is more to see."

Lola followed Salis to the leg of the elephant. It contained a spiral staircase leading to a stage within the elephant's stomach. He told her that dancers perform sensual belly dances for a male-only audience.

"Monsieur Salis, I cannot thank you enough for bringing me here. The Moulin Rouge is a wonderful place! I would be so excited to work here!"

"Excellent! Let us meet Monsieur Zidler. He is in charge of hiring new acts." Salis brought her to the indoor stage. "Monsieur Zidler, this is the young lady I told you about."

Zidler was formally dressed. He had large, kindly eyes and furry mutton-chop sideburns. "It is a pleasure to meet you, Mademoiselle Dupin. Monsieur Salis has told me so much about you." To Salis, he said, "You are right, she is a beautiful young lady." To Lola, he said, "Monsieur Salis has extolled your talents and I am interested to see you perform. Would you like to show us your act?"

Lola's face glowed. "Oh yes, I would love to."

Her performance was the same as at L'antre Du Diable, but she added additional songs and several subtle, provocative dance moves. After the performance, she looked expectantly at Zidler and felt elated when he applauded with a flourish.

"Thank you, Mademoiselle Dupin. Welcome to our entertainment family. Come to my office tomorrow morning. I will introduce you to my staff manager who will help you prepare for your performance." He put his hand in his coat pocket and produced a piece of paper. "When Monsieur Salis recommends someone to me, I respect his opinion. Therefore, I prepared this contract in advance knowing that if he believes in you, so will I. If you would like to sign it, your employment will be official."

Lola scanned the contract and, thrilled with the salary she would earn, signed the contract.

"We are looking forward to having you at the Moulin Rouge. Congratulations and good day."

Lola gushed with appreciation. After Zidler left, she hugged Salis. "Did you hear him? He said I can work here! He even gave me a contract! Monsieur Salis, you are the most wonderful man in the world!"

Upon arriving at Nini's place, she was excited and out of breath when she found Nini. Although tempted to shout out her news with glee, she controlled herself.

Nini frowned. "What is going on? You look like you are being chased by a wild boar. Sit and catch your breath."

Lola sat and gave Nini a weak smile. "I want to tell you how much I appreciate all you have done for me. You took me in when there was no place else for me to go. You taught me how to do *le chahut* and gave me the opportunity to perform. I am grateful to you, but I am sorry to say I must leave now. I have been employed at the Moulin Rouge." Lola braced herself for Nini's reaction to the news.

Nini furrowed her brows and gave Lola a stern look. "Sorry! You say you are sorry! We both know you are not sorry. Perhaps you think I am upset that you are leaving? Not at all. I am surprised you have stayed here this long. Girls come and go all the time. That is the nature of things. Unfortunately, too many girls grow up on the streets. They are more than happy to come here where it is safe for them. I teach them how to dance and hope that will help them have a better life. No, I am not sorry you are leaving and I wish you a good life."

"But what about L'antre Du Diable? Will it cause Monsieur Moreau a problem?"

"You are popular and he will be sorry to see you go. But you are too talented to remain there and he knew you would only be there a short time. Do not be concerned."

Lola felt relieved. "Thank you, Nini. I have one more request. I want to find another place to live and I would like to move right away. Can you recommend a girl with whom I can share an apartment?"

Nini sucked on her cigarette and thought for a moment. "I do know of someone who wants to share a flat. But I am not sure it will be good for you to meet her. She is a sly one. You may want to find other arrangements."

"Please provide me with her information. I have no time to look for a place. I must find one right away."

"All right, if you insist. Her name is Sophie Décharde. She works here from time to time. I will contact her and have her meet you here later. But I must warn you, she is not to be trusted."

"I appreciate your concern, Nini, but I am sure everything will work out with Sophie."

Dance of the Restless Soul

Chapter 17

Lola was eager to meet Sophie and see her new living arrangements, but Nini's warning buzzed in her brain like an angry bee. *She's not to be trusted. Should I wait and find another arrangement? No! I cannot bear to stay at Nini's place one minute longer! If I suspect treachery, I will find another place.*

Sophie arrived at their meeting place and said cheerfully, "*Bonjour*, Lola, it is a pleasure to meet you. I am Sophie Décharde. I used to live at Nini's place, too, and I understand why you want to leave. The other dancers can be jealous and mean. Now that you are moving on, things will be better for you, *oui*? I am happy to have you see my flat. I think you will like it." She linked Lola's arm and said, "Let us go."

Lola envisioned an untrustworthy person to be a rough-talking, hardened, bitter woman. A woman who resembled Hortense in appearance and temperament. When she saw Sophie's ebullient smile and cheerful demeanor, she felt relieved.

Sophie's eyes and hair were soft brown, her makeup restrained and hair fashioned in the latest style. She dressed in a skirt and a shirt with a floppy bow and stick pin bar brooch. Sophie appeared to be only a few years older. Lola thought she seemed a positive, cheerful girl, a girl she might get along with. It would be nice to have a friend. Perhaps Nini was being too cautious.

When they arrived at Boulevard Haussmann, Lola was surprised to see she knew the area well. Throughout the centuries, the center of Paris had become overcrowded, dark, dangerous and unhealthy. In the middle of the nineteenth century, Napoleon III directed Georges-Eugene Haussmann to redesign the area. Haussmann called for the demolition of these medieval neighborhoods and had them replaced with wide avenues, parks and squares, and adjoining handsome apartment buildings that lined the boulevards.

Shops, restaurants or offices often occupied the ground floor of these buildings. The second, or *piano nobile* floor, was the most desirable with its balconies and the largest and best apartments. The blue mansard roof, angled at 45 degrees, had garret rooms and dormer windows.

Sophie directed Lola to one of the buildings. "This is it! Come, my flat is on the second floor. See what you think." When they reached the apartment door Sophie opened it, and with a grand flourish waved Lola in. She said, "Here is your Shangri-La!"

Lola smiled and followed Sophie. The apartment had tall windows allowing bright sunlight into the sizable living room. Sophie went out to the balcony. She beckoned Lola, "Come out and look!" The sights and sounds of Paris below thrilled Lola. The streets were buzzing with activity. Everyone seemed to have somewhere to go. Now she could be one of those pedestrians, shopping or eating at a café, making her own decisions with no one to answer to. *For the first time since I left home, I feel free.*

They continued through the apartment. The kitchen was small but functional. There were three bedrooms. Sophie walked past the first one explaining that was hers but gave Lola the choice of the remaining two. The first was small and bare, with only a bed. Despite the smell of musty wood emanating from the wardrobe, Lola chose the larger of the two bedrooms. She liked the sizeable bed and having both a wardrobe and a dresser with a mirror. The apartment was partially furnished, with a mixture of furniture styles from different periods. A few pieces were new, but most were old and shabby.

"It is too large for just me," Sophie explained. "I met an American several months ago. He told me he was here on business, but I think he was here for pleasure. He fell for me right away and set me up in this flat. He paid the rent for six months in advance, but something came up and he had to leave. I must pay rent soon or I will lose it. I am used to this place with its nice view and spaciousness, so I need help with the rent." Sophie shrugged her shoulders and turned up her palms. "Who knows when I will meet up with another rich American, eh? So, what do you think? It is fine, yes?"

She didn't care that the furniture was old. Lola liked the apartment. Now she would no longer have to put up with Nini's imposed discipline or the pettiness of the dancers. She could finally concentrate on her career. However, she was not sure if she should trust Sophie.

Lola liked Sophie despite Nini's warning. But she would not feel assured until she asked Sophie how much the rent would be, suspecting she might try to take advantage. Lola was pleased and found the price acceptable. "Yes," she said. "This will do."

"So, we share the rent, food and all the expenses, yes?"

"Yes, I agree."

"You will give me money for the first month now, yes?"

Lola reached into her purse and counted out the exact amount and handed it to Sophie who licked her fingers as she counted it once more.

"C'est magnifique! Let us celebrate with champagne." Sophie grinned as she popped the cork. She showed the bottle to Lola and said, "A farewell present from my American friend." She wiped two glasses with a not-so-clean rag and poured the bubbly amber liquid into them.

They sat together at a small round table covered with a wine and coffee-stained threadbare tablecloth. Sophie sat with legs crossed. She leaned her elbow on the table and rested her head on the heel of her hand. Her feline eyes anchored onto Lola's face and studied her. "So, Lola, tell me about yourself."

Lola hesitated. She had not discussed her past with anyone and was not sure how open she should be.

"Do not be shy," Sophie said. "I am sure there is nothing so bad or embarrassing that I have not heard a hundred times before."

Lola looked at the shabby tablecloth and thought about the last time she saw her father. She remembered his face convulsed with anger when he banished her to a convent. Each word made her father's angry face draw nearer. "There is not much I can say. *Papá*, he—" Lola cleared her throat to choke back her tears. "I angered my father when I refused to marry the man he chose for me. And when he found out that I wanted to be an entertainer, he disowned me and kicked me out of the house with nothing."

"That is a sad story." Sophie touched Lola's hand. "I can tell your *Papá* has caused you much pain. Men can be so foolish and cruel. But it is hardly the worst story I have heard. At least you know who your father is."

Lola was shaken. She never thought about what it would be like to not know who your parents were. Just above a whisper, she said, "I think you have a sad story too."

Sophie lit a cigarette and took a deep drag. The exhaled smoke caused her to squint. "You pity me. If you pity me, you must pity all the poor, unfortunate women of the world. My story is not so different from theirs. Nothing new under the sun. I was poor like all the others who lived around me in the dark, narrow, stinking streets and alleys of the Rue Saint-Antoine. I am the eldest of seven starving brothers and sisters—each of us with different fathers. My mother earned her money, what there was of it, on her back. When I was old enough, I did the same. I ran away with the first man who was willing to buy me a good dinner and a pair of shoes. Nothing new under the sun."

"*Mon Dieu!* I am sorry, Sophie. I cannot imagine what it must have been like for you."

Sophie took a long swallow of champagne and licked her lips. "The man, his name was Ramon, said he was a Gypsy from Spain. I did not believe him. I do not believe the stories of men. He said he was a dancer. That was true. He taught me how to dance. At first, I danced in the street for the coins they threw at my feet. Ramon collected the coins and bartered my other talents to the highest bidder. At fifteen, I began dancing in the clubs.

When my dancing improved, the clubs got better and so did the clients. Poor Ramon is gone now. There was an argument. Someone owed him money and refused to pay. Knives were drawn and Ramon was not fast enough. Suddenly Ramon was no more. Nothing new under the sun."

Hearing several loud knocks, Sophie looked towards the door.

Lola asked, "You are entertaining a friend?"

"Entertaining? Yes, I am a tremendous source of entertainment for my friend!" Sophie smirked.

"I do not wish to intrude."

"You are not intruding. Remember you live here now. You understand, I often have men callers here. Do not fear. These men are harmless. But if you are concerned, I will have a lock put on your bedroom door."

Lola thought hard before she answered. *Once again, I am naïve! How could I not realize she would see clients here! What kind of men come here? Are they dangerous? This is a bad idea. However, I love the apartment and I have no time to look for another place today. At least my bedroom door will have a lock. I will stay here for now and look for another place when I can.*

"Yes, please put a lock on my door." Lola frowned. "You say these men are harmless, but how can you know?"

"I can assure you they are. If you will answer the door, you will see the reason you will not be bothered."'

Puzzled, Lola followed Sophie's instructions. She opened the door to find a man standing in the doorway leaning jauntily against the doorframe. Under his peaked cap was a thick mane of black curly hair. He had a swarthy complexion, large seductive eyes, chiseled features and an earring in one ear. His skintight shirt exposed a hard, muscled body. Lola involuntarily sucked in a breath.

"*Bonjour, Mademoiselle,*" he said with an alluring smile.

Sophie drew the man into the room and put a possessive arm around his shoulder. Lola was not sure if the gesture indicated she was keeping him for herself or protecting Lola from him.

Sophie looked at him with a lighthearted smile, but her eyes sparkled with pride and passion. She introduced him. "This is Roccu Faucheur."

He gave Lola a broad, inviting smile, took her hand and kissed it. "Delighted to meet you. I am told you are called, Little Firecracker." His lusty scent oozed sensuality.

Sophie said, "He likes to be called Apash—wild—like the American Apache Indian, *non*? Quite something, is he not? Everyone knows the reputation of Apash. Trust me when I say no one will bother us. He is my lover and my pimp."

Lola withdrew her hand from his. Her eyes widened at such a blatant admission. She was not sure if Sophie said that to shock her or make sure she stayed away from her prize possession. She felt embarrassed and uncomfortable. "I should go to Nini's place and pick up my things." She darted for the door, and said over her shoulder, "A pleasure, *Monsieur* Apash. *Au revoir*, Sophie." She heard their laughter as she ran down the stairs.

Sophie closed the door and rested her back against it. She had a wicked smile.

Apash stepped close to Sophie. With their faces almost touching, he looked into her eyes and grinned. "What scheme is working inside that head of yours?"

Sophie beamed. "My friends at L'antre Du Diable tell me the little fool comes from a rich family. I will find out the name of her family, and when the time is right, we will find a way to take advantage of her. Until then she will be our best friend."

Apash pulled Sophie tight against his body. He whispered in her ear, "You are a wicked bitch!" He kissed her long and hard.

Sophie loved that her cleverness excited him.

Ren'e Fedyna

Chapter 18

It had been six months since Lola moved into Sophie's flat. She became accustomed to seeing male callers, who paid her little attention and had posed no threat. She enjoyed Sophie's companionship and felt the arrangement was working well.

With her living accommodations settled, she could concentrate on her performance skills. Working at the Moulin Rouge was a fantastic opportunity for Lola to watch and learn from the best and most popular performers. Several were known as the divine "unruly girls."

Louise Weber, better known as La Goulue, meaning glutton, so-named because of her voracious appetite for food and sexual pleasure. La Goulue danced on tables displaying a heart embroidered on her drawers. In a turbulent swirl of her underclothes, she lifted her leg and offered an erotic display of bare flesh between her garter and her petticoat. Lola learned La Goulue was once visited by His Royal Highness the Prince of Wales, the future King Edward VII. He came on a private visit to Paris and booked a table just to see her. Recognizing him, she lifted her leg in the air and called out, "Hey, Wales, the champagnes on you!"

Not the only popular performer, Jane Avril became known as Jeanne la Folle (Crazy Jane) because of her contorted dancing. Yvette Guilbert, a famous national fortuneteller who imitated Sarah Bernhardt, became famous for singing raunchy lyrics of tragedy, lost love, and the poverty from which she had come.

Lola's favorite dancer was Lois Fuller. She was known for her graceful, whirling movements in soft, floating silk fabrics under changing colored lights. When she pirouetted and spun amid a mass of gauzy veils, her ethereal, poetic-like dancing presented an image of a flower or a flame.

There was always fun and excitement at Moulin Rouge. One evening a nude Cleopatra surrounded by a procession of young naked women caused a scandal. Another incident occurred during performing the "Dream of Egypt," put on by the writer Colette and her girlfriend, Mathilde de Morny. Colette dressed as an Egyptian mummy. Mathilde dressed as a male archeologist. Mathilde unwrapped the mummy, and they finished the scene with an amorous kiss. Many audience members were so outraged they rushed the stage, forcing the performers to run and lock themselves in the box office until the police arrived.

I love performing at the Moulin Rouge surrounded by today's most famous entertainers. I have succeeded despite my father's disapproval and hindrances. I persevered beyond the petty jealousies of immature young girls and, although I have no close friends, I get along with the dancers here. I earn a living doing what I have always wanted to do. I am desired by gentlemen callers who flood my dressing room with flowers and beseech me to go out with them. Why then, am I so unhappy?

Close to tears, Lola sat in her dressing room holding her head in her fisted hands. Her heart ached for her father's love. He was not here to witness her success. She wanted him to be happy for her. She desperately craved his loving affection. It was hard for her to grasp that no one cared about her. Certainly not the *bouffons* who showed up at her dressing room door. To Lola, they did not differ from the customers at Nini's parlor.

Amid her melancholy, she heard a knock on the door. Expecting it was another admirer she shouted, "Go away. I am not seeing anyone now."

A voice responded, "Sorry, Mademoiselle Dupin, I am Francis, the stagehand. I have a message for you."

Lola jumped from her chair and pulled open the door. She knew better than to expect a note from her father, but she could not help hoping. Francis handed her the note. It was from Salis. She was disappointed but pleased to receive a note from him.

Dearest Lola,

I am happy to hear of your success at the Moulin Rouge. I finally have the chance to watch you perform this evening. Please do me the honor of allowing Francis to bring you to my table. I would like you to meet my friends.

Fondest regards,

Salis

Overjoyed, Lola kissed Francis on the cheek. "Wait just a moment!" She dabbed her eyes and checked her face. "Let us go to see my good friend, Monsieur Salis!" Several gentlemen stood when she approached the table. Lola hugged Salis and kissed him on each cheek. She gushed, "I am so happy to see you! Thank you for coming!"

"You are welcome. Let me introduce you to my friends." He said proudly, "Mademoiselle Lola Dupin, I would like you to meet the famous painter Monsieur Henri de Toulouse-Lautrec."

"Oh, Monsieur Toulouse-Lautrec, I have seen you here many times. I am honored to meet you. The performers often say how appreciative they are that your paintings have added to their fame."

Toulouse-Lautrec offered a warm smile, kissed her hand and said, "I am delighted to meet you as well. I enjoy your performances and perhaps one day you will pose for me."

Lola smiled radiantly. "That would be wonderful! I can be at your disposal whenever you wish."

Salis said, "I would also like you to meet Countess Miralda von Schloss and Monsieur Charles Sloan. Monsieur Sloan is a frequent attendee of the Moulin Rouge and Le Chat Noir."

Lola looked at Monsieur Sloan. Tall and lean with broad shoulders, he had wavy brown hair and captivating blue-gray eyes. Except for long sideburns and a thin mustache, his face was clean-shaven. His strong jaw featured a cleft chin. He looked dashing in his formal attire and had a smile that gave him the appearance of easy self-assurance. The name Adonis came to Lola's mind.

Sloan stared into Lola's eyes. He took her hand and kissed it. "*Enchanté*, Mademoiselle Dupin."

Lola felt a tinge of electricity as Sloan's lips brushed her hand. She found herself speechless for a moment. Then she uttered, "A pleasure, Monsieur Sloan."

His eyes twinkled. "My friends call me Charlie."

Lola heard the countess give a light cough. With difficulty, she pulled her eyes from Sloan to pay deference to the Countess. Her fabulous jewels, splendid clothing and well made-up face did not camouflage the wrinkles and dyed black hair. Lola said, "Countess von Schloss, I am happy to meet you."

Why would he bring an old woman to a place like this? I hope she does not have a heart attack from watching one of the more risqué entertainments!

"The Countess is a friend and my guest for the evening," Sloan said. "We look forward to seeing your performance."

When the Countess scowled at her, Lola, thought that would be a good time to take her leave. She said, "I am delighted to have met you all. However, if you will forgive me, I must leave to prepare for my show. I hope you will enjoy it."

Salis smiled and said, "Please return to us after your performance."

Lola looked at the Countess and saw the annoyance in her eyes. Lola offered a weak smile and nodded. She blew Salis a kiss and hurried off.

On her way backstage, she met Marie, one of the dancers. Lola pointed to the table she had just left and asked, "Do you know the man sitting at the table over there?"

Marie turned toward Salis' table. "Which man are you referring to? The short one, the redhead or Charlie Sloan?"

"Charlie Sloan."

"Oh yes, the American. I know him all right, and so do most of the women in Paris. Especially the old, rich ones. With his dazzling smile and smooth way of talking, he makes you feel like you are the most important woman in the world. *Mon Dieu!* What a good lover he is! Considerate, not like most men who are in a hurry to do their business and leave. The rich old crones are crazy for him. They give him money. He takes it and gambles it away. Do not get involved with that one. He leaves a trail of broken hearts wherever he goes. The only woman he will ever love is the goddess of Fortune!"

Lola was lost in thought for a moment. "Did you say he was a good lover?"

Disappointed to hear Sloan was a lothario, Lola decided to have nothing to do with him. However, during her performance, despite her best efforts, her eyes were drawn towards him and her hips moved with more sensuality than usual. It seemed her mind and body were detached. The more she told herself to ignore him, the more her body disobeyed. When their eyes met, she would quickly shift hers in another direction, but in an instant, they returned.

After her performance, Lola considered not returning to the table but didn't want to disappoint Salis. She changed her clothes and repaired her makeup.

Salis slid back a chair for Lola. "You were wonderful, my dear. Listen to the cheers from the audience. I think you have already become a famous entertainer."

Toulouse-Lautrec said, "Oh yes, I agree."

"They're so right! You were fabulous!" Sloan flashed an engaging smile. "I've seen you perform before, but tonight you were exceptional!"

Her heart fluttered. Her face felt hot. Her throat was dry, and she began to cough.

Salis filled her glass and said, "Here, have champagne. You must be thirsty after your exuberant performance."

She took a sip, but it went down wrong and she continued to cough. Sloan patted her on the back until she caught her breath. He offered her his handkerchief. Happy to accept it, she thanked him. It smelled of his cologne, light and masculine. Reluctantly she attempted to hand it back to him and was pleased when he told her to keep it.

Lola could see the countess' annoyance at Sloan's gesture. He whispered into the ear of the countess and she gave him a seductive smile. He stood and pulled back her chair. Together they walked onto the dance floor.

She watched Sloan wrap his arm around the expansive waist of the countess and hold her close. They danced elegantly together. Lola was unaware she was sniffing Sloan's handkerchief. She wondered, *Why do I feel so angry toward the countess? Damn! I cannot believe I am jealous of an old woman! I cannot let myself fall for him. It would be a terrible mistake!*

"Lola. Lola? Are you feeling all right?" Salis asked.

His voice brought her out of her reverie. "Monsieur Salis, please forgive me. I think I must be tired this evening." She focused on paying more attention to Salis and Toulouse-Lautrec. She chatted with them, but her eyes remained on Sloan and the countess.

She watched with envy when they returned from the dance floor. The couple laughed together and appeared to be having a wonderful time. Once seated, they conversed enthusiastically with Salis and Toulouse-Lautrec. Much to Lola's dismay, Sloan paid little attention to her for the rest of the evening.

That night Lola tried to sleep, but thoughts of Sloan kept her awake. She sniffed his handkerchief imagining it was she, rather than the countess who danced with him. Each time she forced herself to stop thinking of him, his face popped into her head. She hoped she would never see him again! She hoped he would be there tomorrow night!

At her performance the next evening, Lola looked out into the audience. She was both relieved and disappointed Sloan wasn't there. It was the same for the next several evenings. She knew it was best to avoid getting involved with him but feared she would never see him again.

Then one night he was there! Sloan sat at the table nearest the stage. She was delighted he was by himself and gave him a joyous smile. In her performance, she emphasized the movement of her hips and her breasts with the enthusiastic sensuality.

At the end of her performance, Lola rushed to her dressing room with the hope he would come to her room. She hurriedly changed and waited. The minutes passed. She had begun to lose hope when she heard a knock. *"Entrez,"* she said. Her pulse raced. Her body stirred. His smile mesmerized her. "Shall we dance?" he asked.

They walked together to the dance floor, where they waltzed to Charles K. Harris' "After the Ball." She tingled at the touch of his hand. When Sloan put his arm around her waist and looked deeply into her eyes, she thought she would melt. Her breath quickened when she felt his cheek next to hers.

They continued dancing until the musicians packed up their instruments. At the end of the final dance, Sloan smiled sadly. "It's time for you to go home."

"No, it is much too soon," Lola protested.

"I'm afraid we have no choice. The musicians are leaving."

With pleading eyes Lola whispered, "Take me home with you."

"I'm sorry, Lola. That's not a good idea. Let's get your wrap. It's time for you to go home."

They sat together in the carriage. She wished he would look into her eyes. Instead, he looked out the window. Her stomach fluttered. *Should I touch his hand? Should I move closer to him? Why is he paying no attention to me? Why did he insist on taking me home?* She struggled to think what to say but nothing came to her. Before she knew it, the ride ended, and they were outside the door of Sophie's apartment.

Sloan removed his hat. "Thank you. I had a wonderful time." He turned to walk away.

"No!" Lola blurted. "I—I want to be with you!" She leaned her face towards him. "Kiss me."

Sloan rested his hands on her shoulders. His eyes were soft and showed concern. He tilted his head and gave her a kind smile. "Lola, you're not only a beautiful young woman, but I feel there's a specialness about you. The way you dance gives the impression you're worldly-wise, yet there's an innocence about you, a refreshing naïveté. Lola, you're the most intriguing woman I've ever met, and it's taking all of my will power to leave you here tonight. However, you must understand, it's not in my nature to be with only one woman. You can't depend on me, and I don't want to hurt you."

"I do not care. I want to be with you tonight."

"Are you sure?"

"Yes! Yes, I am sure!"

Sloan hailed a cab, and they headed to his apartment. He asked, "I noticed we stopped outside the apartment of Sophie Déchard. Are you friends?"

Lola took in a quick breath. Her tone was sharper than she intended. "How do you know her?"

Sloan chuckled. "I'm not a customer of hers if that's your concern. Paris is a big city, but it's also a small town. I know many people here. We have acquaintances in common, that's all."

Casually he asked again, "So, how do you know Sophie?"

Lola felt relieved. "She needed someone to share her flat. I liked it. So far, it is working out well."

The carriage came to a stop. Sloan looked out the window and said, "Looks like we've arrived."

It surprised Lola that he was living at the Le Grand Hotel, one of the most exclusive hotels in Paris. It had been built in the Baron Haussmann style with its mansard roof and filled an entire triangular city block. The hotel had hosted royalty throughout its long history, including Tsar Nicholas and King Edward VII of England. Lola's former tutor mentioned that, in 1869, James Gordon Bennett, Jr., publisher of the Paris Herald, met with Henry Morton Stanley in the hotel's Imperial Suite to convince him to make his famous journey to Africa in search of David Livingstone.

Sloan helped Lola from the cab and brought her into the building. Inside his suite he asked, "Perhaps you'd like a drink?"

Her eyes flashed with desire. "No, that is not what I want!"

He removed his hat and coat and tossed them onto a chair. He stepped behind Lola and removed hers. She felt a gentle kiss on the nape of her neck that made her spine tingle. She turned, lifted her chin and put her mouth close to his. Their breaths mingled. When he wrapped her in his arms and kissed her tenderly, her world fell away. His lips were soft and warm. They tasted like the finest champagne. It was not enough. She knew he felt it too. Their lips crushed together hungrily. They kissed again and again, each kiss more fervid than the last. Lola's body yearned for more. She felt fiery, passionate and demanding. When his hand slid up the curve of her hip to knead her breast, she welcomed it and covered his hand, encouraging him.

He brought Lola into the bedroom and flicked on the lamplight. She fumbled with her clothes.

"Allow me." Sloan took her hands and whispered, "It will be better this way."

He was her teacher, and she was his ardent student. Lola dropped her hands and surrendered her will.

He unpinned her hair and undressed her slowly. He kissed and caressed her bare skin, lingering in places that would give her the most pleasure. Lola's body awakened to a craving that drove her mad. When the last piece of clothing fell away, he said, "My God, you're exquisite!"

Lola's face reddened from the flattery and the heat from her inner core. Sloan embraced her naked body. Her breasts brushed against the crispness of his shirt fabric. The heat of his rhythmic breath on her exposed skin heightened the intensity of her lust.

He began to undress. Lola helped him. Her fingers were urgent and clumsy. Finally, he stood before her, naked. She sensed he knew this was the first time she had seen a naked man.

Her eyes were wide with wonder. *Has Michelangelo's David stepped from his pedestal to be with me?* No, Sloan felt warm and alive. She could feel his heartbeat when she touched his chest. She could feel the warmth of his skin when she stroked his powerful arms, flat belly, strong legs and his manhood.

He brought her to the bed where they came together in a frenzied embrace. Her mouth was eager for the taste of him. She could feel his fingers squeezing and probing while his hands explored her body. Her undulating hips urged him on. His moist, velvet tongue tantalized her, lunging and darting, teasing her—driving her wild. A moan escaped her parted lips. She loved the feel of him. A tempest rose inside her when she felt him hard against her. She heard him whisper in her ear, "I think this may be your first time. You will feel a bit of pain."

"I do not care!" He was right about the pain, but it was nothing. The excitement of feeling him inside her was intense, almost unbearable. She gripped the bedcovers in her fists. Her body quivered with agonizing delight. Lola's half-closed eyes blazed with ecstasy. She felt him thrust faster and deeper. Her moans grew louder. Their bodies danced in a frenetic rhythm until they shouted simultaneously when their bodies exploded with spasms of pleasure.

She gasped. "*Mon Dieu!* Charlie, what have you done to me?"

"It was a pleasure, m'lady!" They both laughed.

They lay on the bed breathless, sweaty and exhausted. Lola felt satisfied and yet felt she could never get enough of Charlie Sloan.

Dance of the Restless Soul

Chapter 19

Lola stared at Sloan's perfect profile as he lay beside her. She thought, *Am I dreaming? Or have I been made love to by a Greek God?* Her hand caressed his face. "You *are* real," she purred.

"Real? Let me show you how real I am!" He put his hands under the covers and tickled her.

She shrieked and squirmed in joyous delight and tickled him in return. They burst into hysterics. "Stop, please, stop!" Lola pleaded. "My stomach hurts from laughing!"

"All right if you insist. But only if we have breakfast. I'm starving!"

"It is no wonder you are hungry, you have been working all night!" He gave a lighthearted laugh. She loved the sound of his laughter.

They enjoyed breakfast at Café de la Paix. Known for its luxurious Second Empire style décor, the furniture of had been made of ebony, pitch pine, tulipwood and walnut woods coated with black lacquer. The fittings were of gilt-bronze copper, pewter, ivory and mother-of-pearl inlay. The applied porcelain plaques, along with painting on wood and panels, evoked imagery of the Far East, Africa and Native Americans.

Lola and Sloan ate heartily. In between bites, she asked in English, "So, you are American. How is it you speak French so well?"

Sloan's eyebrows shot up in surprise. "I would much rather know how you speak English so well."

Lola smiled and lifted her chin to mock a haughty attitude. "It just so happens I know Spanish and German as well!"

"Well, *Mademoiselle* La De Da, how is it you're so worldly?"

"My father insisted I learn these languages. He said, 'Just in case you ever have an American, Spanish, or German lover, you will always know what he is saying about you.'" Lola smiled at her joke.

"So, how many lovers from these countries have you had?"

"Never mind. It is none of your business. Now, it is your turn. You tell me how you know French so well."

Sloan finished buttering his croissant. He licked a dab of wayward butter from his fingers. "I'm American, but I spent much of my life in France. My father owned a gambling casino in New Orleans. He met my mother when he was on a business trip here in Paris. They fell in love and she moved to New Orleans with him. Do you know of New Orleans?"

"I have heard of it, but I do not know much about it."

"It's an amazing city with lots of great music and Mardi Gras balls and parades. You can ride on a showboat that paddlewheels up and down the Mississippi River. Maybe one day I'll take you for a ride on one."

Lola's heart leaped with delight when she heard him talk of having a future together. "Go to America with you? That sounds so exciting!"

"But what about you? Tell me of your life."

Lola decided not to go into the details of her troubled life. Her memories were still painful. "No, I am interested in your life. So how is it you came to France?"

"My parents married, and soon after, I was born. My mother died when I was seven, so my father sent me to live with my Grand-mère in Clichy."

Lola gave him a sad smile. "I am sorry to hear your mother died when you were so young. It must have been hard for you."

"Yes, it was hard. My mother was a special woman. So is my *Grand-mère*. She's tough and takes no nonsense from me. She is also full of love and understanding."

"So, you were brought up in France?"

"That's true. Although I traveled to New Orleans during the summers and holidays to be with my father until I was old enough to go to college. I left college early to travel around

America. When my father passed away, he willed me our house and his casino. Unfortunately, he left me his debts as well. I had to sell everything to pay his creditors."

"It must have been terrible for you to have lost everything." Lola wanted to ask, *How is it that you're able to afford such an expensive suite if you have no money? And why do you not have a job instead of taking money from old ladies?* Instead, she asked, "Do you ever return to America?"

"Yes, I often return."

"I hope you will not be going back soon."

"I don't know." He dipped his finger in a pot of chocolate mousse and dabbed it on her nose. "I do know I would love to spend lots of time with you."

"Charlie!" Lola feigned annoyance. She wiped the mousse from her nose and chided, "Stop that! *Tu êtes un enfant terrible!*" They laughed together.

Sloan's expression became serious. "Lola, there's something I must tell you. About to take a bite of a chocolate bonbon, she lost her appetite and wiped her sweaty hands on her napkin. "What is it you need to tell me?"

"I want you to know you need not worry about becoming with child because—."

"With child! *Mon Dieu!*" She put her hands to her belly and shouted, then looked to see if anyone heard her outburst. *How stupid am I? How could I not think about that? I do not even know how to prevent it from happening! I feel like such an imbecile! Am I pregnant already?*

"Sweetheart, it's all right! I'm incapable. Relax. You look like you're about to faint!"

She put her hand to her chest and took a breath. "I feel so foolish."

He gave her an affectionate smile. "Are you all right? I didn't mean to upset you. I want you to know we can be together with no concern.

"Yes. I just feel a little ridiculous."

"There's no need for that. You could never be ridiculous."

Calmer now, Lola smiled, "Thank you for the news about your—you know what I mean." She yawned. "I need a bath and to get some sleep before tonight's performance."

"Before you go, there's something I want to ask. You seem to be happy living with Sophie, but have you met Apash?"

"Yes, I have met him. Why do you ask?"

"Be careful around him. I believe he may be a member of a gang of ruffians who follow unsuspecting victims in the streets late at night to rob and even kill them."

"Sophie advised me he that his reputation that makes people afraid of him. I rarely see him and when I do, he is always nice to me. Do you think Apash is capable of killing someone?"

"I don't know. I've only heard rumors and don't know what he's capable of. It may be best for you to find other living arrangements."

Is he suggesting that I move in with him? Should I ask? What if the answer is no? It would be awkward. What will I do if he asks me? I better wait and say nothing.

"Apash has never given me any reason to fear him. I think I will be all right, *non?*" Lola held her breath, *Will he ask me to move in with him?* When he didn't respond, she asked, "Will I see you tonight?"

"Yes, my sweet. I will be there!"

That evening Lola saw Sloan seated at what would become his regular table. He winked at her and she gave him a saucy smile. They spent that night together and every night thereafter. They dined at magnificent restaurants like Maxim's, one of the most fashionable restaurants in Paris. Maxim's had been known for its Art Nouveau style. The elegant interior décor exhibited graceful flowing shapes inspired by fauna reminiscent of butterflies, dragonflies, and birds, and flora like lilies, irises and poppies. The curvy shapes suggested sensual feminine charm.

They danced in fabulous cabarets and enjoyed entertainment at marvelous music halls and he even took her gambling at the most famous and stylish casinos in Paris.

Lola felt giddy with happiness. She had a fabulous career and an amorous lover who wanted to spend all his time with her. Everything was going so well—until the night he didn't appear at his regular table. After several weeks together, he had never once missed her performance. Was *he ill? Had he been injured?* Surely, he would've let her know if something happened unless he was too ill to do so.

During her performance, she could only think of Charlie. She imagined him lying on his bed feverish and near death. When Lola finished her routine, she hurried to her dressing room to change and find Charlie. When she entered, the largest bouquet Lola had ever seen sat on her dressing table. Attached was a note from Sloan. She ripped open the envelope. Her eyes tore past the words.

Dearest Lola,

I had to leave suddenly and I am not sure when I will return. Please try to forgive me. I will always have a place for you in my heart.

Fondest regards,
Charlie Sloan

Chapter 20

Lola read the note over and over, too stunned to process the words. Her pulse pounded in her ears. Slowly, the heavy fog of numbness began to lift. She preferred numbness to the pain she knew she was about to feel. *What have I done wrong? We were having so much fun. Why would he want to leave me? Please, let this be a bad dream.*

The evening's winter chill made Lola shiver. She pulled her cloak tighter while she waited for the carriage that would take her to her home. Yesterday her heart felt light as a balloon. Now it feels like a heavy stone, dragging her into the depths of despair.

Upon arriving, she saw Sophie holding the door open for a short, elderly customer who was leaving. Sophie patted his bald head. He proffered a toothless smile to Lola and left.

"*Bonsoir*, Lola."

Lola bit back her tears. She brushed past Sophie and marched towards her bedroom. Sophie followed and placed her hand on Lola's shoulder. "Why are you so upset?"

"I do not want to talk about it!" She continued towards her room.

Sophie stepped in front of her. "Come, Lola, sit and talk with me. I will make you tea. Keeping troubles inside is like swallowing poison. You will not feel better until you get it out of your system."

Lola looked at Sophie through tear-brimmed eyes. Her voice was small and taut. "He left me."

"Who left you?" Sophie thought a moment. "Charlie left you?"

Lola nodded and scrunched her face. She lost the battle to hold back her tears.

Sophie took her in her arms. Muffling her sobs, Lola's head nestled into Sophie's shoulder. After a few minutes, Lola pulled away and blurted, "Why? I cannot understand. He told me he loved being with me! Why did he leave me?"

She pulled out a kitchen chair. "Sit here," Sophie said and handed Lola a tea towel. "Wipe your face." She turned on the tea kettle. While she waited for the water to boil, Sophie sighed, shook her head and said in a whisper, "Nothing new under the sun." She poured them each a cup of tea and sat next to Lola.

"I am sorry to hear Charlie went away, but he is like that. He probably ran out of money and needed to get more."

Lola stopped crying. She wiped her face and exhaled a ragged breath. She felt a glimmer of hope. "Do you think he just went to get money and will return to me?"

Before she answered, Sophie took her teacup in both hands and took a sip, giving herself time to find the right words. "Charlie is unpredictable, but one thing is certain, he always runs out of money. He treats women as if they are banks that he can withdraw money from. He takes their money and uses it to indulge them like goddesses. But he also gambles with their money, and soon it is gone and so is he."

"But he took no money from me!"

"That is probably because he was using the money Countess Von Schloss had given him. It is likely she returned to Switzerland, and when he used up all she had given him, he left to find another bank."

"But he lives at the Le Grand Hotel! How can he afford to live there if he has no money of his own?"

"Poor Lola, you have much to learn." Sophie shook her head. "The countess owns that suite and lets him live there. She pays all his bills."

Lola remembered Marie had warned her about Charlie. She had not listened, and now she must live with this heartache. But if it were possible to go back in time, she would do it all over again. "Sophie, I hate that he is the type of man who takes money from women, but he means so much to me. What can I do?"

"I am sorry to say there is nothing you can do. Who knows where he is or whom he is with. Most likely, he will return to Paris. But when he does, you must know that sooner or later he will leave again."

Sophie's words slammed against her like a violent ocean wave. A fresh torrent of tears burst forth and Lola covered her swollen eyes with the towel. She cried until she could cry no more. When she lifted her head, she said in a voice thick with melancholy, "Thank you, Sophie. I will have to find a way to deal with this." Lola rose, kissed Sophie on the cheek and went to her room.

Lola struggled to put Charlie out of her thoughts. Yet, during each performance, her eyes scoured the audience with the hope he might be there. Her heart yearned for him. The fire she had felt for him still burned. It seemed every minute she envisioned his beautiful face and engaging smile, the warm comfort of his embrace, the sensual way he had touched her body and how he had felt inside her.

I can no longer bear to be alone. There must be someone else I can care about. Someone who will care about me. But who? I cannot tolerate those gentlemen callers with their wolfish smiles and their disingenuous acts of devotion. This is your fault Charlie. To hell with you! I will agree to be with the next decent person who asks me.

After her performance, she returned to her dressing room and awaited the usual knock on the door from her standard admirers. This time she hoped it would be someone new, someone handsome, charming and exciting. But, the first to come was Alfred Lefebvre. She had rebuffed him many times before, but he was never dissuaded. His girth strained the cut of his tailcoat. His small round eyes were swallowed by his oversized pulpy face and hidden behind a bulbous nose. Alfred's lusty smile was enough to turn her stomach. *No! Oh no! What was I thinking? This will not do!* She shooed Albert away.

Frustrated, she prepared to leave. When she heard an urgent rapping at the door, Lola thought, *Oh no, not another bouffon!* She shouted, "Go away!" The rapping continued. "Go away, I said!" The rapping became more insistent. Lola yanked the door open and was about to reprimand the perpetrator of the insufferable noise when she saw a tall, striking young man dressed in a soldier's uniform. Lola's anger eased as she looked up into his dazzling ice-blue eyes. She asked, "What is so urgent?"

"Excuse me, Mademoiselle Dupin, my name is Baron Freiherr Diedrich von Breckendorf. Please forgive my impudence, but it was imperative I see you."

Intrigued, she purred, "Why must you see me?"

"I have been on leave in Paris for four weeks and tomorrow I must return to my regiment in Germany. I have come here every night to watch your performance. You are the most beautiful woman I have ever seen. I will not be able to live with myself if I do not ask you to do me the honor of joining me for dinner this evening."

Lola was instantly attracted to him with his thick dark hair that accentuated a face carved with high cheekbones, an imperious nose and a chiseled jaw. The form-fitting, dark blue uniform emphasized the breadth of his firm chest and the gilt epaulets stressed the broadness of his shoulders. Everything about him was angular, with strong, sharp edges that embodied a soldier's bearing. So opposite from Charlie's appearance and easy-going manner. Lola thought the change might do her good.

She teased, "If you think I am so beautiful, why have you waited so long to ask me to dinner?"

"It is difficult for a German officer to admit, but rejection is not an easy thing to live with. If you should refuse me tonight, I will at least return with the knowledge that I was courageous enough to ask you."

Lola thought before she answered. *He is German. Papá hates Germany and how they stole Alsace and parts of Lorraine during the Franco-German war.* She looked at the strong face of Diedrich. *Why should I care who Papá hates!* With a vivacious smile, she offered him her hand. "I would not want you to feel rejected!"

Ren'e Fedyna

Chapter 21

Lola placed her forearm atop Diedrich's as they strolled to his table. When seated, he looked into her eyes and said, "I am pleased to have you join me, Mademoiselle Dupin."

"Please call me Lola."

"Well then, I must ask you to call me by my little-known nickname. But you must not laugh." He looked both ways as if about to tell a secret, and whispered, "My parents call me Deke. It is only to special people that I admit this name. So please do not tell any of my fellow soldiers, as they would make fun of me."

Lola's lips curved into a pleasant grin. She reassured him, "Have no fear Deke, your secret is safe with me!"

Diedrich asked, "Have you ever been to Germany?"

"When I was a girl, my father took me to Berlin. But I cannot remember much about it."

"I hope you will see Germany again. It is a beautiful country. The people are decisive, competent and eager to make Germany the greatest nation on earth. Everyone strives to do their best, whether a soldier or a waiter—." Diedrich eyed a passing waiter. "You there! Come here! We wish to place our order." When the oblivious waiter walked passed their table Diedrich shouted, "You! Come here now!"

The waiter approached Diedrich. Perturbed, the waiter said, "Pardon Monsieur, how may I help you?"

Diedrich's face was fierce. He snapped, "You must be attentive. I expect you to make sure we are well taken care of! Do you understand? Bring us champagne and plenty of it! I want our glasses full at all times." Diedrich placed the food order for both of them without asking Lola what she wished to order.

When the waiter left, Diedrich's face relaxed. He gave Lola a good-natured smile. "Forgive me, Lola. I am spoiled and cannot tolerate incompetence. I hope I did not make you uncomfortable."

Lola felt uncomfortable with his haughty attitude. However, she realized that as a military officer he would expect immediate obedience. She gave him a weak smile.

Diedrich lowered his eyebrows and focused on Lola's face. "I cannot help being curious. You appear to be an intelligent and sophisticated woman. Why do you work in a place like this?"

She gave him a sharp look. "And what is wrong with this place?"

"You appear to be from an aristocratic family. You must have many admirers of a similar class. I expect your admirers would have fought to be the first to swoop you up and make you their bride."

Annoyed to hear once again what was expected of her by society, she stated, "I have no interest in these so-called admirers. My interest was to become a performer. It was difficult to go against my father's wishes, but I achieved my goal."

A broad smiled appeared on Diedrich's face. "Ahh! I admire a woman with spirit! Come, let us toast to your success!"

During dinner, Lola was a jumble of mixed emotions. She enjoyed their conversation and Diedrich treated her with the utmost respect, but she sensed a cold rigidity about him. She wished it was Charlie she was sitting with. Determined to put Charlie out of her mind, she compelled herself to have a good time with Diedrich.

After consuming a great deal of champagne, Lola felt more relaxed. Diedrich surprised her with his sense of humor and she found herself laughing often. After dinner, they danced. She enjoyed how he held her against him.

During their dance, Diedrich whispered in her ear, "*Schätzchen*, would you like to join me in Hell?"

Lola pulled back from him and blurted, "What! What did you ask me?"

Diedrich laughed. "Oh, *schätzchen*, have you never heard of the place? It is a cabaret. A most unusual cabaret not far from here. He pulled her close and said, "I think you are a daring woman. You would enjoy something different, would you not?"

Although it was not far from the Moulin Rouge, Lola never heard of the cabaret called Hell. Feeling tipsy and carefree, she thought trying something different would be fun. "If you are you challenging me to join you in Hell, I accept!"

Diedrich smiled with gusto and said, "Excellent! Let us be on our way."

It was a pleasant winter evening. They walked arm in arm along the busy streets enjoying the many textures of Paris. The dazzling lights and aromas from busy cafes; street musicians showing their skills; hawkers exhibiting their wares; and the bustling crowds in a hurry to arrive to their next destination.

They walked past a few shops and cabarets until Diedrich stopped in front of the Hell Cabaret. He announced, "Here we are. What do you think?"

Lola caught her breath when she saw the cabaret. Projecting from its façade was a gruesome display of stone monsters above an enormous hideous face. Crimson lights blazed from its wild, bulging eyes. The large nose appeared swollen. The huge fanged mouth was the passage into the cabaret. Lola gaped at this macabre display in disbelief. She asked, "This is where you want to take me?"

He laughed and said, "You accepted the challenge. If you are too frightened, we do not have to go. It can be scary and I would not want you to have nightmares."

"A promise is a promise, so let us go in." She swallowed hard and steeled herself for her passage into the unknown.

She hugged Diedrich's arm as they passed through the large, ugly mouth into the fierce red glow of Hell. The walls appeared to gleam with flaming coals. A little red imp guarded the throat of the monster and made a great show of stirring the fires. The imp opened a heavy metal door for their passage and wailed,

"Ah! Still, they come! Oh, how they will roast! Enter and be damned, the Evil One awaits you!"

A suspended cauldron hung above what looked much like a genuine fire. Within it was half a dozen devilish musicians, male and female, playing a selection from 'Faust' on stringed instruments. Imps with red-hot irons prodded those musicians who lagged in their performance. Crevices in the walls displayed caverns lit up by smoldering fires and vapors emitting sulfurous volcanic odors. Thunder rolled through the caverns. Lola jumped and laughed when surprised by flames that burst from clefts in the rocks. Red imps were everywhere, darting about noiselessly, carrying beverages for the thirsty lost souls, stirring the fires or turning somersaults. Everywhere she saw a high blur of motion.

They were directed to one of the many red tables sitting against the fiery walls. An imp came to take their order of two cognacs. The imp shrieked, "That will be two brimstone intensifiers!" When he returned with their order he said, "This will season your intestines, and render them invulnerable to the tortures of the melted iron that will soon be poured down your throats." The glasses glowed with a phosphorescent light.

Splendid in his imperial red robe and bedecked with blazing jewels, Satan strode into the cavern. With a grand flourish, he brandished a sword from which fire flashed. His black mustache was waxed into sharp points and turned upward above lips. He paraded through the audience selecting patrons at random to bestow upon them a withering stare and laughed maniacally when they cowered in fear.

Lola lowered her eyes in hopes he would pay her no attention. To her dismay, he stopped in front of her. The devil made a mocking bow. His evil eyes locked onto hers. His lips spread into a mischievous grin. He pointed his sword at her and in a booming voice he taunted, "Ah, you! Why do you tremble so? Is it that you fear the consequences for all the men you have sent hither to damnation with those beautiful eyes and those tempting lips?" He burst into a shrieking, malevolent laugh that unnerved Lola. It rattled through the cavern with a startling effect. Lola shivered and snuggled closer to Diedrich. As the night continued with similar spine-tingling entertainment, they fortified themselves with several more cognacs.

Ren'e Fedyna

Chapter 22

The next morning Lola rubbed her blurry eyes. Her tongue felt like a woolen overcoat and her head felt as if her brain had been replaced with an incessantly pounding drum.

What place is this? She rose onto her elbows to get a better view of the room. *How did I get here? And damn it, why am I naked?*

The small and sparsely furnished room contained an inexpensive dresser, a desk, and the lumpy bed on which she lay. Except for two cheap framed imitations of works by Eugène Delacroix, the drab white walls showed no adornment. A pair of thin shabby drapes covered the only window. The space between the drapes allowed a view of the shuttered brick building next door. Lola heard the percussion of rain beating against the window. The drumming, out of sequence with the throbbing in her head, made her headache worse. She groaned, closed her eyes and eased her head back onto the pillow. To block the daylight, she covered her eyes with her forearm and tried to remember how she got there, but her mind was too muddled.

Desperate for a drink of water, Lola saw a hand towel atop the dresser alongside a pitcher and two glasses nestled inside a washbasin. She forced herself to stand, but it made her dizzy so she leaned against the wall for support. Holding her hands to her queasy stomach, she noticed her clothes lay strewn along the floor. *Someone must have brought me here, but who? And why? Is it because I am sick?* Bewildered, she put her questions aside. Drinking a glass of water was all that mattered. On unsteady legs, she made her way to the dresser.

After quenching her thirst, she washed her face and looked in the mirror. Her gray complexion and wildly mussed hair frightened her. She looked like she had come back from the dead and felt like it.

She needed rest. When Lola turned towards the bed, she noticed sitting on the desk was an envelope leaning against a candlestick. She couldn't make out the writing and lumbered to the desk. The envelope was addressed to *Schätzchen.*

Lola tried to remember the significance of the word, but the pounding in her head intensified. She looked inside and read the note written on hotel stationery.

Schätzchen my darling,
I told you yesterday that I must return to my regiment and leave for Germany early this morning. But I want you to know you gave me the best night of my life! Your beautiful face will be etched into my mind forever.
With affection,
Deke

The fog began to lift. *Deke, yes! I remember dining and dancing with him, and that horrible Hell cabaret. He must have brought me here after we left the cabaret. Oh yes, all of that alcohol I drank! No wonder I feel terrible.*

Lola looked down at her naked body and realized she hurt in places that had nothing to do with drinking too much. Her breasts and groin were sore, much more so than she ever felt when with Charlie. She also had scratches and bruises.

I remember laughing and kissing Deke as we made our way to the room. And how we tore away clothes to have sex. She rubbed her sore arms. *I enjoyed myself until he got rough. It was all about his needs. There was no pleasure for me. That scoundrel!* She tore the letter to shreds and tossed it into the wastebasket.

Lola dressed and left returned home. She locked her bedroom door and went to bed fully clothed. Grateful she wasn't scheduled to perform that evening and fell into a deep sleep.

The following day Lola went back to work at The Moulin Rouge. *Why do the men in her life—Papá, Charlie and now Diedrich—disappoint me? Maybe someday I will meet a man who is right for me. But for the time being, I am through with men!*

Over the next several weeks, Lola began to feel out of sorts. She found herself to be edgy and crying for no apparent reason. She felt bloated and her costumes were tight. When she began to retch every morning, she thought she must be seriously ill. She refused to allow herself to consider any other cause for her ailments. When she did not remember the last time she had her monthly, she broke into a cold sweat. *Could I be...No! No! Please do not let it be so.* In her heart, she knew she had to face the truth.

Diedrich, you bastard! You made me pregnant!

Chapter 23

Lola paced in her room. Soon after she had moved into Sophie's flat, she spent much time and money to make her room cheerful and welcoming. New paint, curtains, duvet and furniture. Now these embellishments meant nothing to her.

She couldn't sleep or concentrate on anything but the fact that she was pregnant. *What shall I do? Do I give up my career to raise a child? I do not want to give up my career. To give up my career means I will have no money to support the child. I have spent lavishly on myself, purchasing anything I want without thought of the cost. I have some savings from working at the Moulin Rouge, but how long will that last once I have another mouth to feed? What will happen when my belly grows too big? I will have to give up my position. What happens if Monsieur Zidler refuses to take me back when I am ready to return?*

What of the child? I know nothing about rearing children. Should I hire a nursemaid to take care of the baby while I work? No! A child must have a mother. Mamá died when I was born. I have been so sad having no Mamá in my life. I do not want my baby to be as sad as I have been!

With little sleep and no appetite, Lola began to lose weight. Until now, her complexion had glowed with a creamy, soft, pink tinge that radiated good health. She had been proud of her large, expressive, sapphire blue eyes and remembered how her chaperone Teresa loved to brush her thick, lustrous, black hair. Men always admired her full-figured body.

Now Lola was reluctant to look in a mirror. Her skin was pallid. Hollow cheeks made her cheekbones more prominent, giving her a ghostlike appearance. Her glassy eyes were sunken above dark shadows and her hair was dull.

I am driving myself mad. I must decide what is best for the baby and me!

Her thoughts turned to her father. *I love him and miss him so. Maybe time has softened him. It would be wonderful if he loved this baby and forgave me. We could all live together as a happy family. I could continue working and Papá would help me raise the little one. Yes! I must write him a letter now!*

She sat at her dressing table and began to write:

Dearest Papá,
I hope this letter finds you in the best of health. Since I have seen you last my life has changed considerably. I hope you can forgive me for disobeying you and we can make amends. It is most important now because you will soon become a Grand-père.

Lola stopped writing. She threw down her pen with force. *What am I doing?* She grabbed the letter, tore it to shreds and threw it in the wastebasket.

He will never agree to see me. He is too proud and too stubborn and will never forgive me. No! I will not give him the opportunity to refuse me. Instead, I will confront him. I want to see his face when I tell him he will be a grand-père.
Lola wasn't looking forward to the confrontation with her father. No matter how hard she tried to imagine him happy to see her, she knew he wouldn't be. She thought of many reasons to delay, but her belly was growing and she could put it off no longer.

Pleased the heavy rains of yesterday had passed, she hoped today's bright blue sky would be a good omen. She closed her eyes and lifted her face to the warmth of the sun. She took a deep breath, then headed on her way.

For the entire carriage ride to her father's house, Lola tried to think good thoughts. She imagined her *Papá* playing with her child, the way he had often played with her. She remembered how he delighted her when he sang lullabies and surprised her with little treats. But as the carriage drew near to the house her thoughts darkened. Lola envisioned her father's angry face and put her hand to her belly as if to protect her baby.

Now that stood at her father's front door Lola's throat tightened. She stared at the doorknocker and felt faint. Steeling herself, she threw back her shoulders and with sweaty fingers, grabbed the doorknocker. Her nerves caused her to use more force than she intended. It took all her willpower to resist the urge to run away. But she clung to the hope he would welcome her and the little soul growing in her belly. No matter how great her humiliation, she would go through with this.

Joseph, the footman who had been with her family for years, opened the door. It surprised Lola to see how much he had changed since she saw him last. He once stood proudly erect, but now his shoulders curled forward. The bags under his eyes were more pronounced and his jowls sagged, making him look like a tired, old hound dog.

His jaw dropped open. He gasped, "*Mademoiselle* Lola!"

Lola gave him a weak smile. "*Bonjou*r Joseph, it is good to see you again. Is *Papá* at home?"

"*Oui*, Mademoiselle Lola. But we have strict orders—."

"Just tell him I am here!"

"But—."

"Never mind! Lola pushed past Joseph and headed towards Émile's study. Joseph hurried behind on his old legs.

Her father sat behind his desk with his head down, buried in paperwork. He must have heard their footsteps because he lifted his head and looked at them. She was so happy to see his face, the face she had missed so much. Lola wanted to embrace him, to squeeze him tight, to push out all the poison and replace it with her overflowing love.

She stepped closer to the open door but stopped before entering. Émile looked at Lola and his eyebrows raised in surprise but he said nothing.

Joseph broke the silence. He wheezed, "I am sorry *Monsieur*, I told her you would not see her." Then he scurried off.

Émile glowered at Lola through dark, dangerous eyes. A cold, thick silence hung in the air like an impending avalanche.

Lola stepped inside his study. "Oh *Papá*, how good it is to see you!"

He snarled, "You are not welcome here!"

Lola used her little girl voice. "But *Papá*, I have missed you so much, did you not miss me?"

Émile's voice rose. "You are not welcome here.

Lola forced herself to hold back her tears. "But, *Papá*, I have news for you—important news."

"I have no interest in anything you want to tell me," he shouted.

Lola approached him. She knew she wouldn't have much time. Her lips moved but no words came out. She licked her lips and uttered, "My dearest *Papá*, you will soon be a *Grand-pére*."

His face reddened, a vein bulged from his forehead. For the first time in her life, he raised his hand to slap her face. She recoiled in horror when she saw his hand rise against her. But his hand stopped in midair and then he lowered it. Even though he didn't slap her, her face stung as if he had.

Émile shook his head and lowered his voice, but the contempt in his words was worse than his shouts. "You are a disgrace to me. I gave you everything, my love and my trust, and this is what I get in return? You are a slut, a whore who sells her body for a few cheap baubles. I disown you. I want nothing to do with you or your bastard child!"

"*Papá*, you are wrong about me. I am not a whore! How can you say that about me? I am your daughter, your flesh and blood. Do you not love me at all?"

His voice softened. "I loved my dear, sweet, unblemished Lola." His expression hardened. "I cannot love the ugly tramp you have become. Leave my house. Never return or contact me again. If you do, I will have the police remove you."

Lola pleaded, "But *Papá*—"

His face was as cold as the words he spat, "I have no daughter. Lola is dead."

"How can you say that?"

"Get out! Get out now!" he screamed.

Her tears blinded Lola as she ran from the house. She ran down street after street, bumping into people in her path, ignoring their curious stares. Horses whinnied in fright when she surprised their carriage drivers and forced them to avoid running her down. She ran until she was overcome with nausea and stopped to vomit. No matter how hard she ran, she couldn't run away from her father's angry face or those ghastly words, "Lola is dead!"

Exhausted and breathless, Lola stopped and sat on a park bench in the Bois de Boulogne. A vast expanse of fountains, flowers, lush lawns and shaded glens surrounded her. There was a fountain with a huge basin where children sailed toy wooden sailboats, an ancient carousel and a marionette theater. But she had no interest in her magnificent surroundings. In despair, she covered her face with her hands and tried to shut down her brain. She didn't want to think or remember, only to feel nothing.

Suddenly, sweet words filled the air. "Why are you crying?"

Lola dropped her hands to see a little girl watching her. She had large, blue-green eyes and long, beautiful, coppery ringlets. Her mouth was covered with chocolate candy.

She wiped her tears and smiled at the child.

"Why are you so sad?" She asked.

"I am sad because someone hurt my feelings."

"Oh, I understand. My brother hurts my feelings all the time. He is just a big buffoon. I bet whoever hurt your feelings is a big buffoon too!"

Lola offered a brief smile. "Yes, you are right. He is just a big buffoon!"

The little girl grinned, exposing the space where two front teeth were missing and asked, "What is your name?

"My name is Lola. What is your name?"

A nursemaid rushed up to the little girl. "I have been looking all over for you." She took the little girl's hand and pulled her along, "Never run from me again!"

As she was being led away, she turned her head. Her darling face beamed. She said, "My name is Rita!"

Lola said as she watched Rita leave, "I am going to have a baby and I hope she is just like you!"

She remained in the park watching mothers hold their babies as they snuggled and kissed them. Watching the children play, she listened to their laughter. When a child fell down and began to cry, Lola picked her up. She embraced the child and sang her a lullaby. When the little girl smiled, Lola's heart melted. The child's mother came to fetch her. Lola kissed the little girl on the cheek and reluctantly returned the little girl to her mother. A strong maternal instinct awoke from deep inside Lola. She realized having a baby would fill a void she didn't even know she had.

Chapter 24

Lola returned to her apartment with her mind buzzing. Having a baby was no longer a burden, but a joyous event. *How wonderful it would be to have a baby to love me, and for me to love in return.* Still, she had no solution for how to bring up her child as a mother alone.

Lola saw Sophie wearing her long, brown houndstooth cape unloading groceries onto the kitchen table. She greeted Lola with a smile that kept the dangling cigarette between her bright red painted lips. On the table lay a baguette, cheeses, olives, salami and pâté. The food aromas wafted from the table, making Lola's stomach churn. She rushed from the room. A short time later, she returned to the kitchen.

She gave Sophie a gloomy smile and wiped her sweaty brow with a handkerchief. Her body felt heavy and clammy. She slumped into a kitchen chair and shut her eyes. She heard Sophie's voice and opened her eyes to see her standing before her with arms crossed against her chest like a schoolteacher scrutinizing a disobedient student.

Sophie asked, "So, tell me, my little lamb, how long have you been pregnant?"

Lola's eyes widened. "How do you know?"

"Ha!" Sophie laughed. "I have seen many pregnant women in my day and I can always tell. You have a pregnant face."

"A pregnant face! What does that mean?"

"It means either you have a dreadful disease or you are pregnant! Which is it?"

Lola sighed. "Yes, I am pregnant."

"I knew it!" Sophie shook her head. "And where is the father? Busy making wedding arrangements?"

Lola stared at her hands.

Sophie continued. "See! I told you, there is nothing new under the sun. It happens every day. For love or money, it does not matter. Most of us will get pregnant without the so-called glory of marriage. Why do you think there are so many squealing orphan brats around, eh? And why have I heard nothing from you about this man? Is he married? He refused to marry you, *oui?* Have you told him? You told him, did you not? Please do not say you are in love with him."

Lola felt overwhelmed by her questions. She went to the sink where she patted her face with a damp towel. Then she turned to Sophie, "No, I do not love him. I do not even like him! I certainly do not want to be married to him. Oh, how I hate men! I do not want to marry anyone!"

"Well then if that is the case, I know someone who can take care of your…eh…condition. But it will cost a lot of money."

"What do you mean?" Lola thought for a moment. "No! I cannot! I will not do that! I have a little life growing inside me. I want to have the baby." Her voice softened. "I must find a way to deal with it. I want to be a full-time mother, but I also want to continue my career. I have no idea what to do."

Sophie raised an eyebrow. "Are you sure you want to keep the baby? Perhaps someone else would want your baby, someone rich."

"Give my baby away? No, never!"

"*Give* the baby away?" Sophie's jaw dropped. "Oh no! There are those who will buy—"

An angry heat rose within Lola as she glowered at Sophie.

Sophie cleared her throat. "So, you will have someone watch the baby while you are working?"

Lola ran her fingers through her hair. "I do not know. I am so confused."

"Have you told the father yet? Is he willing to help you?"

"He does not know. Nevertheless, I would not accept his help. There is something mean about him. I think he would not be a good father. Besides, he is a German soldier and has already returned to Germany. There is no use thinking about him."

Sophie tapped her lips with her forefinger. "Is there a way you can contact him? Is he an officer? I know people. If he is a high-ranking officer, we may be able to find out more about him. And if he is married, we may be able to convince him to offer you and the poor little bastard his help."

Lola shouted, "Do not call my baby that name! That is what *Papá* called the baby."

"*Papá?* You went to see your father?" Sophie waggled her finger at Lola, "That was a mistake. Since he threw you out, it is unlikely he would support a fatherless child."

"Yes, it was a mistake. I do not understand him. He used to love me so much!"

"Love, hah!" Sophie laughed. "Love is such an easy word to say but it can be the cruelest word in the world. We women give up everything when a man, be it lover or father, tells us they love us. We would give our money, our life and even our soul to that man. And what do they give us? Heartache and pain. They twist our hearts into knots and squeeze until there is no blood left. If your *Papá* loved you, he would love you no matter what you do and only want the best for you."

Tears flooded Lola's eyes.

Sophie continued in a tender tone, "Now, *ma petite*, it is not the end of the world. Do you have anyone who can help you? Anyone who will give you money?"

Lola held her face and sobbed.

"Stop blubbering foolish girl! You must think. There must be someone."

Lola's took a ragged breath. "No one I know would want anything to do with me, I am *déclassé*."

Sophie refused to give up. "What did your father say before he threw you out?"

Lola's stomach swam with acid. "He told me I was dead to him. He said if I ever returned, he would call the police!" Her voice became shrill. "How could he do this to me? Once he was my beloved *Papá* who read me fairy tales and kissed my forehead each night before I went to bed. Once he gave me everything. We rode our horses together in the Bois, and we danced at summer balls." She wiped her eyes and blew her nose. Her voice hardened. "But he only cares about his reputation. He cares more about his position than he cares for me. Just because I would not marry the imbecile, he pledged me to, I am no longer good enough for him."

Sophie's eyes lit up. "Position? Who is your father? What does he do? I always meant to ask you your real name. Lola Dupin is a stage name, is it not?"

"I cannot tell you, *Papá* does not want me to say."

"Your *Papá!* What do you care what your *Papá* says? Did you not just say your *Papá* does not love you? Why are you protecting him? He cares nothing for you or your little bas— baby."

Lola began to cry again.

"Now Lola, stop crying, you must think of the little one. We will need money to bring him up. If your *Papá* can give you money—"

"No! I want nothing from him! I will bring the baby up myself. I will find a way!"

Sophie's patted Lola's hand. "All right my sweet, you need your rest. Go to bed now. I will help you through this. I promise we will work together to solve your problem."

Lola kissed Sophie's cheek. "Thank you. It is good to have you for a friend."

Sophie's eyes sparkled. She said, "It is good to have you for a friend too, *ma chérie.*"

Chapter 25

Sophie felt relieved when she saw Lola close the door behind her as she left to perform at the Moulin Rouge. To be sure Lola was well on her way, Sophie stepped onto the balcony and watched the busy traffic below until she saw Lola enter a Hansom cab.

She smiled as she reached into her *décolleté* to remove her key to Lola's bedroom. Although she had seen this room from time to time as it was being re-decorated to Lola's standards, she had never seen it completed. *This girl has taste!*

Lola's cheerful room had walls painted buttercup yellow with tassel-trimmed curtains and tiebacks in a muted gray-and-yellow paisley print, a matching luxurious duvet, an elegant dressing table, and full-length mirror.

Sophie jumped onto Lola's comfortable bed. She lay there thinking, *I would have to work six months on my back to afford the changes she made to this room. That stupid little bitch! She has everything, but all she does is whine. Oh, Charlie! Oh, my baby! Oh, poor me! She would rather share a flat with a prostitute than live in rich surroundings with her father. What is wrong with her?*

She searched the room beginning with Lola's dressing table. On the dresser top lay various ornate sterling silver Repoussé Cupid combs and brushes. Perfume bottles of various shapes and sizes were lined up like pretty little soldiers. Sophie sniffed each one. She dabbed her neck and wrists and between her breasts with the ones she liked. She made ugly faces at the ones she didn't. How delicious it felt!

She opened a large trunk-shaped jewelry box of doré metallic silver and gold, with intricate work on all four sides. The handle was attached to a bombé-shaped lid. Within the box were necklaces, bracelets, hair combs, hatpins and rings made with fine gemstones. Sophie tried them on. *So, this is what she has been doing with her money! What a fool!* She let out a chuckle. *She is lucky she does not live with dishonest people or this would all be gone.* She examined each drawer. Nothing there but expensive makeup.

Sophie went to the chest of drawers and opened each drawer. She ran her fingers over the undergarments made of fabulous silks and linens. It made her mouth water. *Mon Dieu! If I had underwear like this, I would never take it off—unless I was working.*

From there Sophie opened the doors of the Stephanoise Louis XV armoire made of blond walnut from the city of Saint Etienne in the French Loire Region. The paneled doors had S-shaped moldings. The frieze had a simple carving of a sunflower in its center and the cornice had a double *chapeau de gendarme.* Sophie gasped at the magnificence of Lola's wardrobe. There were dresses, hats, shoes and scarves fashioned by famous designers such as Worth, Lanvin and others. She marveled at the lace, silk ribbons and brocades, velvets, chiffon flowers, feathers, braids, beadwork and embroidery before her. One gown was by the famous designer Doucet, known as the King of Haute Couture, with its rare *gros point* de Venise lace.

How many times had she drooled over fashions like these displayed in store windows? She had been envious seeing Lola wear these dresses. Now they shouted to her: "Try me on, you will be so beautiful!" Sophie pulled out each dress and held it against her as she looked into the full-length mirror.

She tried on the ones she thought beautiful. The dresses piled up on the bed and soon the armoire was bare of clothes. Sophie sighed. *Get back to work!* On the upper shelf sat a carpetbag. She brought it down and found several personal papers. Sophie perused each one until she found what she was looking for. She discovered a tear-stained letter, dated two years prior, from Lola's father, written on official government stationery.

Sophie's eyes popped as she shouted, *"Bordel de merde!"*, *I know who Lola's father is! This is better news than I could have imagined. A gold mine has fallen into my lap! I must find a way to—I will find a way, and we will be rich!*

She sat on the bed and thought about how she could take advantage of this wonderful news. It all centered on the baby. *That baby will make us a fortune!* It was just a matter of how to make it work.

Think! Think! Wait—yes, that is it! It will be dangerous, but if I plan it right it will be foolproof. Too bad, I have to wait until Lola is ready to give birth. But that will give me time to set the plan in motion.

Sophie couldn't wait to get dressed and tell Apash the news. After applying Lola's makeup, she selected a red silk print dress by the famous designer Paul Poiret. The high-waisted, slim, straight skirt showed off her figure. She added a brimmed floral hat and black patent leather Derby shoes with wide laces and a long, narrow duckbill toe. They were a size too small, but she forced her feet into them. She admired herself in the mirror and applauded. *One day soon, I will have clothing like this in my closet!*

Sophie hurried to the Omnibus stop and waited impatiently for the double-decker horse-drawn wagon. When it arrived, she stepped in and found a seat on one of the two long wooden benches that faced each other. She preferred to sit atop in the open air, but the breeze would mess her hair, and she wanted to look posh when she gave Apash the good news.

She arrived at L'antre Du Diable. Sophie saw Apash as soon as she entered. Her heart broke when she saw him sitting at the bar with his tongue in the ear of Paulette, one of his street sluts. She should be used to this by now, but she loved him so much the pain never abated.

He took no notice of her until she approached him and said, "Apash, I have to talk to you. It is important!"

Apash demanded, "What are you doing here? Why are you not working? And who did you steal those fancy clothes from?"

Sophie wasn't surprised that he didn't compliment her appearance. "What I have to tell you cannot wait. It is the best news you will ever hear!"

Paulette's face became a mixture of irritation and disappointment when Apash pushed her away and shouted, "The room is full of customers waiting for you! Go to work!"

He asked, "So what is this news? It better be worth the money you are not making for me today."

Sophie took Paulette's seat and gave the letter to Apash. Expecting praise, she said, "Read this and you will see how we will become rich!" After a moment, she squirmed and hollered, "Ouch! Apash stop! Why are you pinching me?"

"You cow! You are making fun of me! You know I cannot read!"

"I am sorry, I forgot. Forgive me!"

"Why are you here? You better have a damn good reason."

"Lola is the daughter of Monsieur Émile La Fontaine. He is the Finance Minister! We can blackmail him and make ourselves a fortune!"

"You think there is a way we can become rich from this man?"

"Oh yes! But I am still working on the plan. It will be necessary for Lola to stay at my flat until she has the baby. We must make sure she believes we are only interested in helping her and do everything we can to keep her satisfied. Once she has the baby, our lives will be happy forever!"

He wrapped his arms around her and whispered, "You are a smart bitch!"

Ren'e Fedyna

Chapter 26

Lola sat in her dressing room, applying makeup. Her new dress had been designed to hide her growing belly. She knew it wouldn't be much longer before there was no disguising it. If her calculations were correct, she would have to stop working in eight weeks.

She felt a kick from within her belly. She looked down and smiled. "Your legs are strong, my little one. I think you will want to be a dancer!" She rubbed her belly and whispered, "I cannot wait to see you. Do not worry. I know that I must work so I can give you all the things you deserve and I will find us a new place to live where it is just the two of us—."

A knock on her door interrupted her. "*Entrez,*" she said.

Monsieur Zidler entered. It was unusual for him to come to her dressing room. She feared the reason for this visit. *"Bonsoir, Monsieur* Zidler. Please have a seat."

"No, thank you. I will not be staying. How are you feeling this evening?"

"I feel very well, thank you. Why do you ask?"

His face was kind, but his eyes were earnest. "It has come to my attention that you have changed your act and no longer dance, but only sing. As you are aware, that is not our agreement. You are popular with the audience. However, I have been advised that our patrons have expressed disappointment with your new routine. I am sorry, but this is not acceptable. I do not mean to be indelicate, but your appearance has changed considerably, and it is obvious that is the reason you changed your act."

Lola blushed. *"Oui,* it is true I am pregnant, and will need a little time away when I give birth. Monsieur Zidler, you have been very good to me and I meant no disrespect. Please forgive me for not speaking to you about this, but I feared you might dismiss me. I would very much like to continue to perform here after the birth of my child. Is that acceptable to you?" She held her breath waiting for his answer.

He cleared his throat. "Lola, you are a valuable performer with a great deal of talent. However, I cannot promise you we will hold your position open. There are a great many talented people in Paris. I assume your time will come soon. Continue to perform here for as long as you are able. Advise me when you are ready to return. If possible, we will have you as a guest performer on occasion, and if the crowd demands it, we will hire you again."

Lola felt like she was about to drop through the floor. "Thank you, Monsieur Zidler, you are very generous."

She allowed herself several moments of self-pity before she walked to the mirror, pinched her cheeks to add color and said aloud, "The show must go on!" Lola put on a brave face during her performance, but could only think about what would happen after the baby was born.

The next afternoon she sat at the kitchen table sipping coffee. Lola's finger circled her cup while she thought about the plans she made. Sophie entered the kitchen. Her hair was mussed, and she wore a bathrobe that hung off one shoulder. The bathrobe was made of lustrous cobalt blue and black Chinese silk with dragons and patterns in gold.

"*Bonjour,* Sophie. My, that is a beautiful dressing gown. Is it new?"

Sophie stretched and yawned. She regarded Lola through bleary eyes. She shuffled to the table in her feathery gold slippers. In a hoarse voice, she said, "*Bonjour, ma petite.*" Sophie looked at her robe as if this was the first time she had seen it. Her face registered remembrance, and she gave a little laugh. "Ah, *oui!* I received this present last night from a rich and grateful Chinaman."

Lola poured them each a cup of coffee. "I need to speak with you."

Sophie took a seat "Ah, coffee! You are an angel!" She added several spoonfuls of sugar into the steaming cup and took a swallow. Then took a cigarette and tapped it on the case, lit the cigarette and took a deep drag. With eyes closed, she lifted her head and exhaled in a moment of reverie. She struggled to focus her eyes. "So, what is it you need to tell me?"

"I have been doing a lot of thinking. It will not be long before my baby is born. I have to prepare for the birth and my new living arrangements."

Sophie flicked cigarette ashes into the ashtray. "New living arrangements? What arrangements are these?"

Lola rested her hands on her belly. "You understand I cannot bring up a baby here where you—uh—work. I must find a new apartment right away."

"My little dove, you have been doing a lot of thinking, but maybe you need think more. There is no need for you to find another place until after the baby is born. If you were to move out now, who would look out for you?"

Lola shouted, "I do not need anyone to look out for me. I can take care of myself!"

Startled by Lola's outburst, Sophie quickly recovered and said, "What I mean is, it is a bad idea for you to move out now and live on your own. Who will help you when it is time to give birth? If you stay here, I can deliver your baby."

"You? I was planning to have the baby in a hospital, or I will find a good doctor."

Sophie looked horrified. "The hospital? Oh no! That is the worst thing you can do! If you live on your own, will you run to catch a cab for the hospital when your labor pains make it difficult for you to stand? And to give birth in the hospital is ridiculous! Do you have any idea how many women die giving birth in the hospital? Have you heard of Puerperal fever?"

With widened eyes, Lola she shook her head.

"Whether in a hospital or by a doctor, men do not wash their hands and women die every day from infection. Men know nothing about taking care of a woman properly. It is best you remain here, where I can help you give birth safely."

Lola knitted her brows. "But I fear for my baby and I fear for myself. My *Mamá* died after giving birth to me. I must be sure I have the best care."

Sophie took Lola's hand and looked at her with sad eyes. "I am sorry about your *Mamá*. You know how fond I am of you. I assure you I will let nothing happen to you. Stay here. I will find someone to stay with you, and when the time comes, I will help you give birth. I am the oldest of seven children. I know more about birthing babies than any doctor."

"I appreciate that you have so much experience. Please forgive me, but if it cannot be a hospital or a doctor, I want a midwife. A woman who does this every day."

"Hmmm. A midwife?" Her face brightened, "Oh, yes!! I have just the woman for you, Madame Rosalie. She has been a midwife for many years. She is well known in her profession. She has even performed her duties for many of the rich and powerful. So, what do you say?"

Lola rested her face in her hand. "I am so confused. Is she expensive? No, it does not matter. I will pay any price to be sure we are safe. But I found out yesterday I may not be able to work at the Moulin Rouge after my baby is born. I have savings, but that will have to do for me until I can find other employment."

Sophie looked relieved. "That is no problem. You can stay here rent-free until the baby is born. You can even stay until you find another cabaret where you can perform. I will find someone to watch the baby while you look for work. I told you, I would help you. You *do* trust me, do you not?

"Yes, I trust you."

Dance of the Restless Soul

Chapter 27

Second guessing her plan, Sophie headed towards her pre-arranged meeting with Madame Rosalie. *It is a dangerous decision to let the Madame in on the plot. Apash will be angry with me for including her. I am headed for pain with that man, but what else can I do?*

Her knock on the door was answered promptly by a maid who brought her into the parlor. Sophie had never been to the Madame's home before. Everywhere she looked the furniture and décor was of Egyptian style, embellished with details of gilt bronze fittings shaped like sphinxes, winged lions, lotus blossoms and scarabs. Egyptian scenes of pyramids and hieroglyphics were woven into the seating fabrics. Exotic plants filled the room.

Sophie knew that the Egyptian style came and went over the years. Each time an event like the opening of the Suez Canal in 1869 and the excavation of Tell El-Amarna in 1887 put Egypt in the press, the style became popular again. But she had never been in a place where this style surrounded her.

She sat on a polished bronze and mahogany settee adorned with a winged sphinx at the end of each arm. She wondered if Madame Rosalie felt like an Egyptian goddess amidst this outlandish decor.

Madame Rosalie entered the parlor.

Anxious to complete her business, Sophie said, "Please close the doors and sit. We must get down to business right away. I have to discuss a sensitive matter, and no one must know about it but us."

Madame Rosalie closed the double doors and sat across from Sophie. She leaned her body forward and said, "I must say your note piqued my curiosity. You say you have a lucrative proposition for me. What is it?"

Although Sophie had done business with her in the past, she had never noticed Madame's appearance. Madame Rosalie was short and plump. Despite her shape, she took pains to look captivating. She had neatly groomed black hair, flawless porcelain skin and perfectly shaped eyebrows. She wore makeup to highlight her almond-shaped light green eyes. The extravagance of her clothing enhanced every aspect of her look.

It surprised Sophie to see Madame Rosalie wearing a kaftan. Although Sophie read in the newspaper that Alix of Hesse, Empress of Russia, had worn one during her coronation, it was uncommon for a Parisian woman to wear one. The Madame's black velvet kaftan had been embellished with pearls and adorned with silver metal thread on the hem, cuffs and collar. Multiple rings, necklaces and bracelets added to her fashion statement. Her perfume clung to the air like a heavy blanket.

Sophie took a deep breath. "Madame Rosalie, you have a reputation for discretion. You must promise me what I am about to tell you will never leave this room."

The Madame frowned. She thought for a moment, leveling her eyes at Sophie. "Yes, I promise. Now tell me, what is this proposition?" After listening intently to Sophie's scheme, she paused in thought. With a stern expression, she asked, "Are you sure you want to do this dangerous thing?"

Sophie replied, "All my life I have scraped by, providing pleasure for others, receiving nothing but misery in return. A man has always owned me and told me what to do. Now, at last, I can release my chains. With this money, I can be free to do whatever I want. I must do this! Will you help me?"

The fierceness of Madame Rosalie's stare unnerved Sophie. The tap, tap, tap of her perfectly manicured fingernails, as she drummed them against the wooden arm of the sofa, sounded like a hammer against Sophie's head. Her future was in Madame

Rosalie's hands. Sweat rolled down her back as she waited for an answer.

Madame Rosalie shook her head. "No. There is too much risk involved. I see no reason why I should put myself in danger."

"My dear Madame, I came to you because you have a reputation for taking advantage of any situation where you will be handsomely rewarded. This is such a situation. Your risk is minimal. You only have to deliver a baby. Beyond that, you have no responsibility except to tell no one of your involvement. For this, you will be paid well. I do not understand what your concern might be."

Madam Rosalie's glare was like searchlights beaming into Sophie's soul. She narrowed her eyes and asked, "Are you telling me everything?"

In a strong voice, Sophie said, "I am telling you everything you need to know."

"I want no surprises. I will not protect you if you get yourself into trouble!"

Sophie countered, "There is no need to be concerned. Your job is to deliver the baby, nothing more. Do we have an understanding?"

"What of Apash? Is he capable of doing his part? He has a reputation as a thief and a murderer, but this situation takes clever timing. Are you sure he is up to this…uh…task?"

Sophie smiled. "If this is your major worry, I assure you Apash will do what is necessary. It will not be a pleasant thing, but he has no distress about fulfilling his role. He wants this as much as I do, and he will do whatever is required."

Madame Rosalie leaned back. She tilted her head exposing her several chins. She appeared to be analyzing her odds. Then she looked at Sophie and said, "Yes, we have an understanding, but it will cost you. I want two thousand francs in advance."

Sophie raised her voice, "Two thousand francs! How do you expect me to get that kind of money?"

Madame Rosalie scowled. "Hush! Do you want the world to know of your plan?"

Sophie blanched. She ran to the parlor doors and opened one to peek out. Looking relieved. *"Rendre grâce à Dieu*! No one was there." She returned to her seat and in a muted voice she pleaded, "Madame Rosalie, that is an outrageous sum of money. Your job is important, but that is so much more than you charge for delivering a baby."

"But I am not delivering just any baby. You said it yourself. This is the grandchild of *the Minister of Finance*. It is a dangerous plan. I will not consider one *sou* less!"

Sophie hesitated. "All right! I will give you a deposit of one thousand francs and the rest when the job is done."

Madame Rosalie crossed her arms. "That will not do! Do you think I will be able to collect my money after the guillotine removes your head? No, you must pay all of it in advance!"

Sophie wrung her hands. *Where will I get the money? Apash? He would break my neck before he would give me that kind of money! My savings are not enough. I must find a way.* "Yes Madame, I will get the money, but remember, we must convince Lola that she is dying. It is good her mother died when she was born, so her fear is strong. We can use this to our advantage. No matter how bad her pain, be sure not to give her the chloroform until I tell you. Do you understand?"

"Do not worry Sophie. I am an expert at this."

Sophie left Madame Rosalie's home with a heavy heart. This was the best opportunity she would ever have to make a better life for herself, but where would she get 2,000 francs to make it happen? She would have to empty her bank account, but even that would not be enough, she needed more. She was afraid to ask Apash, and certainly, none of her customers would give it to her. She smiled and said aloud, "Of course! I will get it from Lola!"

Chapter 28

Sophie was surprised to see Apash seated on her living room sofa. He had a key, but he seldom visited without advance notice. She knew she was in trouble for not being with a client when he arrived.

It didn't matter. He always found some reason to be angry with her. He was dangerous, and that frightened her, but that danger excited her, too. She remembered the day they had met. Sophie had been a streetwalker, standing at her station in the rain with the other prostitutes. He hadn't even looked at the other girls. He walked straight to her and ushered her into the nearby alley. He seized her umbrella and threw it to the ground. Rivulets of rain streamed down his curly black hair onto his unshaven face. His pungent scent aroused her, like a magnificent animal. He'd taken her hard. She'd never been so excited.

Afterward, he told her he'd just come from Corsica and needed to make money. He was looking to set himself up as a pimp, and if she worked for him, he would set her world on fire. She didn't believe him, but looking into his large, obsidian eyes, she knew she would be his.

Sophie told him she already had a pimp named Claude who would never release her. "Take me to him," he insisted, and she did. Apash put a knife to Claude's throat and made it clear that Sophie would not be working for him anymore. Claude later sent his thugs to waylay Apash and seek revenge. In Corsica, vendettas were commonplace, and he was taught as a child how to protect himself in an ambush. His knife skills were exceptional. He was too fierce for them and they fled. Apash returned to Claude's lair and cut him deeply in the stomach, nearly killing him. He never bothered Apash again. No one had ever fought for her before. It was the most thrilling thing that had ever happened to Sophie.

Her juices began to flow just thinking about those moments. However, Sophie could tell by the scowl on his face that Apash was angry. Her body tensed. To assuage his anger, she flung off her coat and began to unbutton her dress. She put on her sexiest expression, sauntered over to him and said enticingly, "What a happy surprise to see you, my love. Are you here because you missed me?"

Apash stood when she approached him. She was about to put her arms around his neck when he put his hand on her chest and shoved her hard. "Where have you been, you slut? Why are you not working?"

Sophie fell backward and grabbed the couch to keep from landing on the floor. "I am working, but in a better way than you think. I have been making arrangements. When Lola has the baby, we will be rich. But I must make many plans so that everything runs smoothly."

He scoffed, "So that is your excuse! These plans, they take all day?"

"I am expecting a customer here in an hour." Sophie approached him and continued to unbutton her dress. Her eyes flashed with sensuality. "That will give us a little time together, no?"

Apash drew Sophie into his arms, and whispered into her ear, "My wicked little bitch." He pulled her dress down, exposing her shoulder, and kissed it hungrily. Sophie closed her eyes and let her head fall back. She was absorbed in the pleasure of the moment, until he asked, "Are you telling me everything? You would not keep anything from me, would you? You know what will happen if you try to keep secrets from me."

She murmured in his ear, "Um…my sweet, there is one little thing—"

Apash pushed her away, "I knew it! I knew you would do something to screw this up!"

She was frantic. "No! My love, it is just a little thing."

He growled, *"Putain de vache!* All right, out with it! What did you do?" Apash locked his fingers on her wrist and squeezed hard.

Sophie tried to pull away, but he was too strong. She pleaded, "Let me go! It is nothing! I have already taken care of it!"

He dropped her wrist with disgust. She rubbed her wrist and said, "The little fool insists on using a midwife other than me."

"Other than you? You stupid cow! Why could you not convince her to use you as the midwife? You said you had her eating out of your hand!"

Sophie reached into her purse to grab a cigarette. She lit it with shaky hands. "Lola is so stupid! Everyone knows it is best to use a midwife. Everyone but her! She wanted to go to the hospital or a doctor. I talked her out of that. I told her I should deliver the baby, but she insisted she have the best. I told her I was the best. But she said, no. The only way I could keep her here was to agree to find her a midwife. But it is all right, *mon cher*, Madame Rosalie will do it. The Madame knows how to keep her mouth shut."

Apash shouted, "Madame Rosalie! How much do you have to pay her? She does not come cheap!"

"Do not worry about that. I have already made a deal with her. She will be no trouble. As for the money, I will get Lola to pay the Madame by pawning her jewelry, and she will be glad of it! You should also know I had to make plans for a wet nurse. I spoke to Adele and she will wet nurse the baby. She has no idea who she will be nursing and has no interest in knowing, so long as she is paid. You see my sweet. I am doing everything that needs to be done."

He rubbed his ear and shook his head. "I do not like it. I do not like having others in on this. It is risky enough as it is! We must call it off. I will not go to jail because you are a stupid bitch!"

Sophie pleaded, "*Mon coco*, please! There is no problem." Sophie stepped closer to Apash. She soothed his face with her hand and spoke in a motherly tone, "Think of the money. Remember, when this is over, we can have anything we want. We will have everything we have ever desired. I promise you it will go smoothly. You must trust me. I will take care of everything."

"Does that mean you have figured out the entire plan?

"Not quite. I must still determine how to get Lola out of Paris after the baby is born."

Apash pulled a dagger from his jacket pocket. He smirked as he twirled the point of the dagger against his forefinger. "That is no problem. I can make Lola disappear for good!"

Sophie's eyes grew wide. She crushed the cigarette in an ashtray. "Put that away!" Although she knew Lola was at work, she looked anxiously towards the door as if expecting her to walk in. "I do not want to resort to that unless we have no choice. Do not worry. I have an idea.

Apash returned the knife into his jacket pocket. "So, you will take care of everything? No more mistakes?"

"Yes, my darling. I guarantee everything will work out perfectly. Just wait and see."

He smiled at her. "Ah well, then I guess I have nothing to worry about." He tenderly put his hand to her throat.

Sophie relaxed in anticipation of the carnal delight to come. But her eyes popped with terror when his grip tightened. "I want to make sure you understand there will be no mistakes." He commanded, "Say it, say there will be no mistakes!" He released enough pressure so she could speak.

She coughed and sputtered, "There will be no mistakes!"

Apash released his grip and put his arms around her. "That is all I wanted to hear." He kissed her hard and led her into her bedroom. "We must hurry before your client arrives."

Chapter 29

Sophie looked up from reading her magazine when she heard Lola enter the flat. She smiled and said, "Now that you are no longer performing, it is good for you and the baby that you are still getting exercise.

She surveyed Lola's body to predict how long it would be before Lola would give birth. Now that the time was growing near, Sophie was especially vigilant. "Your belly has dropped Lola. I think you will be having the baby soon. How are you feeling?"

Lola yawned. "My back hurts and I am ready for my afternoon nap. But the way this little one kicks, I am not sure I will get much rest." She laughed and headed towards her bedroom. "I think she wants to come out dancing!"

Sophie was entertaining a client when she heard Lola's urgent knock and shout outside her bedroom door. "Sophie! Sophie! Hurry! It is time. I am having the baby!"

Sophie cursed under her breath. "Lola," she shouted, "go back to your bedroom. I will be there in a few minutes." Then she turned to her surprised client and demanded, "Sam, you must go now. This is an emergency!"

Sam growled. "What is going on? Who is having a baby? I had nothing to do with it! This better not be a swindle!"

"This is no swindle. It has nothing to do with you. Now get out of bed. I have to leave!"

"Leave? What are you talking about? I did not get my money's worth. We must finish!"

Sophie reached under her bed. She pulled out a rolling pin and held it high. "Get out of bed now, or I will smack your head with this!"

Sam grumbled and rose from the bed. "This is no way to treat a good customer!"

She put down the rolling pin. "I am sorry. I will make it up to you next time. But you must leave now!" She threw on her robe, helped Sam get dressed, and hastened him to the door. She blew him a kiss and said sweetly, "*À bientôt, mon cher.*"

Sophie hurried to Lola's bedroom. With knitted brows, she asked, "What is happening?"

"I am in pain. I think the baby is coming right now!"

"How many contractions have you had?"

"I just had a second one."

"A second contraction? Only two?"

Lola nodded.

"*Ma chère*, you're not ready yet. It will hours. Try to relax. I will fetch Madame Rosalie." Sophie sucked in her bottom lip. Then uttered, "But—"

Lola gave Sophie a sharp look. "But? But what!"

"Dearest Lola, I am sorry. I forgot to tell you she must be paid in advance. You must pay her three thousand francs."

Lola raged. "You forgot to tell me Madame Rosalie wants three thousand francs! How could you forget such a thing? This cannot be what midwives charge! She is surely taking advantage of me! I never thought…I just assumed the price would be reasonable. How foolish of me!"

Sophie pretended to be hurt and said, "I am sorry. You asked for the best midwife. If you think that is too much, I can deliver your baby for free."

Lola shouted, "No! It must be Madame Rosalie. But I do not have sufficient money now. Can I pay when I have recovered?"

"No, she will only come if you give her the money first. What do you want me to do?"

"You should have told me sooner. I cannot understand why she needs the entire amount first. Are you sure she is the best?"

"I told you, she is the preferred midwife of royalty and aristocrats, and she knows all the latest methods of child birthing. But, if you wish, I can try to find someone else. I am not sure I can find someone before you give birth, but I can try."

"No! I insist on Madame Rosalie, but what can I do?" In desperation, Lola looked about the room. Her eyes fixed on her dressing table. "There, in the jewelry box. Take what you need! Give her the jewels. There is more than enough to cover her fee."

Sophie offered a sorry smile. "Are you sure you do not wish me to deliver your baby?"

"Yes, I am sure!" Lola put her hands on her stomach. "My baby may come at any moment. I want her here when it happens."

She helped Lola onto her bed and brushed her hair from her sweaty face. With her back turned away from Lola, Sophie selected an exquisite black opal diamond and cluster ring, a fabulous gold platinum pendant, a gorgeous diamond swirl brooch and a beautiful gold charm bracelet. She smiled with self-satisfaction and thought, *Lola you are a fool, but I love you for it!*

"I am leaving now. Try to relax. I will be back with Madame Rosalie long before the baby is ready to enter the world."

Lola swallowed tears. "But what if my baby comes before you return?"

Sophie patted Lola's hand. "I know you are afraid. It is a frightening thing to have a baby the first time. Trust me. I know exactly what must be done. I promise we will be back in time." She kissed Lola's forehead, dressed and rushed down the stairs.

She hailed a Hansom cab and told the driver she would be making several stops. Sophie's first stop was at L'antre Du Diable. She spotted Apash chatting with the bartender as he sat in his usual seat at the bar. Sophie smiled. She ran to him and said with pride, "Apash, wonderful news! She is having the baby today! Everything is going as I expected!" She touched his arm. "But we must hurry, her time is near!"

Apash looked puzzled for a moment, then his lips grew into an evil smile. "Ah, *très bon*! Let us go!" They left the cabaret together.

Her next stop was to a pawnshop she frequented. Sophie negotiated a good deal and got 3,000 francs. She put 1,000 in her coat pocket and the remainder in her purse. Sophie gave Madame Rosalie's address to the cab driver and shouted, "Hurry!"

She asked the cabbie to wait once more. Her nerves were on edge. She pounded the door until it was opened by the maid. "My name is Sophie Décharde. Tell the Madame it is time. I must see her now!"

The maid showed no surprise. She appeared to be familiar with frantic callers shouting urgently for the Madame to come and deliver a baby. The maid brought Sophie into the parlor. "Wait here," she said and left.

Sophie was relieved the Madame was at home but was still concerned for time. She shouted after the maid, "It is an emergency! Tell her to hurry!"

A few minutes later Madame Rosalie appeared. She asked, "What is the emergency? Is Lola all right?"

"Yes, she is. Get your coat. There's no time to lose. The baby will be coming soon!"

The Madame raised an eyebrow, "Did you bring the money?"

"Yes! Yes, of course!" Sophie handed the 2,000 francs to Madame Rosalie and waited as she counted the money twice. The Madame smiled and said, "Wait here. I must get my kit. I will be right back."

Sophie tapped her foot impatiently. Finally, the Madame returned. "Do you have everything you need?"

Madame Rosalie said, "Yes, of course!"

"We must leave at once. A cab is waiting."

As they left, sheets of rain poured down. The Madame wanted to return to her house to get an umbrella, but Sophie insisted, "We have no time for that!" She grabbed the Madame's arm and pulled her to the cab. Sophie shouted to the driver, "Take me home, now!"

The heavy rain snarled traffic. The ride back to the apartment took much longer than Sophie expected. She feared Lola would give birth before they got there. She repeated the plan several times to Madame Rosalie during their ride.

The Madame grumbled, "Yes, yes I understand! Do not worry so much, you are giving me a headache! Anyone would think you are having the baby!"

The apartment was dark when they entered. Sophie froze when she heard a terrifying scream from Lola's bedroom. They rushed into her room. The darkness was shattered by a brilliant flash of lightning that exposed Lola's sweaty face, twisted with fear, as she lay with the sheets tightly clenched in her fists.

Chapter 30

Sophie lit the lamp. The raging storm rattled the windows. A crash of thunder followed by lightning in the shape of bony fingers. Lola cried. "I am dying! Sophie, help me! I am so frightened!"

Madame Rosalie threw off her coat then went to the kitchen to scrub her hands.

Sophie caressed Lola's face. "Hush, my little dove. Do not worry. The Madame is here to take care of you. Remember, I told you she is an expert."

"But I am so—"

"Do not think about it. Just know soon you will be holding your precious babe in your arms."

Madame Rosalie returned from the kitchen and began to examine Lola. After a few moments, she nodded to Sophie, indicating that Lola was doing well. The Madame moved to the dressing table to prepare for the birth. She cleared the table, opened her kit to remove a starched white cotton sheet and laid it upon the dressing table. She put on an apron and placed a baby blanket, forceps, scissors, and various apparatus onto the sheet.

Watching the Madame lay strange and scary objects on the sheet, Lola's eyes widened. Sweat beaded her upper lip. "Those things look like medieval torture devices. Must you use them on me?"

The Madame sighed. "Lola, you must understand these devices are important aids in the delivery of your baby. They may look scary, but I know how to use them properly." She gave Lola a reassuring smile and moved to the foot of Lola's bed to watch over her.

Sophie filled a basin with water and put several towels under her arm. Water sloshed from the basin as she rushed to Lola's room. She was dabbing Lola's sweaty face with a moist towel when she felt a vice-like grip on her arm.

"I know I am dying, I know it! You must tell my *Papá* so he can take care of my baby after I am gone." When another contraction overcame her, Lola released Sophie's arm. Her eyelids were clamped shut and through gritted teeth, she grunted, "You must call for my P*apá*!"

Sophie said "It will do no good. He will not come."

"Please! You must bring him to me!"

Sophie continued to dab the sweat from Lola's face, chest and arms, "It is useless to think about him. He is too stubborn."

"Dearest Sophie, you must send for him. At least he should know I am having the baby right now. Maybe that will soften his heart."

"He has no heart to put you through this alone. It will do no good. Nothing will make him come to you, unless—"

"Lola gasped, struggling for breath. "Unless what?"

Sophie protested, "No, it is not right. We cannot…it is too terrible!"

"Please, please! I am frightened. I need *Papá*!"

"If you want him to come, you must write him a cruel letter. You must tell him you will kill yourself if he does not come. It is cruel, yes, but he has been cruel to you. He is like a stone, and the only way you can make him come to you is to break his heart the way he has broken yours."

Lola shrieked. Intense pain caused her back to arch. After the pain passed, her limbs were like jelly. She shouted, "Madame Rosalie, my pain is unbearable! Is there nothing you can do?"

Madame Rosalie approached Lola, "Yes, I will give you a potion but we must make sure the time is right. It will be soon, my dear."

"*Mon Dieu*, it hurts so much!" In a heavy breath, she muttered to Sophie, "I should tell him I…will kill myself? Do you think that will work? It seems cruel."

Sophie said, "You are right, it is too cruel, you may hurt his feelings. Anyway, he has already told you that you are dead to him, so we should forget the idea."

"I cannot think straight. If you believe it will make him come, I will write anything you say."

With eyes hooded like a cobra, Sophie smiled at Madame Rosalie. She brought Lola paper and a pen and recited the letter she had repeated to herself every night before she slept as if it were a lullaby. She cleared her throat and dictated, "Now, write exactly what I tell you."

My dearest Papá,
All my life I have loved you and never meant to hurt you. But I was a foolish girl, and I have made many mistakes. Mistakes I can never undo. I can no longer live in a world without your love, and I cannot live with the shame I have caused you. The only way I can end your pain and mine is to end my miserable life and start a new life through my little one. The little baby that I am giving birth to, even as I write this letter My dear friend Sophie will bring this innocent child for you to raise after I am gone. I pray you raise my baby to be a better person than I have been. I will love you through my child better in death than I have ever been able to love you in life.
Pray for me and please, please forgive me.
Your loving daughter,
Lola

The pen fell from Lola's hand. She dropped back onto the pillow exhausted.

Sophie read the letter and with a sorrowful expression, she said, "Have no fear, he will see how distressed you are to write to him when you are in so much pain. This will convince him how desperately you need him." Sophie looked at Madame Rosalie and winked. "I will have this letter sent right away."

Madame Rosalie examined Lola and acknowledged, "The baby is ready to come. I will give you chloroform. It will put you to sleep. When you wake, your beautiful new baby will be ready for you to hold." She placed a porous cloth over Lola's face and dripped chloroform one drop at a time until Lola drifted off and then began the birthing procedures.

Sophie paced the floor and kept looking at the clock. She grumbled, "Where is Apash? He should be here by now!"

The Madame announced, "Everything is going well with the birth. The baby is coming. I hope for your sake, Apash is on his way."

Relieved to hear tapping at the door, Sophie's face brightened. *"Rendre grâce à Dieu!* Apash is here!" She ran to the door. "Do you have it?"

Apash held a bundle wrapped in a blanket. "Of course!"

Sophie asked, "How did you get it?"

"Do you really want to know?"

Sophie bit her lip and shook her head.

Apash whispered, "How are things going? Has the baby been born yet?"

Sophie took the bundle from Apash and pulled the blanket down to take a peek., "A girl," She sighed. "Not yet." Suddenly she heard a smack and a baby's wail. She and Apash both looked towards Madame Rosalie, who expressed a broad smile.

Sophie laid the infant bundle on the living room sofa and hurried to Madame Rosalie. She took Lola's baby from the Madame, wrapped it in a blanket and returned it to Apash. She instructed him, "Take this baby directly to Adele. Be careful. Let no one see you."

Sophie asked the Madame, "Is Lola all right?"

"Of course, she is all right! I am an expert. Let's get on with it. I want to leave and forget everything about this."

They cleaned Lola's room, and Sophie unwrapped the bundle brought by Apash. Sophie smeared the infant with Lola's natal blood. She walked over to Lola and shook her shoulder until she woke. "How are you feeling, *ma chèrie*?"

Lola tried to remember what happened. Her face brightened. She broke into a smile. "How is my baby?" Lola raised herself onto her elbows and looked around the room. "Where is my baby?"

She looked into Sophie's solemn face. "My sweet, you had a little girl. I am sorry to say I have sad news. The poor creature is dead."

Chapter 31

"Dead? *Dead!* No! That is not possible!" Lola grimaced as she pushed herself to sit up. "I felt her kick inside me many times. She was so alive!" Tears filled her eyes. "She…she…." Lola's words caught in her throat, "She cannot be…dead!"

"Madame Rosalie, what is Sophie talking about?"

The Madame put on a sad face. "I am so sorry, my dear. It was a difficult birth. The umbilical cord wrapped around her little neck and strangled her. There was nothing I could do. I am very sorry."

Lola's eyes narrowed. "I do not believe you! I heard her cry." Her eyes combed the room. "Where is she? Show her to me!" She pounded the bed "Why are you hiding her? Is this a cruel joke?" Lola pointed her finger at Sophie. "Bring her to me at once!"

"Poor dear, it is best you do not see her."

Leaning forward, Lola's eyes bored into Sophie with menace. "Bring her to me! *Now!*"

Sophie sighed and went into the parlor where she had left the dead infant. She picked it up and brought it to Lola.

Lola put her hand to her mouth as she sucked in her breath. "*Mon Dieu!* Oh, no! This cannot be!" She removed the blanket and examined the baby. The infant's skin was velvety soft but cold. Her mouth was slightly open. The sweet delicate lips were blue. She could see bruises on the infant's neck. Lola kissed the infant's fingers, toes and cheeks. She replaced the blanket and cradled it in her arms. Tears slid down Lola's face. She rocked the baby and sang a lullaby. Lola wiped her tears as they fell onto the baby's face.

Sophie whispered, "It is time. We must put her to rest."

She allowed Sophie to take the baby away. Her wet, dull eyes and a trembling chin expressed her deep pain,

Madame Rosalie handed Lola a pill and a glass of water. "Take this for the pain." She placed the bottle on the dressing table. "You will need one every six hours."

Madame Rosalie hurriedly packed her things and was about to walk out the door, when Lola screamed, "Wait!" Overcome with grief and anger she shouted, "I do not understand! If you are such an expert, how could you let this happen? I think you are not the expert you claim to be!" She screeched, "You are an imposter! A charlatan! If you were a good midwife, you would not have let my baby die!"

The Madame's face turned red. She was about to shout back at Lola when Sophie intervened. "Dear Lola, you're understandably upset. Of course, you are angry. I am angry too, and so is Madame Rosalie. It was an act of God. No one could possibly know this would happen. This was not the Madame's fault. We are so very sorry for you. Please, you must rest." Sophie nodded her head to indicate the Madame should leave. She sat next to Lola and put her arm around her.

Lola rested her head on Sophie's shoulder and said, "*Papá* did not come. Did you give him my letter?"

"*Ma chèrie*, I hate to tell you that I gave him your letter. He tore it into little pieces. When I tried to explain, he would not hear it. He rudely dismissed me. I did my best. I feel so sad for you." Sophie patted her back while Lola cried on her shoulder. She eased Lola onto the pillow and said, "Rest now. The pill will help you sleep." Sophie beamed. *This went perfectly! Now, how do I get rid of Lola?*

Chapter 32

"When are you getting rid of her?" Apash stood in Sophie's living room with arms crossed against his chest. He glared at her. "I am losing patience! If you do not get rid of her, I will!"

Sophie grabbed Apash by the arm and hurried him into her bedroom. She closed the door and whispered, "Hush! Lola's sleeping in the other room.

The springs squeaked as Apash slumped onto the edge of the bed. He lowered his voice. "So, what are you doing about Lola? It has been ten days. Every day she lays in bed feeling sorry for herself. You keep telling her the only way she can forget her bad memories is to leave Paris and move on with her life! But she is still here! I will give you until the end of the week, or she is finished!

Sophie stood over him with her hands akimbo. She said, "Do not be hasty. We must be careful! Everything has gone perfectly. We do not want to ruin it now!" With a sly smile, she added, "Besides, I have good news, *mon coco*. I read in the society column that her lover, Charlie Sloan, is back in Paris."

She moved closer to him and put her arms around his neck. She pressed her large, rounded breasts against his mouth. "I told you I will take care of everything." The moist heat of his lips against her thin cotton blouse made her nipples harden.

Apash's arms tightened around her waist. He nuzzled her and bit her playfully. "What difference does that make?"

She brought her lips close to his ear and said, "I will get Charlie to convince Lola to leave Paris, and perhaps even to leave France!"

He laid back onto the bed, pulling her down on top of him. His hands roamed her body. He kissed her and rolled her onto her back. He lay atop her, with their lips almost touching and asked, "How do you plan to do that?"

Sophie found it difficult to concentrate on anything but his hardness as he gyrated against her. She uttered, "Do not worry about that. I have an idea."

"So do I," he said and unbuttoned her blouse.

That evening, Sophie knocked and entered Lola's room. Lola lay in bed lost in thought.

"Lola, you are so sad. You need cheering up. Tonight, I am going to a ball. Why not join me?"

"Cheering up?" Lola's sardonic laugh sounded like broken glass. "I am in no mood to go anywhere, especially a ball."

"Are you sure? It would be good for you to have some fun."

"No, I am not interested," Lola said in a flat voice. "I hope you have a good time."

Sophie sat on Lola's bed and brushed back a wayward lock of hair from Lola's pale face. "*Ma cherie*, I have a problem. I need an elegant dress, and my meager wardrobe is inappropriate. Would it be all right if I borrowed one of your dresses?"

"A dress? Yes, of course." Lola waved a disinterested hand towards her closet. "Help yourself. I have no use for them now."

Sophie's heart raced as she reviewed the beautiful dresses. She chose an evening dress of lemon-colored satin, painted with La France tea roses. The lemon color would go well with her skin tone. The flounce was of lemon-colored mousseline draped over a ruffle of *plissé* mauve-colored fabric. The sleeves and corsage were made of jeweled butterflies. Sophie removed it from the closet and hurried to the mirror to hold it against herself. "So, Lola, what do you think? I look beautiful, *oui*?"

Lola gave a brief smile and replied dully, "Yes, Sophie. You look beautiful."

"May I have accessories as well?"

"Help yourself." Lola turned her face to the wall as Sophie left the room.

Sophie prepared herself, then went to see her friend Jacques Richard at his chateaux. It had been remodeled into a gambling establishment, exclusive to high rollers. When Charlie Sloan could afford the high stakes required, he frequented Jacques' gambling establishment

Sophie pressed the doorbell. A moment later, a smartly dressed butler opened the door. "I am a friend of Jacques Richard," she announced. The butler nodded and said with a sweeping gesture, *"Bonsoir, madame. Entrez, s'il vous plait."*

Sophie walked through the gaming establishment looking for Charlie. The atmosphere was sophisticated and lavishly appointed with crystal chandeliers, Italian marble pilasters and several grand bars. Some waiters carried trays of champagne-filled glasses. Others carried trays of various hors-d'oeuvres, including anchovies in puff pastry, eel served in its own liquor, caviar in small, silver timbales and various tartlets.

Above the classical music played by a small orchestra, she heard laughter, shouts of celebration and groans of disappointment, as the gamblers succeeded and failed in their attempts to outsmart the roulette wheels.

Sophie's stomach tightened with jealousy as she passed the ostentatiously-bejeweled, elegantly coifed ladies who hung on to the arms of their male companions. *Thanks to Lola, someday I will have a place like this.*

Charlie was nowhere to be seen, so she looked for Jacques Richard. She knew him well. He had been a client of hers before he inherited family wealth and opened the successful gambling club. She found Jacques and strode to him.

"Bonsoir, Jacques. I can see things are going well for you." Jacques was tall and slender, with a fine-featured face, slicked-back black hair and the air of relaxed confidence that comes with success.

"Bonsoir, Sophie." He held a glass of champagne in his hand and kissed her on both cheeks. "It has been a while. I have missed you!" He took her hand and stepped back to look her

over. "I must say, you are looking stylish. Things must be going well for you, too."

Sophie's eyes twinkled as she gave an evasive smile. "*Oui, Jacques*, things are looking up."

"Are you here to try your luck at the tables?"

"Thank you, no. I am looking for Charlie Sloan. I read he is back in Paris, and I would like to speak with him."

"Charlie? Oh yes. Poor Charlie, I am afraid things are not going well for him." Jacques frowned. "Do you know he is no longer with Countess Miralda von Schloss?"

Sophie read in the society column that the Countess had returned to Paris on the arm of another man. She assumed Charlie was between bankrolling biddies and hoped she could find him before he found another one. She shook her head and said, "No, I did not."

Jacques said, "Sadly, she threw him over for a younger man. He was here the other night. Um, Sunday, I think. He was unlucky. He drank too much and was about to leave with empty pockets. So, I offered him a loan, which he appreciated."

"I am sorry to hear that but I have news that might cheer him. Do you know where I can find him?"

Jacques scratched his neatly trimmed goatee. I think when Charlie's luck is bad, he usually goes to Le Pied du Lapin. Do you know it?"

"Ah, yes, I do. *Merci*, Jacques. If you really do miss me, why not come and see me?" She winked. "You know we will have fun!"

Jacques laughed and kissed her hand. "I may just do that!"

She left and hailed a cab to Le Pied du Lapin. Sophie had been there several times on the arms of various clients. The neighborhood was not fashionable, nor was the gambling den. She knocked and was greeted, not by a smartly dressed butler, but by a pot-bellied, greasy-faced man, sucking a toothpick.

He looked her up and down and sneered. "What do you want?"

"Is Charlie Sloan here?"

"Who wants to know?" he growled.

"I am Sophie Décharde. Tell him I have good news for him!"

He looked over his shoulder, and back at Sophie. He rolled the toothpick between his thumb and forefinger. Removing it from between his fat lips, he tossed it outside and hiked his thumb over his shoulder. "Tell him yourself. He is over there!"

Sophie walked past the man into the large, dingy, smoke-filled room. There were several roulette tables surrounded by men in the process of drinking, smoking and calling out their favorite numbers. She could hear the whirrs of spinning roulette wheels and the rattle of the ivory balls as they bounced from pocket to pocket. Sophie recognized Charlie's back as he leaned over a roulette table. She remembered his lean physique, broad shoulders and wavy brown hair. She tapped his shoulder and said, "*Bonsoir,* Charlie, it is good to see you again!"

Charlie had been in the process of making a bet and too preoccupied to hear her.

"Charlie! It is Sophie! I need to talk to you!"

Charlie turned to face her. "Sophie! What are you doing here?" He turned back to hear the croupier call out the winning number. Charlie punched his fist against his palm. "Shit!"

"Come with me," Sophie demanded, "I have something urgent to tell you."

Charlie hesitated, then grabbed his few casino chips and followed her.

She led him to a poorly lit, windowless room. It had a well-worn wooden bar and smelled of cigarettes and stale beer. The room was empty of patrons, except for the bored-looking bartender, and a man sleeping head down at a distant table, his empty glass still in hand.

They sat in a corner. Charlie waved the bartender over and announced. "We'll each have a *Tremblement de Terre*!"

"What is that?"

"I think you'll enjoy it. I had it at one of the parties thrown by Toulouse-Lautrec. You stir cognac and absinthe, add a lemon twist, and *voila*! It's potent but delicious. You know, aside from being a fabulous painter, he's also quite the chef. His feasts are famous for their excellent food and crazy antics."

Sophie said, "That is fascinating, but I have important news to tell you."

He leaned forward, resting his head in his hand. Peering into her eyes and with a half-smile, he asked, "All right, what's so important?"

Sophie could tell he was trying to appear unperturbed by his plight, but she knew better. "Charlie, it looks like you might be down on your luck. I have a proposition that will make you happy."

"A proposition for me?" He sat back in his chair. With narrowed eyes, he asked, "What kind of proposition?"

"It concerns Lola."

"Lola! How is she?" He reflected for a moment. "You know, she's the only woman I ever cared for."

"I am happy you care for her, Charlie. She needs your help."

"My help? What can I possibly do for her?"

"She has been ill."

Charlie frowned. "What? How ill is she?"

The bartender arrived with their drinks. Sophie waited until he placed them on the table and left before she responded. "Lola had a baby, but it was strangled by the umbilical cord and was dead when she gave birth."

"A baby! The baby died! How terrible! Is Lola all right?

"Yes, she is all right physically, but she needs your help."

"My help? I didn't even know she was pregnant! Does she believe I'm the father? It's not possible! I can't—"

"She knows it is not yours. The father is not in the picture. He is a German soldier who is no longer in France. She did not love him, it just happened. Lola wanted to keep the baby, but it was not meant to be. She is sad and barely eats or gets out of bed. She needs cheering up, but more than that."

"What do you mean, more than that?"

"Lola has had a bad time of it. Were you aware her father is the Minister of Finance?"

Charlie looked shocked. "No! I had no idea. But what does that have to do with anything?"

"Lola loves him with all her heart. Yet, when he found out she was pregnant, he disowned her. Now she is heartbroken. I am concerned for her. Between the loss of her baby and the rejection of her father, I am afraid she might want to kill herself. I keep telling her she needs to leave Paris and start a new life elsewhere. Maybe in America. But she will not go!"

"I'm sorry to hear that. But what can I do?"

"Take her away. You often go to America. This would be a good time for you to go and take Lola with you." She could see by the way Charlie avoided her eyes that he was not ready to make a commitment.

"Charlie, listen to me. You say you care about Lola. If you really care, now is a good time to show it. Take her to America with you. Take her to New Orleans. You can get her work as an entertainer there, *non*?"

"Sure, no problem. However, I have no money now. My luck has been so bad I would like to leave Paris too. But if I can't afford to take myself to the states how can I afford to take us both?"

Sophic smiled, "That is the good news! Lola can afford to pay the passage to America for both of you, and she can afford much more! She has made a great deal of money at the Moulin Rouge. She has lots of jewelry and clothing. I am sure she would sell it all to be with you in America. She misses you so much! I think you are the only one who can save her life and maybe doing this good deed will change your luck. What do you say, Charlie?"

Chapter 33

Lola had held the cold body of her poor baby in her arms, yet knowing it was impossible, she felt her sweet little daughter was still alive.

Every time she heard the house key jiggle in the front door lock, she imagined it was Sophie, who would come rushing into her room, holding a baby in her arms, shouting, "It was all a mistake! Here is your beautiful little girl, alive and well! And I have another surprise for you, your *Papá* has come for you!"

Lola fantasized herself holding and kissing her baby, as her *Papá* sat at by her side, embracing them both. She could see his sad face as he apologized. *Lola, my sweet. I have treated you so badly. I have been a stubborn fool. Can you ever forgive me? Please, come home with me and bring your sweet daughter, my granddaughter, with you. I will take care of you both forever.*

She knew this could never happen. But she kept seeing these images over and over, and each time her heart ached more. Each time she reached for another pain pill.

Lola lay on her bed. Once again, she heard the key in the latch and was about to reach for her pills. This time, she heard Sophie hasten towards her bedroom, followed by what sounded like a man's approaching footsteps. Lola thought she was dreaming when she heard Sophie shout, "Look who's come to see you!"

She strained her ears to hear those words she had longed for. But when Sophie entered her room, she held no baby in her arms, and the man standing with her was not Lola's father. The man's face was hidden behind a dramatic display of large, beautiful, dark red roses that immersed the room in their sweet, intoxicating perfume. It smelled like spring. It smelled like love.

For a moment, Lola felt lifted from her melancholy. However, she quickly deflated, realizing it was just a flower delivery. Suddenly, the man opened his arms and dropped all of the roses on to her bed. Confused, she looked up at the deliveryman. She felt a shockwave go through her when she saw the man's bright blue-gray eyes, his well-defined jaw and the playful smile that accentuated the cleft in his chin. She gasped, "Charlie? Is it really you? These roses! *Mon Dieu,* they are gorgeous!"

The roses scattered when Lola jumped from the bed and put her arms around Charlie's neck. She felt the strength in his arms as he lifted her and swung her in a tight embrace.

"Oh, Charlie, I missed you so much!"

Sophie stepped from the room, but stopped just outside the doorway, craning her neck to observe their encounter.

"*Ma belle*, I missed you, too!" He put her down and looked into her eyes with a somber expression. "You don't look well. I'm worried about you. I hear things have been tough for you. I'm so sorry."

Lola murmured, "It is true, things have been bad for me."

Making a place for them to sit, Charlie brushed the remaining roses from the bed. With his thumb, he wiped a lone teardrop making its way down her cheek. "I hate to see you like this. It's time for you to cheer up. Cheering people up is my specialty."

"Charlie, the roses are so beautiful, but I do not think I can ever feel happy again."

"Don't say that. I tell you what, throw on some clothes and let's go out. We'll have a great dinner and lots of wine to cheer you up. We'll have fun just as we did before. Remember the good times we had together?"

"Yes, I remember well. That sounds wonderful. But I cannot."

"Of course, you can! I want to see that beautiful smile of yours." He tickled her under her chin.

She held on to his fingers. "No, I cannot. I am sure Sophie told you about the baby. I am too upset. I am not ready. I am not sure I will ever be ready."

Charlie pursed his lips. "Look, Lola, the fact of the matter is, I'm leaving town. Actually, I'm going back to America, to New Orleans."

Lola tried to hold back her tears. The lump in her throat felt as big as a lemon.

Charlie took her hand. With a soothing voice said, "Lola, I'm telling you this because I want you to come with me. I really care for you and we can have a great time. Just think how much fun we can have crossing the ocean together. Then we'll be with each other in New Orleans. I know great joints there. Come with me. Forget the bad news, let's enjoy ourselves."

Lola took a deep breath. "That sounds wonderful, but no. I just cannot."

"Why do you keep saying you can't? What's stopping you? Would you rather stay here and be miserable? Don't you want to be with me? I thought you liked me."

"Of course, I like you. But—"

"But what?"

Lola's mind circled back to the evening she returned to her dressing room at the Moulin Rouge. Waiting for her there was an incredible bouquet of flowers sent to her by Charlie. She remembered the shock of pain and despair she felt when she read the note attached to the bouquet. The note that said he had to leave and wasn't sure when he'd return.

Lola looked into Charlie's eyes. *Can I trust him? Will he leave me again? Will it be worth the pain I will feel if he deserts me?*

She saw no answers there, and said, "I need time to think."

Charlie frowned. "Lola, the last thing you need is time to think. You need to change your life. Come with me. We'll be great together."

Lola burst into tears.

Charlie put his arms around her. "*Ma chèrie*, what's the matter? Don't you want to go?" Charlie pulled her back and stared into her face. His voice was stern. "Lola, I won't take no for an answer. I'm afraid for you. If you stay here, you'll get sick. There's nothing left for you here. You must come with me. It's the only way." He removed a handkerchief from his pocket and handed it to her. His voice softened, "Sweetheart, please say yes."

Lola felt as if she was falling off a cliff. Now that he was near her, she began to feel alive, but Charlie might hurt her again. She needed to feel his arms around her. She needed his kiss. No matter the future consequences, she needed happiness now.

Lola dabbed her eyes and sniffled. "I would be a terrible bore."

"Lola, you are many things, but you could never be a bore."

"All right, but—"

"No buts! I'll be back in a few days. That will give you time to settle your affairs and to pack. I'll come to pick you up and the fun will begin." Charlie took Lola into his arms and gave her a slow, deep, sensual kiss. He picked up a rose, and, with an encouraging smile, handed it to her before he left the apartment.

Sophie rushed into the room and said cheerfully, "How wonderful—to be off on such an exciting adventure, and with such a handsome rogue. Lola, I am so happy you have this opportunity. Charlie is right. If you stay here, you will surely make yourself sick. Now you have something marvelous to look forward to, *oui*?"

"I hope I am not making a mistake."

Sophie looked surprised. "A mistake? Of course, it is not a mistake! You and Charlie are going on a great journey. So be happy, be very happy. But Lola, *ma chèrie*, there is something you should know. Charlie has had bad luck. He has no money now, and cannot afford to go to America unless you help him."

Lola frowned. "He cannot afford to go? Then why—? You mean he is taking me with him because he wants me to pay for his passage? Am I just another dalliance? Just another bankroll? I really am making a terrible mistake!"

Sophie shook her head, "No! No, of course not! Charlie told me you are the only woman he has ever cared about, and he truly means it. What does it matter who pays for the journey? He wants to be with you. That is what matters. What do you have here? Only bad memories. Think about starting a new life in a fabulous country. A young country, where everything is possible. Where you will no longer have to put up with a pompous society and its hypocritical morality. You will be free! Free to do as you please. Surely, that is what you have always wanted, freedom to be who you really are?"

Lola was simmering. She thought over what Sophie said, and realized she was still holding the rose Charlie gave her. She inhaled its aroma. She could still feel his embrace and taste the magic of his kiss. She wanted to believe Sophie—she needed to believe her.

Chapter 34

Sophie was in Lola's room opening drawers and cabinet doors. "We should get started immediately. We have much to do in a short time."

"What is the hurry? I am not sure I am ready to leave yet."

"Lola, what are you saying? You just heard Charlie say he will be back in a few days. You need to decide what to pack and what you wish to sell."

"Sell? Why should I wish to sell my belongings?"

"Do you have enough money to pay for the voyage for both you and Charlie?"

Lola sat on her bed and smelled the rose in her hand.

"You are planning to go to America with Charlie, are you not?" Sophie stepped in front of her. With arms akimbo, she stared down at her and demanded, "Lola! You are going to America with Charlie?"

Lola looked pensive. "I am not sure. I want to, but I do not know if I am ready for such a big change in my life."

Sophie sat beside Lola on the bed. She put her arm around her and with her other hand, she gently turned Lola's face towards her. "Listen to me. I am telling you this because I care about you. Your father does not love you. He thinks you are a tramp. You have just lost your baby girl. You told me they would replace you at the Moulin Rouge, so you would have to find work elsewhere." Sophie's eyes glittered. "Just think, if you have to find another place to work, why not find a place in New Orleans? Which do you prefer? You can stay in Paris and be miserable, or you can move on with your life. Why not have a wonderful affair with Charlie? I guarantee he will make you happy on your journey to New Orleans. Do you want to be happy?"

She hugged Lola. "I am so happy for you to have this fabulous opportunity. I wish I could be with you and see New Orleans with a handsome lover. So, let us go through your things and take out what you want to sell. I can help you get a good price." Sophie held her breath awaiting Lola's response.

Chapter 35

Over the next few days, Lola grew more cheerful as she and Sophie completed the preparations.

Charlie arrived at Sophie's flat. He nodded to Apash and Sophie as he entered, but walked to Lola with a big smile and handed her a small bouquet. "Are you ready to leave?"

Lola threw her arms around his neck. "Yes! I am ready for you to whisk me off to a wonderful new world!"

Charlie kissed her. His jaw dropped when he saw a great deal of baggage. He laughed. "Are you planning on opening a clothing store in New Orleans?"

"*Au contraire*. This is all I have left after selling my things. I want to make you proud when you show me off in New Orleans!"

Charlie leaned forward and kissed her hand. "*Ma chérie*, you always make me proud. Besides, it's your beauty everyone will be admiring."

Apash grabbed some bags and demanded, "Come, we must leave if we are to get to the dock on time."

Charlie and Apash helped the driver load all of Lola's baggage into the cab that would take them to the train station. Sophie insisted she and Apash accompany Lola and Charlie on their ride to Le Havre seaport. Sophie was taking no chances. Before she could put the final phase of her plan into action, she needed to confirm Lola was aboard the ship that would carry her to America.

Along the harbor crowded with travelers, seafarers and dockworkers were baggage handlers pushing carts with stacks of luggage, creaking boats tugging on their moorings, shouts of stevedores dragging their cable-like ropes in various directions, the squawk of gulls circling under cloudy skies and the briny smell of the sea, mixed with emissions from ship smokestacks.

They hugged and kissed each other goodbye. Lola thanked Sophie for all she had done. After one more round of hugs, it was time to board.

Sophie saw Lola and Charlie wave from the ship's deck. She returned their waves and waited dockside until the ship departed. She said to Apash, I can feel the money in my hands. Soon we will be rich!"

Apash looked doubtful. "You mean soon we will lose our heads to the guillotine!"

That night Sophie had a nightmare. She dreamt Monsieur La Fontaine called the gendarmes to drag her away to prison. At the trial, the jury heard how she had a baby killed for greed. She could see the disgusted visages of jurors as they decreed she face the guillotine for her rapacious crimes. She could hear the angry cries of the courtroom attendees when they called out for her blood, "She is a baby killer! Cut off her head!"

In her dream, she resisted the unyielding arms that dragged her to the scaffold. She spit at the twisted faces of the outraged crowd who cried out for her death.

Holding her baby, Lola stood at the top of the scaffold, her face twisted into a mask of revulsion. "You stole my baby and now you will die!"

Monsieur La Fontaine stood beside Lola with a diabolical smile.

They tied Sophie's body to the bench, forcing her head into the lunette. She struggled when she saw the basket that would catch her fallen head. Swoosh went the blade.

Sophie woke and screamed, "No! No!" She jumped from her bed and rubbed her neck. "Wake up you fool! It is just a stupid nightmare!"

For the rest of the night, she paced the floor. To wipe the horrible dream from her mind she thought how she will spend her new riches. *I will open a brothel, the best in Paris. A place where the rich and famous will spend their money on earthly delights. Maybe even Monsieur La Fontaine will allow himself to be entertained there!*

Chapter 36

Monsieur Émile La Fontaine, Finance Minister for the Government of France, sat at his breakfast table. A pall of gloom consumed him as he read the daily newspapers. *Le Temps, Le Petit Journal, Le Matin,* and others lay scattered about the table. Each had stories about Daniel Wilson, the son-in-law of President Grévy, who had just been arrested. The police accused him of managing an agency that sold recommendations for honors in the Elysée Palace. There were rumors the President was involved.

Émile knew the President had nothing to do with this affair but the newspapers were always ready to stoke the fires and fan the flames. Radicals were making trouble and they may try to bring down the President. Émile feared for his position, but he was more concerned that there would once again be violence.

France suffered much bloodshed in Émile's lifetime. The Crimean War, The Second Opium War, The Franco-Prussian War, and the worst of it, when Parisian fought Parisian during The Paris Commune when 50,000 Parisians died or were executed.

Besides war, France was still reeling from several scandals over the past few years, including corruption, murder and suicide, and a case of spying that nearly caused another war with Germany. France could not tolerate another scandal.

Émile left for his office. He always enjoyed the walk from his home to his place of work. Not today. He took the path which crossed over the Place de la Bastille. Émile tread lightly as he passed the spot where the infamous Bastille Prison had stood, when on July 14, 1789, an outraged mob stormed it and began the revolution that changed the nation. Of the Bastille, nothing remained. It was demolished a few days after it was taken during the start of the French Revolution. Under his feet was the dried blood of thousands of Parisians who died, not only during the French Revolution but during decades of turmoil over politics, national pride and power.

When he arrived at his office, he saw an unmarked envelope on his desk. He had a bad feeling about the contents and debated if he should open it. Curiosity got the better of him.

Your Excellency, Monsieur La Fontaine,

It is of great importance I meet with you concerning the fate of your daughter. Believe me when I say your political future is at stake. When you know what Lola has done, you will understand the danger you are in. I will be at your house at three pm today. Do not disappoint me, or you will regret it.

In all sincerity,

Madame Sophie Décharde

Émile furrowed his brows. "What insolence!" He crumpled the note and tossed it aside.

He worked at his desk but like a bee buzzing in his ear, he couldn't ignore the note. *Who is she and what does she know? How does it concern my political future? What does my daughter have to do with this? Lola, have you not caused me enough humiliation?*

He looked at the crumpled message. *It must be a joke! Of course, if Lola is involved, anything is possible. All right! I will see what this nonsense is about!*

Chapter 37

Émile hurried home and marched into his study. From his liquor cabinet, he removed a bottle of Courvoisier L'Esprit de Cognac, the cognac both he and Emperor Napoleon preferred.

He poured a small amount of the precious amber liquid into a tulip-shaped glass. Under normal circumstances, he would have warmed the cognac naturally as he held the glass in the palm of his hand and inhale its fragrances of cinnamon, apricot, honey and the smoke of a fine cigar. But he was impatient. He swirled the glass, brought it to his lips and sipped. He relished the complex texture of the liquid fire as it rolled over his tongue, flowed down his throat and pooled into his belly.

The taste brought back memories of his carefree days as a young man. When he and his university comrades enjoyed fine liquor and cigars, singing songs, admiring women, and debating over politics at the local taverns.

But this pleasure did nothing to relieve his anxiety over Lola. Émile decided if Madame Sophie did not arrive exactly on time, he would dismiss the letter as a prank and return to his office. However, promptly at three o'clock, his footman entered the study. His hand held a small round silver tray with a calling card that smelled of cheap perfume. Émile could see the name Madame Sophie written in a grandiose flair. He regarded it as if it was a filthy rag and refused to touch it. "Show her in," he commanded.

To disguise his apprehension, Émile sat behind his desk and busied himself with some papers. The footman showed Sophie into the study. Émile ignored her approach to his desk.

He heard her say in a harsh voice, "Monsieur La Fontaine, I am not here to play games with you. I am here to discuss urgent business."

Émile lifted his head. He could see by her attire and demeanor she was of the peasant class, and most likely a whore. "You are a foolish woman to threaten me. Do you realize who I am?"

Sophie announced with devious delight, "*Oui*, Monsieur La Fontaine, I know exactly who you are. I am here to tell you your daughter Lola is dead!"

"What are you talking about?"

"Lola is dead. She killed herself because of you."

With a caustic stare, he spat out, "Are you playing a joke? You had better get out of here before I have you arrested!"

Sophie snapped, "This is no joke, Monsieur La Fontaine. Your daughter is dead!"

Émile sprang from his desk chair. It skidded back and crashed against the bookcase. "That is impossible! Lola would never kill herself!"

Sophie smiled. "Oh yes, she is dead. I saw her myself as she jumped into *La Seine*."

"Dead!" His face contorted with rage. "You are either mad or a damnable liar!"

"I am not mad. You need not believe me. However, you will believe your daughter. She has provided you with the proof!" Sophie removed the letter from her purse that Lola wrote in childbirth at Sophie's direction. She presented it to Émile. "I found this note on her desk. Lola wrote this for you before she died. I am sure you will recognize your daughter's handwriting."

He glared at Sophie and grabbed the note. His hands trembled as he read Lola's words. Émile stomach twisted and the letter slipped from his hands. "When did this happen?"

Sophie scooped up the letter and said, "Last week."

"Last week! Why have I not heard of this before?" The blood hammered his temples in time with his pounding heartbeat.

"Oh, now you care!" Sophie's voice was hard. "When she came to you alone and with child, you called her a *putain* and said you never wanted to see her again. You were cold and cruel to her. How do you think she felt when you told her she was dead to you? What difference is it to you now that she is dead? You did not care then, why should you care now?"

"My relationship with Lola is none of your business! You have no knowledge of my feelings for her. You are in no position to judge me."

"So, you do have feelings for Lola."

"You say she drowned in *La Seine*? Where is her bod—where is she?"

"She has not been found. Many people drown in La Seine and are not found for weeks or months, sometimes never."

He paced the floor, turned and asked, "You say you saw her drowned. Are you sure it was her?"

"Of course, I am sure! She was staying with me when the baby was born. The next day she ran from the house like a madwoman, screaming and crying that she shamed her *Papá* and could not live without your love. I ran after her, but I was holding the baby and could not keep up. I saw her jump. There was nothing I could do. Now you are a *Grand-pére*. You must take care of your *petite-fille!*"

Émile thought back to the last time he had seen his daughter. *Yes, I was angry that she expected me to take care of her and her bastard. But to kill herself?*

Sophie slammed her fist onto the desk. "*Grand-pére!* What about the baby! You must take her!"

"The baby? I cannot—I will not take care of a baby!"

"I thought that would be your response. You turned Lola from your house, now you would let her baby starve in the streets? Did you not read Lola's words? She wants you to love the poor little one. Have you learned nothing from Lola's death?

"I am too old to care for a baby and too tired." He ran his fingers across his balding head. "What about the baby's father?"

"He knows nothing of the baby and would never believe it was his."

"Have you spoken to him? Perhaps he would want the child."

"You talk like a fool! Let me make this simple for you. You have no choice. You will take care of Lola's baby or I will tell the newspapers everything. I will tell them you cast out your only daughter because she became a can-can dancer. I will tell them that when she told you she was pregnant, you said she was dead to you. I will tell them she killed herself because of you. Then I will tell them you will let your grandchild starve in the streets because you do not want it to dirty your pompous world. That should make quite the juicy scandal. What do you think, Monsieur Le Minister? What will Monsieur Le President think, *eh,* when he finds out about his important cabinet minister? Do you think this news will make the headlines?"

"If you try that, I will have you thrown in the darkest dungeon in the Le Conciergerie Prison!"

Sophie threw her head back with a hearty laugh. "You can try, but I have many friends who know your story just as well as I. They will tell the newspapers, and if you try to throw them in jail, they have friends who will tell. So, you see, I have helped you make your decision, *oui?"*

He hated Sophie for putting him in this untenable position. But he knew Sophie was right. He could not afford a scandal, certainly not now. He had enough to worry about without Sophie giving him more problems. He sighed. His words came slowly and in tired defeat, "Bring me the baby. I will have it taken care of."

Sophie's words flowed like a cobra's venom, "Do you think I am doing this from the kindness of my heart?"

He felt hot blood surge to his face. "I should have known, you are nothing but a mercenary slut."

"Your words mean nothing to me. I have been called names you have never heard in your clean, little world. You may have the baby and my silence for fifty thousand francs."

"Are you insane? I will not give you even one franc!"

"All right, suit yourself. I will be happy to deliver the newspaper to you tomorrow. I am sure you will not need your spectacles to read the headlines." Sophie turned to leave.

Émile shouted, "Wait! Wait! Come back!"

"So, you have come to your senses, Monsieur La Fontaine?"

"Yes, all right. But that is too much money. I will give you half of what you ask for!"

"So, you wish to bargain with your granddaughter's life? Shall I just drop her in the street, where she will live with the other poor homeless bastards? Or maybe, I will sell her. There are plenty of men who would pay me a large sum for your beautiful granddaughter."

Rage consumed him. He wanted to thrash Sophie, but he held back. Instead, he capitulated. "I will pay what you ask, you miserable bitch. When do I get the child?"

"Tomorrow you are to come to the Cafe Pisse d'ane on the Rue d'Abouler. Do you know where it is?"

"I will not be there. André my manservant will come in my place."

"I do not care who comes, but he must have the money. Remember, fifty thousand francs, not one sou less—or you will not get the baby, and I will bring her to the newspaper office as proof when I tell them all about you. Do not try any tricks, Monsieur Le Minister."

"I will not trick you. Now *get out of my house!*"

Chapter 38

Lola and Charlie looked at the wharf from the promenade deck. Lola had tears in her eyes.

"*Ma belle-aimée*, why are you crying?"

Lola shook her head. "I am both happy and sad. I am happy to start a new life in America but I love Paris. It has always been my home. Although I have been unhappy there, I am sad to leave.

Charlie hugged her. "This is no time for crying. Dry your tears. It's time to have fun, so come on, let's enjoy ourselves! Is that all right with you?"

Lola's face brightened. "Yes, Charlie, that is definitely all right with me!"

Their stateroom pleased Lola. She said to Charlie, "I have never been on an ocean liner before. The accommodation is more comfortable than I imagined it would be. It resembles a grand hotel." She walked around their cabin and ran her fingers over the smooth, polished oak and mahogany woodwork, the lustrous silk draperies and matching comforters. "Look Charlie, the lower berth! It is extended to accommodate two people! There is a nice large wardrobe and a sofa!" She opened the door. "We even have toilet conveniences."

"Of course!" Charlie grinned. "These are modern times, you know! Would you like me to give you a tour? I've been on this ship before, so I know my way around."

"That would be wonderful!"

He presented her his elbow. "Follow me for the grand tour, *mademoiselle*."

They walked to a wide staircase. It was handsomely ornamented with plush handrails and balusters of a rich and fanciful wrought iron pattern.

Charlie began the tour with the Library. They entered through folding mahogany doors. Surrounding the expansive open area were several alcoves and cozy corners adapted for reading and conversation. A large number of bookcases bounded the end of the room. The light came from above through an octagonal skylight. The ceiling treatment displayed broad panels of scroll ornaments in low relief. The tables, bookcases and chairs were of dark mahogany. Lola joked, "This is a beautiful room, Charlie. Do you think we will spend most of our time reading?"

"I rather doubt that."

Next was the elegantly appointed smoking room with paintings hanging against dark wood paneling. There were a number of small tables. The divans covered with Moroccan leather, and a liberal supply of similarly covered, exceedingly comfortable armchairs. Charlie said, "This is a cozy room for after-dinner coffee."

Lola pointed. "I think you would be more interested in that refreshment bar than coffee, no?"

Charlie smirked.

They proceeded to the music room on the promenade deck. The inviting room was painted in a cheerful yellow and well-adapted to social gatherings and concert hours. Lola walked to the piano, tinkled a few keys and hummed. Charlie said, "Maybe you'll entertain us one night."

Lola smirked. "The only entertaining I wish to do is in our bedroom."

Charlie asked, "Do you think there's enough to do on this ship?"

"Yes, I believe we will never have a boring moment. But what about the dining room?"

"You'll just have to wait for supper to see that room."

They returned to their cabin. Lola couldn't stop talking about how impressed she was with the luxuriousness of the ship. They sat together on the sofa when she noticed push buttons attached to the wall in several places around the cabin. "What are the buttons for?"

"Why don't you press one?"

Lola furrowed her brows in mock jest. "Will it make the ship sink?"

He presented a sly smile. "Try it and find out."

Lola tentatively pressed a button. "Shall I hold my nose as we go under?" She giggled.

Moments later they heard a soft knock on the stateroom door. Lola opened it to see a steward.

Charlie said, "I think we should celebrate our voyage with a toast. Shall I have him bring us a bottle of champagne?"

"Is it not rather early for a cocktail?"

He smiled, "Not in New Orleans!"

Lola laughed. "But we are not there yet."

"Who cares? Go, young man, and fetch us a bottle of your finest bubbly!"

The steward returned with the champagne, opened the bottle, set it in an ice bucket and left.

Charlie poured them each a glass and toasted, "As they say in New Orleans, *laissez les bons temps rouler!*"

They clinked glasses and sipped.

Lola said, "That is not any French I know. What does it mean?"

"It's Cajun French for 'Let the good times roll.' It means it's time for us to have fun!"

"Cajun French? What language is that?"

"It's a long story. But in the last century, people emigrated from France to Canada. Originally, they were called les Acadians, but eventually became known as Cajuns. When the British took over French Canada, the Cajuns were expelled and many eventually settled in the Bayou area of New Orleans. Cajuns have their own way of speaking and their own culture."

"Cajun French? Bayou area? Oh, I have so much to learn!"

Charlie laughed. "New Orleans is a wonderful place with people of all cultures and nationalities. It might take a little time to get used to, but I think you'll enjoy being there."

"I expect you are right. But, since I will live in America, from now on speak to me only in English, so I can practice. Umm…how do you say in English? Umm…okay?"

Charlie smiled, "Okay!"

After the champagne, they helped each other undress and made love. Then slept until the steward knocked on their door and announced it was time for supper.

Lola and Charlie each selected their attire. He chose a fashionable black wool tailcoat ensemble. Fitted to his body, the tailcoat had a straight waist and peaked lapels faced in black silk and a watch chain hung from his white silk waistcoat. The white formal shirt had a stand up rolled collar with a white silk bow tie worn with dress studs and cuff links. His trousers had a stripe at the side seam. He wore black patent leather shoes with pointed toes and carried a black silk top hat and white kid gloves.

Lola dressed in an evening gown of white taffeta with a small design of pink roses through it. The skirt draped over her hips. The waist had a fichu of white chiffon fastened with an immense artificial pink rose, whose leaves and buds reached to the point of the bodice. The sleeves were close-fitting to the elbow and were finished with a ruffle of white chiffon, which, like the fichu, it was edged was pink satin ribbon. Atop her head, she had a small hat decorated with plumage of exotic birds. Her glacé kid gloves came below the elbow and her satin slippers matched her gown.

Charlie finished dressing first and watched Lola standing at the mirror fussing over her finishing touches. She could see Charlie's reflection in the mirror as he stood behind her. "Why are you looking at me like that?"

"Lola, you're so beautiful! I want to remember you as you look at this moment for the rest of my life."

She laughed and wondered what he might be trying to tell her. Lola wasn't sure how she felt about Charlie. *Did she love him? Did he love her?* She asked, "Why? Do you think there'll be a time when you will forget how I look?"

"*Ma chérie,* I can never forget you."

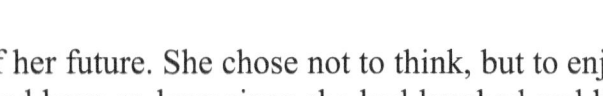

Lola felt unsure of her future. She chose not to think, but to enjoy each moment. It had been so long since she had laughed and had fun. She decided to wait until the end of their voyage to examine her feelings for Charlie. For now, she planned only to enjoy herself.

They entered the grand dining hall through the Palm Court, a long hall lined with palm trees sitting on a marble floor. There were groupings of renaissance style chairs and small tables.

The dining hall had a domed stained-glass skylight. The ceiling was done in white and gold Lincrusta, and the walls were superbly paneled with elaborate figures, rich carvings and moldings. Khiva silk patterned carpets conjured up exotic images of Asia's Silk Road. The general effect of the dark rich mahogany walls, the graceful arches and the paneled ceiling in white and gold, surmounted by a great crystal dome rising through the two decks to a height of thirty-three feet, along with the dark russet velvet upholstery, suggested a palatial structure on terra firma rather than a floating temple of luxury.

A small orchestra played soft music adding brilliance and festivity to the room. After the couple had been seated, they were handed menus and treated attentively by several waiters. They enjoyed hors d'oeuvres, a fish consommé, duckling with green peas, sweetbread croquettes, cauliflower, boiled new potatoes, assorted pastry and orange ice cream dessert. They drank champagne and claret and finished their sumptuous meal with a brandy.

After dinner, they strolled to the ballroom where they danced to a full orchestra playing vibrant music. Later they retired to a night of sexual delight.

Their days were filled with pleasant walks along the promenade deck, playing shuffleboard, reading and enjoying the pleasant weather as they lay in deck chairs. For Lola, their evenings were the most exciting. Although dining and dancing, sometimes under the stars, kept them up into the wee hours, what Lola enjoyed most was their all-consuming passion when they made love.

The week of their voyage passed quickly. Before she knew it, Lola realized it was the morning of arrival at the port of New Orleans. They lay in bed naked after another night of lovemaking. Charlie was still asleep. Lola leaned her head on her crooked elbow watching him. She admired his beautiful face and fine physique. She felt wonderful. Charlie was always attentive and ensured she had been happy and comfortable. He frequently flattered her and made her laugh. He knew how to arouse her sexually and always satisfied her. *Does he treat me so well because he cares for me or because I'm paying for everything? How does he feel about me? Will this end badly for me?*

Lola and Charlie waited on the deck while the porter collected their bags. The port was much longer and busier than the port at Le Havre. She could see the busy wharves, warehouses, factories, and office buildings of the Central Business District. Barges, dredgers, tugboats, and many banana ships crowded the port. All manner of ships and boats, flying flags from many nations, were departing, arriving or docked. She had her first view of ornately trimmed paddle wheelers with their roaring engines, belching smokestacks, distinctive whistles and splashing paddlewheels.

Lola hugged Charlie's arm. Her body tingled with excitement. She looked at him with wide eyes and said, "I can't believe we're actually in America! I feel like I'm leaving sadness behind and beginning a wonderful new life."

Charlie covered her hand with his and smiled. "I hope your new life is all you desire it to be."

Before she could respond, the ship bells rang to indicate it was time to disembark.

Making their way down the gangplank, Lola heard the shouts of sailors as they tied giant ropes and chains to the dock. Heady aromas of bananas and coffee filled the air as the port pulsated with a never-ending procession of men carrying banana stalks or sacks of coffee hoisted onto their shoulders.

Lola waited on the pier for Charlie while he left to fetch a porter and a carriage. The exhilaration of the hectic activity fascinated her until she had an uncomfortable feeling that caused the hair on the back of her neck to stand. She tried to shake off the feeling, but it remained. She scanned the dock to determine what made her feel so agitated. She caught sight of an old woman standing on a loading platform about six meters away. *Is that woman staring at me?* The woman wore a shawl, dress and an elaborately twisted turban all in white, contrasting with the color of her deep brown skin. Around her neck were many varicolored necklaces and hoop earrings dangled from her ears. The old woman's large amber eyes were like pinpoint beams of light burning into her. Lola turned away, but she continued to feel the glare.

Charlie returned, driven in a carriage loaded with their luggage. He jumped from the carriage and put out his hand to help her. Lola stopped him and pointed in the old woman's direction. She asked, "Do you have any idea who that woman is?"

He turned his head. "Which woman?"

"That woman—." Lola searched the crowd. "I...The old woman...where is she?"

Chapter 39

Charlie helped Lola onto the seat of the landau carriage and announced the address to the driver.

Lola's eyes combed the crowd.

"Are you still looking for that woman?"

Lola frowned. "She was staring at me as if she knew me. It wasn't a pleasant stare."

"I wouldn't worry about it. She was probably trying to find someone. You say she's old? Her eyesight's probably poor and she may have thought you were a woman she knew."

"I suppose you're right." She shrugged. "No matter, she's no longer there."

Lola appreciated the charm and character of New Orleans. "The air smells so sweet here, like a thousand flowers. And look at all the shops!"

"That's because we're riding along Canal Street, the main shopping district of the city." He pointed to a building. "You see the St. Charles Hotel over there? It's the grandest hotel in the South. When it was built, it was considered the finest piece of architecture in the new world. Half the business of this city is transacted there. It's quite a historic monument for the entire state of Louisiana. And see that corner? That's where the flower-women sit."

Lola took a deep breath and enjoyed the multitude of fragrances. She saw women along the outer edges of the arcaded sidewalk, surrounded by flowers of every variety.

She marveled at seeing the quaint shops and restaurants, the buildings adorned with lacy iron fenced balconies and archways that revealed partially hidden courtyards. "I can see why people become enthralled with the mystique of New Orleans."

They arrived at the Lower Garden District, a charming area with a variety of housing styles. Charlie's house sat with a view of Coliseum Square, a lovely tree-lined park with fountains, curved walks and a fish pond.

Charlie announced, "Here we are!"

Lola saw a two-story Greek Revival style townhouse with three tall openings across the front on both the first and second floors. There was a scrolled-iron fenced balcony and a front garden perfumed by an array of camellias, magnolias and jasmine.

"Oh, Charlie! Your house is wonderful!"

Charlie opened the door and said, "Thank you, but it's not my house. It belongs to my Aunt Marie, my father's sister. She lives on a plantation out of town, so she seldom uses it. She lets me live here when I am in New Orleans. Oh, but there are people you must meet." Charlie called out, "Esther! *Grand-père* Samuel! We're here!"

A black woman with kindly eyes and pleasing features approached them accompanied by a grey-haired black gentleman with a cane. He had small facial scars and the milky eyes of a blind person. They smiled and nodded with deference. "*Bienvenue*, Mademoiselle Dupin, Charlie advised us you were coming. It's a great pleasure to meet you."

Charlie announced, "It's important to Lola to practice, so please be sure to speak to her only in English.

Samuel nodded his head politely and said, "Welcome, Mademoiselle Dupin."

Lola said, "*C'est un Plaisir...*" Lola paused, blushed and giggled. She continued, "Err...It's a pleasure to meet you, also."

Charlie placed his arm around Esther and kissed her on the cheek. He said, "These wonderful people are my family."

Lola looked confused. "Your family?"

Charlie laughed. "Although we're not related, they are closer to me than any of my natural-born relatives. As you know, my mother died when I was young and my father was seldom home.

Esther's mother, who has sadly passed, took care of me as a child. Now Esther takes care of me like a mother. *Grand-père* Samuel is Esther's father. They live here and attend to the house."

Charlie asked Esther, "Where are your children?"

"They're in the kitchen. I'll fetch them." She returned accompanied by two handsome young people.

Samuel smiled proudly. He placed his hand on the shoulder of the boy, "My grandson's name is Alphonse and my lovely granddaughter is Monique. Children, say hello to Mademoiselle Dupin, but say it in English so she can practice."

Monique curtsied. She appeared to be about seventeen years old. She was tall and slim with a sweet face and lively brown eyes. The boy bowed and smiled at Lola. He was about fourteen with bright white teeth and large hazel eyes. "Pleased to meet you, Mademoiselle Dupin," they said in unison.

"Take the luggage to their room."

"Oui, Grand-père."

"Why don't you get settled while I prepare dinner?"

"Good idea, Esther!" Charlie turned to Lola, "Esther is the best cook in New Orleans, so you're in for a treat!"

<hr>

Later that day, Monique knocked on their bedroom door and announced to Charlie and Lola that dinner was ready. They came downstairs to see a table laden with delightfully prepared dishes of smoked oysters, turtle soup, gumbo and bread pudding. After dinner, Lola exclaimed, "Everything was delicious! I believe Charlie is correct. You must be the best cook in New Orleans!"

The young ones cleared the table and washed the dishes. The adults enjoyed coffee and sherry in the parlor. They chatted for a short time when Charlie announced, "Lola, my sweet, I must leave for a while. You can stay here and talk with the family. They can entertain you with information about New Orleans."

Lola asked, "You're leaving? But why?"

"I have business to attend to and I'll be back late."

"May I go with you?"

"Trust me, you'd be bored. You'll have a much better time with Esther, *Grand-père* Samuel and the children. Tomorrow, I'll show you around New Orleans. You'll love Vieux Carré and the French Quarter, and we'll have a wonderful dinner at Antoine's."

Disappointed and hoping to be wrong, Lola assumed Charlie was off to gamble. Deciding to make the best of it, she said, "If you must leave, I'll be delighted to spend time with your family." She had feared this might happen, but rather than make assumptions, she decided to be patient.

"So, *Mademoiselle* Dupin, you're from Paris?" Samuel asked.

She forced a gentle smile and said, "Please call me Lola. Yes, I'm from Paris but I'm excited to hear about New Orleans."

Esther announced with pride, "My *Papá* is a historian. But I must advise you once he gets started talking about history, he finds it difficult to stop."

Samuel chuckled, "My daughter is opinionated and forthright but I have to admit she's right. Please stop me when you find yourself bored with my chronicle. I won't be offended."

"Monsieur Samuel, I'm sure I will be fascinated. Although I'm from France and have a bit of knowledge of the history of the 'New World', there's much I do not know, so please begin."

"As you wish." He cleared his throat and took a sip of coffee. "Most likely you're aware of the abundance of exploration and colonization fever that took place during the late Middle Ages. Kings and Queens were always trying to enrich their war chests and the discovery of the 'New World' made their eyes dazzle with the possibility of untold riches. Spain led the way, pillaging the Americas, followed by other European powers."

Lola wanted to hear what Samuel was saying, but her mind kept wandering. *Where did Charlie go? Why was it so urgent that he leave?* Her attention to Samuel waned in and out.

Samuel continued, "France, unlike Spain, didn't find gold and precious gems in the New World. Facing bankruptcy from years of war, France had little money or interest in developing the Louisiana Territory called New France. That was until 1718 when a Scotsman by the name of John Law, a professional gambler—"

Lola interrupted, "Did you say gambler?" *Was Charlie gambling at this very moment?*

Samuel nodded, "Oh yes, he was a quite the gambler! He was also a convicted murderer and a prisoner escapee. But he was a brilliant economist, who came up with a scheme to make himself rich."

What if Charlie doesn't come back? What shall I do?

Samuel coughed. "Pardon me," Samuel said. "My daughter tries to get me to stop smoking and one day I may listen to her. If you wish we can do this another day."

Lola felt embarrassed for ignoring Samuel. "Oh, no, please go on."

Samuel continued, "Let's see, where was I? Oh, yes. He was desperate to apply the French policy of forced emigration that had previously been used in Canada. Sadly, John Law turned Louisiana into a French penal colony.

Gendarmes deported their undesirables, emptying French prisons and sweeping the streets for smugglers, thieves, beggars, and the depraved. Also, prostitutes and female criminals, who had the fleur-de-lis branded on their shoulders to mark them as under life sentence, were rounded up for exile to Louisiana.

Many prisoners were set free under the condition they marry prostitutes and go with them to Louisiana. The newly married couples were chained together and taken to the port of embarkation. They were treated no better than the African slaves who were forced to come to the New World. The difference being the prisoners' children were not born into slavery as were the African children."

Lola took in a breath. "How terrible! It makes me angry when anyone is forced to give up their liberty and be at the mercy of the rich and powerful. I'm sorry for the interruption. Please carry on and, if you would, I would like to know about your family."

"No apology necessary. I'm happy you're interested."

Esther said, "I think maybe that'll be enough of a history lesson for one day. Lola's had a long day."

Lola was tired, but she knew she wouldn't be able to sleep until Charlie returned. Determined to listen carefully, she insisted, "Oh, please, I really would like to know about your family. But if you would not mind, Esther, I would love more coffee."

Samuel began again. "It's fortunate the French kept careful records, so there was quite good information about the many Africans who were brought to the New World colony. That's how I became aware of the life of my ancestor, Louis Sinegal. He was captured in Upper Guinea, Africa, and brought to the French Louisiana Territory in 1723. At that time, the territory was nothing more than a tiny village with only a cluster of huts in a poorly drained swamp area. Yet it became the capital city, New France.

Louis Sinegal arrived as a slave from an area near Senegambia, where the people were known to have a sophisticated culture and they were famous for their artisanship. Louis was one of the many African farmers who knew how to cultivate rice. The white settlers of the time didn't know about rice cultivation. Eventually, rice developed into a staple of the Louisiana diet. The slaves not only provided manual labor but also came with the knowledge and skills crucial to keeping the white settlers of Louisiana from starving."

Monique and Alphonse entered the room. Monique announced, "Kitchen's all clean!" She leaned her head on her mother's shoulder as she sat next to her on the sofa.

Alphonse sat on the floor next to his grandfather who rubbed his head playfully. He looked up at his grandfather, "Are you telling those old stories again, grand-père?"

Esther reprimanded him, "Mind your manners, Alphonse. Someday you'll be telling your children about your history."

"Yes, *Mamá*, I'm sorry."

Samuel turned his head towards Lola, "Have I bored you thus far?"

Lola shook her head. "No! Not at all Monsieur Samuel."

"Very well." Samuel took out his pipe and lit it. After a few puffs, he began again. "In those early years, it was possible for slaves to buy their freedom. Louis Sinegal's master loaned him to other landowners to help dig drainage canals, for which he was paid. Most of the money went to his master, but eventually, Louis Sinegal was able to buy his freedom. He believed in education and taught himself to read and write French. He married and sent his five sons to Paris for an education. They returned and over the generations, became farmers, doctors, lawyers and businessmen. Things went well for the Sinegals, but they did have their share of troubles.

"During the Civil War, my family fought along with 10,000 black soldiers, both free and slave, in The Corps d'Afrique. Of the fifty men in my family who joined the Union to fight, ten died during the war. I myself was wounded and lost my eyesight. We won the praise of President Lincoln for our valor and skill. But after the war Union troops burned our farms and properties. The same happened to white folks. Though scattered we may be, the Sinegal family lives on."

It seemed like Charlie had been gone forever, and she was beginning to think he wouldn't return that night—maybe never. Suddenly, there was a loud bang. The sound caught everyone's attention. Charlie kicked the door open. He leaned against the doorframe, his clothes were disheveled and blood oozed from his nose and mouth.

Esther hurried to fetch a rag and water basin. Lola shouted, "Charlie, what happened?"

Chapter 40

Charlie took the damp cloth Esther offered and wiped the blood from his face. "Please don't be concerned. I'm fine. It's nothing. I just ran into a bunch of hoodlums trying to rob me. Unfortunately, New Orleans can be a dangerous place."

Lola said, "We should send for the police!"

"No, it won't do any good. The culprits are long gone by now. Please, I'm perfectly fine. I'm just tired and want to go to bed."

Lola could see the worried look in Esther's eyes as she asked, "Charlie, "Are you sure you're all right?"

Charlie kissed Esther on the forehead, "Yes, I'm fine. I just need rest."

<hr>

After lying awake worrying most of the night, Lola drifted off. It seemed like she had only slept a few moments when Charlie roused her.

"Good morning, sleepyhead. Let's get breakfast, I'm starving!"

Lola saw Charlie standing by the bed dressed, except for bruises, he looked bright and cheerful. "Shouldn't you take it easy after what you've been through last night?"

Charlie scoffed, "I've been in a scuffle or two in my day, much worse than what happened last night. Forget about it and let's enjoy the day."

She was happy to know Charlie wasn't seriously injured and hurriedly dressed. "Will Esther be making us breakfast?"

"Not today. We'll be eating at a special place this morning."

Before she knew it, they were on Decatur Street in the French Quarter, sitting at a table in Café Du Monde. "This place smells wonderful," Lola said as the waiter brought two steaming cups of coffee and two plates, each with three small pillow-like pastries covered in a heaping amount of powdered sugar. "What do you call these?"

Charlie lifted one off his plate and blew the powdered sugar at her.

"*Vous bête*! What are you doing?" Lola brushed the powder from her face and clothes. "Did the knock on your head scatter your brain?"

He laughed. "They're called *beignets* and the tradition is to blow the powdered sugar at a first-time visitor to Café Du Monde."

"I don't like that tradition." Lola took a bite and licked sugar from her fingers. "But the beignet is delicious! I wonder what other interesting things are in store for me in New Orleans."

"If you're ready, let's go and see." They went off arm in arm as he took her sightseeing

Leaving Café Du Monde, they could see the statue of Andrew Jackson atop his rearing horse. As they approached Lola said, "This Square is designed much like Place des Vosges in Paris, do you think? That is, except for the man on the horse."

"You're right. It's called Jackson Square. That statue is of a man called Andrew Jackson. He was the hero of a war we fought with Great Britain in 1812 and became the President of the United States."

"It's interesting that the statue represents the United States and yet the square is still so French!"

"That's New Orleans for you. If you're ready, there's more to see."

They approached the corner of Chartres and St. Louis streets where there was a house with an octagonal copper-clad cupola set on a steep-pitched hip roof.

Lola asked, "What's the significance of this place?"

"This is known as the Girod House and also the Napoleon House."

"Napoleon House? Are you saying Napoleon lived here?"

"Well no, but if he lived long enough, he might have. Nicholas Girod, the owner of this house, was a one-time Mayor of New Orleans. He devised a plot, along with men associated with the pirate Jean Lafitte, to rescue Bonaparte from the island of St. Helena and bring him here. Girod designed this house for Napoleon to use after his rescue. The plan was well underway but Napoleon died before the rescue could take place.

Lola joked, "Do you think the little corporal would have liked this place?"

"I understand it's quite nicely furnished."

Lola smirked.

"But there's another house I'd like to show you. It's quite different from this one."

Charlie brought Lola to see a tall, imposing mansion at 1319 St. Charles Avenue. He pointed to the mansion and said, "There are many places in New Orleans believed to be haunted, but this one is my favorite."

Lola scanned the façade. "What is so special about this one?"

"This place is called The Devil's Mansion."

Lola feigned fright. "The Devil's Mansion—oh my!"

"Old-timers say the devil built it in the late 1820s as a home for his lover, a stunning Frenchwoman named Madeline Frenau. She was said to be an exotic creature with white skin and dark hair. He dressed her in the finest silks and presented her with priceless jewels. She wanted for nothing. However, there were no servants in the house. The spirits of the dead kept the place clean and served Madeline her meals. One day, Madeline disappeared without a trace, and the house was abandoned.

"Around 1840 the house had been sold. Soon after the new owners moved into it, they began to speak of ghosts. They complained that when the sun began to set, an enormous dining table covered with white linen appeared with two place settings.

One place was for a man, and the other for a woman with dark hair and alabaster skin. Although the phantoms appeared to be in deep conservation, no voices were heard. Suddenly, the eyes of the woman flared. She sprang from her seat and, snatching up a cloth napkin from the table, pounced on her companion. She wrapped the twisted napkin around his neck and pulled tight. His face turned crimson and blood burst from his mouth. When he collapsed onto the table, the woman stared at him with satisfaction. When she saw her hands had been stained with the man's blood her eyes widened in horror. She tried to wipe the red gore from her hands, but no matter what she touched, she left red streaks behind. Finally, she ran from the room and vanished without a trace.

"This terrible scene replayed itself repeatedly, year after year. Each new tenant who moved into the house soon abandoned it."

Lola laughed. "Is the house for sale? It comes with its own entertainment!"

Charlie's eyes twinkled. "Come to think of it, you and Madeline look alike!"

"That would make you the devil. Hmmm, maybe you are the devil!"

After a fun day of roaming the French Quarter, it was time for dinner. Charlie brought her to Royal Street and showed her a small window. "Take a peek in there."

Lola peered in, "Is that a wine cellar? *Mon Dieu*! It seems to go on forever. How many bottles of wine do you think are in there?"

"Maybe about 25,000. This is Antoine's Restaurant. They're famous for many things, including a fabulous wine selection!"

"This is making me thirsty. Shall we go?"

They entered Antoine's Restaurant. The maître d'hôtel greeted Charlie with a smile and a handshake. "Good to see you again, Charlie."

Charlie replied, "Please meet Lola Dupin."

Lola smiled as the maître d'hôtel took her hand and said, "A pleasure to meet you, *Mademoiselle* Dupin."

Charlie asked, "Would you let Albert know we're here?"

"Yes, of course!"

In a moment, Albert greeted them and showed them to Charlie's regular table. They passed through the main dining room, Lola noticed the beautiful chandeliers and the dark wooden fireplace sitting against the deep, rich, red-colored walls. Their table was dressed in a white tablecloth and a vase of fresh-cut flowers in the center.

Lola exclaimed, "What a lovely restaurant!"

When Albert pulled the chair for Lola to sit, he explained, "Antoine's is the oldest family-run restaurant in the United States. It was established in 1840 by a Frenchman named Antoine Alciatore."

Lola giggled and looked at Charlie. "Another Frenchman in New Orleans? With everyone speaking French in New Orleans it's almost as if I never left Paris. I am more comfortable than I could have imagined."

"I'm glad you think so. I would like to introduce you to the splendid epicurean delights Antoine's has to offer. I've been here many times, and although everything on the menu is delicious, there are several dishes they are famous for. Would you mind if I order for us?"

"Please do, I cannot wait to taste it all."

"Albert, please bring us my standard order."

Albert smiled, "Yes, of course," he said and hurried off. In a few minutes, he returned with two short glasses of amber liquid and a lemon twist hanging from the glass.

Lola asked, "Is this Absinthe?"

"Yes, but it's Absinthe New Orleans style. It's called Sazerac and was born at Antoine Amédée Peychaud's pharmacy. Peychaud created the bitters used in this drink. It also contains cognac and a simple syrup of sugar water." Charlie raised his glass and said, "Lola, a toast to you. Welcome to New Orleans!"

The sommelier arrived with the wine and, soon after, Albert placed the first dish on the table. Charlie announced, "Before you are Oysters Rockefeller, named, of course, for the richest man of all time. When Rockefeller dined here, he ordered a dish of French snails but, due to a shortage, locally available oysters were substituted for the snails. The dish consists of oysters on the half-shell topped with a sauce and bread crumbs, but the actual recipe is a secret."

Lola tasted them and said, "I love this!"

Soon Albert appeared with the next course and placed it before them.

Charlie explained, "This dish is called Pompano en Papillote. It was created in honor of the Brazilian balloonist Alberto Santos-Dumont. It's a filet of pompano baked in a sealed parchment paper envelope with a white sauce of wine, shrimp and crabmeat. The steam puffs up the parchment suggesting a hot air balloon."

"This is delightful! Monsieur Alciatore is a quite clever chef indeed!"

Charlie beamed, "And now it's time for the *pièce de résistance*! The dessert is Mousse au Chocolat, and, of course, we must have Café Brûlot." Alfred appeared at tableside, and with much showmanship, prepared a flaming Grand Marnier coffee drink, mixing dark brown sugar, cinnamon sticks and whole cloves with strong New Orleans chicory coffee. He used a sterling silver ladle to strain out the fruit peel and spices used in the concoction.

"What a fabulous evening! In fact, the entire day was fabulous. Thank you so much, Charlie."

"Oh, but we're not done yet. I have a surprise for you."

"No, please, no more food!"

"I promise no more food. We have someplace else to go."

Charlie paid the bill with the money Lola had given him. A carriage, called for by the maître d'hôtel, was waiting for them upon their exit.

Lola couldn't imagine what more there was to see after a day filled with the excitement of New Orleans. She was delighted at the thought of a surprise. But when the carriage stopped and Charlie helped her down, she asked, "What is this place?"

Charlie chuckled. "It's called the Dew Drop Social and Benevolent Association. I know it doesn't look like much on the outside, but just wait until you hear what's going on inside."

In the room packed with patrons, Lola heard music she had never heard before. "What kind of music is that?"

"Do you like it?"

"I love it! What is it called?"

"It's called jazz. It's new, and as you can see by the enthusiasm of the crowd, it's popular. It's a combination of many musical styles."

"I don't understand it, but I like it!"

"Let's have a seat. The band will be taking a break soon, and there's someone I want you to meet."

"Who?"

"Be patient and enjoy the music."

As predicted, the band took a break and a short time later a man walked to the table. Charlie stood and shook the man's hand. "I'd like you to meet Lola Dupin."

"Lola, this is Frenchie Baudin, the trombonist and bandleader."

Frenchie bowed as he reached for Lola's hand and kissed it. "*Enchanté, Mademoiselle* Dupin."

"Please call me Lola."

Frenchie was a tall, slim, light-skinned Negro, with short, curly, black hair, a neatly trimmed mustache and a goatee. He wore a bright red cravat. "I'm delighted to meet you."

"Have a seat, Frenchie," Charlie pulled out a chair. He turned to Lola, "Obviously, Frenchie's from France. He and his band have been in New Orleans for a while and he's looking for a singer, right Frenchie?"

"That's true. Lola, I've seen you perform at the Moulin Rouge and I thought you were spectacular! I can't believe you're here in New Orleans. It's a wonderful coincidence!"

"You've seen me perform? I'm pleased you enjoyed my show."

"Are you familiar with jazz? It's an exciting music style."

"This is the first time I've heard it. I love it!"

"Lola, would you like to sing with us?"

"'Sing with you? Now? I don't know jazz."

"Don't worry about learning jazz, I'll work with you. I think you'll be good at it. Please sing for us tonight."

"No, that's not possible."

"Of course, it is. I guarantee you'll know the next song we play. Come with me."

"I don't think—"

Charlie stood and helped Lola from her chair. "Go on, Lola. Enjoy yourself."

"But—"

Charlie took her hand and brought her to the stage. All the while Lola protested, "I am not ready for this, Charlie!"

Before she knew it, she was center stage. She saw Frenchie turn to the band and call out words she couldn't hear. When the band began to play, Lola smiled. They played La Marseilles, the French National Anthem. Lola broke into song. It felt good to sing in front of an audience again.

She was having a great time until, in the middle of the song, the music changed into a jazz rendition. She didn't know what to do. But she could feel the music. Lola began to sway her hips in syncopation to the beat and she sang within the rhythm. The audience applauded enthusiastically and Lola's love of performing bubbled within her. When Frenchie announced her as the newest band member she was surprised and grateful. She hugged Frenchie and beamed with appreciation, thanking Frankie and the audience.

Frenchie told her, "Lola, you were magnificent! I'll contact you tomorrow so we can get together for rehearsal."

"I would love that. But are you sure? I have much to learn about jazz."

"I'm sure. The enthusiastic applause of the audience after your performance tells me you'll be a great asset to the band."

She hugged Frenchie and ran back to her table.

"Charlie, did that really happen? He wants me in his band!"

Charlie grinned, "I know you'll enjoy working with Frenchie and his band."

"But Charlie, if I work with Frenchie, I won't have much time with you. Will that be all right?"

"Yes, it will. I'm happy this is working out for you. In fact, I'm so happy you like New Orleans and living at my Aunt's house, and, especially how comfortable you are with my family."

"You have made it easy for me to be comfortable in my new life."

With a solemn expression, Charlie looked into her eyes and said, "I'm glad to hear that because tomorrow I'm leaving New Orleans."

"What did you say?"

"I'm sorry, but I must leave right away. I know this is a shock to you, but I have no choice."

"I don't understand. What do you mean, you have no choice?"

"If I stay here, I'll be killed!"

"Killed!" A wave of fear washed up Lola's spine. "What are you talking about?"

Charlie put his hand inside his coat pocket and pulled out an envelope. He bit his bottom lip and hesitated. "Esther gave this envelope to me yesterday. She said it arrived several months ago. It was slipped under the door the night I left for Paris."

His face was grim as she took the envelope. It said it was to be opened only by Charlie Sloan. She removed the letter and let out a loud gasp.

Drawn on the page was blood flowing from a heart where a knife had pierced it. Instead of a signature, there was the imprint of a hand in thick black ink. It said: *Pay us $6,000. or you die!!*

Lola paled. "Who sent this? Why are they demanding money?"

"I know it seems like everyone in New Orleans is of French descent. But Lola, there are many nationalities here, one of which is Italian. Among the Italians, there's a syndicate called 'The Black Hand.' They're ruthless. They have a reputation for kidnapping, extortion and murder."

"But why are they threatening you?"

"I made a mistake."

"What kind of mistake?"

He lowered his eyes. "I borrowed money from them. I shouldn't have. I knew I wouldn't be able to pay them back, but I couldn't help myself. I just kept borrowing money and gambling it away. When they wouldn't give me any more, I fled to Paris. Now that I've returned, they're after me to pay the money back."

"Is that what last night was about?"

"Yes. I went to them to ask for more time. The beating was a warning. If I don't pay them in three days, they'll kill me!"

"Charlie, this makes no sense. Why did you bring me here if knew you'd be in danger?"

"Sophie told me if I didn't take you away from France, you'd commit suicide."

Lola's eyes narrowed. "Sophie told you I would *kill* myself! Why did she tell you that? It's true I was sad, but I never told her that I would commit *suicide*."

"Sophie said I was the only person who could save your life. When I saw you at your flat, you were so miserable. I believed you were capable of committing suicide. I was more concerned for you than I was for myself."

"I don't understand. We could have gone anywhere together, why would you bring me here knowing these men were after you?"

"It doesn't matter where I settled in the U.S. The Black Hand would find me. I brought you to New Orleans because here you have a place to live rent-free, and my family will help you with anything you need. Now you have a job as a singer. If I brought you anywhere else, I couldn't provide you with those things. I did this because I care about you. Now, look at you. You're beautiful and happy. You said you love New Orleans and you looked so overjoyed when you sang. I'm glad to have helped you return to your wonderful self!"

"This was unnecessary. I can take care of myself. If you told me, I would never have let you put yourself in danger. Charlie, I am not sure you're telling me the entire truth. I feel as if you used me to pay for your trip to the United States and, now that you're here, you're leaving me so you can find a rich woman to fund your gambling!"

Charlie took a deep breath. "No, that's not it. It's true I'm a gambler who never had a real job. I've always depended on women to support me. However, I don't want to live that way any longer. I want to earn my own money and now I have an opportunity."

"What kind of opportunity?"

He looked around and leaned closer to Lola. Just above a whisper, Charlie said, "There's been a gold strike in Arizona, a big one! I'm going there to stake my claim. Once I make my strike, I'll send for you. After that, we can go to San Francisco or live anywhere you want. All I need is for you to loan me a little more money so I can stake my claim."

Covering her eyes with her hand, Lola exhaled loudly. She didn't know whether to cry or scream at him. With frustration, she said, "Charlie, you said you don't want women to support you anymore, and yet the first thing you do is ask me for money!"

"Lola, you're my only hope. I brought you here at the risk of my life. Now I need to leave. I have no money and no way to get any. Besides, this is just a loan. Soon as I make enough money, I'll send for you and pay you back."

"How do I know you will not gamble away whatever I give you?"

"Because I've changed, Lola. I've learned my lesson. You brought about this change in me. I care about you. No other woman makes me feel like you do. Please give me a chance to show you my feelings for you are real."

Lola felt like she was about to dive off a precipice. She knew she would be making a mistake to give Charlie money, but if she didn't, he might be killed. "How much money do you need?"

"Just enough to make my way to Arizona and get supplies."

"Tell me, how much?"

Charlie cleared his throat. "About three thousand francs."

"Three thousand francs! Charlie, you know I sold many of my things to pay for our journey here. I am not one of those rich women you are used to being with. I have little money left!"

"But at least you have a job and a place to live. Esther will be happy to cook for you. This will be only until I make my strike. Afterwards, we can be together."

"What if I come with you?"

"No, Lola, that's not possible. There are no hotels or restaurants there. You would have to sleep on the ground in a tent. The work is hard and dirty, and no place to bathe except maybe a cold stream. That's not a life for you."

Arching an eyebrow, she replied, "You would be surprised what I am capable of, and I am not afraid of hard work."

"You may not be afraid, but I'm afraid for you. It's too dangerous. Prospectors are not gentlemen. They're rough, violent men. Some have been in prison. I couldn't be with you every minute and I'd be frightened to leave you alone. It's best you stay here."

Lola pushed back her chair. It's time to leave!"

Charlie looked at her. His voice was meek, "Lola, will you give me the money?" When she gave him no response he pleaded, "You won't let them kill me, will you?"

Chapter 41

The following morning, Lola awoke to see a note on the dresser. She knew it was from Charlie. He thanked her for the loan and promised to send for her when he made his strike.

Lola crumpled the note and tossed it away. *He is probably on his way to meet a rich old crone, dying to get his hands on her money.* She felt the icy fingers of loneliness clutch her heart. *I am such a fool. I gave him my money and will never see him again.*

After bathing and dressing, Lola made it down to the kitchen. Esther was washing dishes. *"Bonjour*, Esther. May I ask you a question about Charlie?"

"Bonjour, Lola," she replied. She wiped her hands with a dishtowel and walked to the stove. "Would like coffee? It's fresh made."

"Thank you, I can really use it."

She filled two cups and placed them on the kitchen table. "Have a seat," Esther said as she pulled out a chair for herself and asked, "What do you want to know about Charlie?"

"You've known Charlie since he was a child, but I haven't known him long. In fact, I hardly know him at all. Charlie says he cares for me but he's unpredictable. He brought me here from Paris and now he's gone. I know he gambles and he told me bad people were after him. I care for him, but I don't trust him."

Esther said, "We love Charlie and I don't feel comfortable talking about him. But I understand your concern. Charlie is a complex man. He's kind, charming and quite affectionate. He's also like a butterfly, fluttering from Paris to New Orleans to parts unknown. He can't seem to find himself, but I think he's making an effort."

"Maybe so. He got me a job performing with Frenchie Baudin and said I can live with you until he sends for me. But he plans on prospecting gold in Arizona. I can't imagine that's true. I don't know what to do."

Esther gazed at Lola with kind eyes. "I understand your frustration. If I may make a recommendation. Give yourself time to adjust to your new surroundings. Charlie must care for you. After all, he arranged for you to live here and he's never done anything like that before. If he doesn't contact you in a reasonable amount of time, I think you'll know what to do."

"Thank you, Esther. You may be right. I will wait for a while and see what happens. By the way, Charlie arranged for me to sing with the band. Are you familiar with Frenchie Baudin, the trombonist and bandleader? He plays music called jazz."

"Oh, yes, Monique talks about him all of the time. She loves that music."

"I will be meeting Frenchie later today. He will be teaching me how to sing jazz. Would you and your family like to come to my performance tonight? I am new at this, so I cannot guarantee I will be the best jazz singer you have ever heard, but I would be delighted if all of you would come."

"We would enjoy hearing you and the band. But it would only be me and Monique. My father will stay here with Alphonse."

"Excellent! I will be singing at the Dew Drop Social and Benevolent Association. Do you know it?"

"Very much so."

"Frenchie will be sending for me, but I do not expect that will be until much later today. Is there anything I can do for you?"

"No, thank you." Esther thought for a moment. "Monique is about to go to the French Market to purchase items for supper. Would you like to accompany her?"

"Absolutely!"

"Good," Esther said. She called for Monique, who entered the kitchen a few moments later. "Lola will accompany you to the market."

Monique smiled. "If you're ready, we can leave now."

Enjoying their walk to the market, Lola said, "The weather is so pleasant here."

Monique laughed. "Pleasant? It's autumn now, so the weather's comfortable. You haven't experienced a New Orleans summer. It gets so hot and sticky. You'll feel like you're in a steam bath. People who can afford it leave town. Also, you have to be careful not to catch yellow fever."

"Yellow fever? Sadly, many French soldiers died in Africa from that terrible disease. I am sorry to know it is prevalent here."

"Unfortunately, many people have died from it here too, including my father."

"I am so sorry."

"It was a long time ago. Soon after Alphonse was born."

Lola said wistfully, "It must have been difficult growing up without a father."

"I wish I had known him. But *Grand-père* has been a father to me."

Lola asked, "So, are you a student?"

"Yes, I attend the Phyllis Wheatley Sanitarium and Training School for Negro Nurses."

"Excellent! But is it a nursing school only for Negroes?"

"Of course! Negroes and whites aren't allowed to work together."

"Really? I thought the Civil War had changed things for Negroes?"

"It did at first. We even had Negro members of Congress. But things gradually changed. White congressmen implemented unreasonable voting requirements so that few Negroes were allowed to vote. Recently there was a Supreme Court ruling that upheld the state law allowing the railroads to segregate black and white people. The Court said that, as long as blacks and whites were treated equally, separate facilities didn't make a black person inferior. So now lots of institutions, including schools, hospitals, restaurants, hotels, parks, and even cemeteries have separate facilities, just so white people don't have to be with black people."

"That is ridiculous!"

"Maybe it will change in the future. For now, there's not much we can do about it. Here's the French Market."

The expanse of the crowded market amazed Lola. Among the shoppers and hawkers, she heard a confusion of tongues. In addition to French, she recognized German, Italian, Spanish, and other languages she didn't recognize.

Aromas from an array of flowers, produce and grocery goods, as well as the butcher's market and fish market, filled the air.

Lola thought the produce looked fresh and beautiful but she was unfamiliar with many types. She pointed to a green, strangely-shaped vegetable. "What is that?"

Monique giggled. "Okra. It was in the gumbo *Mamá* made for us. But let me show you other things unique to New Orleans." She was in the process of describing candies, spice blends and various condiments when a wizened old woman sidled up to them. In a raspy voice, she said, "Ya be needin' me soon!"

Lola's mouth dropped when she recognized the woman. She was dressed in the same white outfit and elaborately twisted turban she wore when Lola saw her last. Just as before, her large amber eyes bored into Lola.

Placing a protective arm around Monique, Lola blurted, "You are that woman who was at the pier when I arrived! Who are you? What do you want?"

The woman waggled her finger at both Lola and Monique. "Ya don knows it yet, but you soon be needin' ma hep. When da time comes, you find me waitin' for ya at midnight at da grave of Marie Laveau."

Monique shouted, "Go away, old woman! Leave us alone!"

The woman cackled and disappeared into the crowd.

Lola questioned Monique, "Do you know that woman?"

"She's just a crazy old hoodoo woman. Pay her no mind."

"Hoodoo? What is that?

"Let's get our purchases and go home. *Grand-père* can explain it all to you."

Chapter 42

Monique shouted when she placed their purchases on the kitchen table, "*Mamá*! That old hoodoo woman bothered us!"

Esther turned from the stove and faced her daughter. With lowered eyebrows, she asked, "Who'd you say bothered you?"

"You know, that crazy lady who dresses in white and wears a turban."

"What did she do?"

"She said Lola and I will need her help soon and should meet her at Madame Leveau's gravesite when the time comes."

Lola added, "That woman is quite peculiar. I saw her at the pier when I arrived here. Now she was at the French Market. I think she's following me. I can't imagine why."

Esther returned to her cooking and said, "Monique may be right about that woman being crazy. I would avoid her."

Lola asked Esther, "Do you know what hoodoo is?"

"I think it has to do with black magic. But to me, hoodoo is nonsense."

Samuel entered the kitchen just as Esther was finishing her sentence.

"Nonsense? So, Monique, you've had an encounter with Madame Charlot?"

Lola looked at Samuel. "You know her? Who is she?"

Samuel said, "I know of her. I believe she's a practitioner of hoodoo. As you can see, my daughter is a skeptic, but there's more to it than black magic. Lola, if you'd like to join me in the parlor, I can give you more information about hoodoo and Voodoo."

Esther demanded, "Now *Papá*, don't you go giving Lola lectures again. Lunch is ready, so you all go sit at the table."

Esther looked around the kitchen. "Where's Alphonse? Monique, go find that boy. Lola, would you mind setting the table?"

"I would be happy to," Lola said. She picked up the plates sitting on the sideboard.

After they gathered at the dining table, Ester served steaming bowls of crawfish bisque and cornbread infused with bits of onion, bell pepper and spicy andouille sausage. On the table lay a dessert platter of cherry bread pudding with rum sauce, walnuts, raisins and cinnamon.

Lola was admiring the luscious food display when she heard Samuel ask, "So, would you like to know about hoodoo?"

She was about to take a spoonful of bisque but stopped to observe the family members to see if they might object. "Is it all right with everyone if we discuss it now?"

Alphonse let out an exuberant "Yes! I want to hear all about zombies and Voodoo dolls and how they cut off chicken heads!"

Esther reprimanded him. "Alphonse! Mind your manners!"

With a sheepish expression, Alphonse apologized, "Yes, *Mamá*. I'm sorry. But I still want to hear about it. *Grand-père,* please tell us!"

Samuel grinned at the boy. "I won't go into that now, but I'd like to tell you more about the difference between hoodoo and Voodoo if you'd like to hear it."

Lola looked to Esther and saw no objection in her face. She turned to Samuel and said, "Absolutely! Voodoo and hoodoo are such exotic mysteries to me!"

Samuel nodded, "As they are to most people. Now, what I'm about to explain is a simplified version of complex belief systems. In addition, the rituals may be different, depending upon the areas in which they're practiced. Voodoo and hoodoo share African roots and mixed beliefs, including pagan traditions, worship of ancients, use of trances to communicate with spirits, healing arts of Native Americans, and elements of European religions. When African slaves were torn from their native lands, they brought with them their beliefs and regional practices. Their slave owners thought of them as savages and forced them to be Christianized. The slaves realized the similarities between their beliefs and those of the Catholics, as when the Catholics prayed to their Saints to intercede with a higher god in their favor. The slaves recognized the existence of one god but substituted Catholic saints with their own powerful spirits. To survive, they masked their rituals and beliefs in Catholicism."

Alphonse butted in, "*Grand-père,* can't we hear about the interesting stuff?" With a sharp look from Samuel, Alphonse lowered his head and went back to eating.

"The word Voodoo means 'spirit of God'. The practice of Voodoo is a way of dealing with life, which heals and destroys. It's both good and bad. Voodoo reflects the dual nature of the rattlesnake, whose poison is toxic, but its poison is also needed to heal."

Lola drew in a breath, "Rattlesnake! *Mon Dieu!* Monsieur Samuel, I am both frightened and fascinated! Please, go on."

"Unlike Voodoo, which is an organized religion with established practices and whose main purpose is to protect or heal, hoodoo is folk magic. The purpose of hoodoo is to allow people access to supernatural forces to improve their own lives. Herbs, animal parts, and the possession of an individual's bodily fluids are used extensively in these practices."

Alphonse looked at his grandfather. "Now you're getting to the good stuff!" After receiving an admonishing look from Esther, Alphonse lowered his eyes and offered, "Sorry, Grand-père."

"Hoodoo is known for conjuring, that is, contact with ancestors or other spirits of the dead. Practitioners of hoodoo access supernatural forces to help or hinder a person in various aspects of life, including luck, love, evil, or restraining enemies."

"Animal parts and bodily fluids! Monsieur Samuel, this is quite unsettling. If this woman, Madame Charlot, is a practitioner of hoodoo, do you think she is planning on doing me or Monique harm?"

Samuel took a deep breath. "I don't know. I am an outsider who's only learned about this by studying about it. These practices hold many secrets and mysteries. Hoodoo isn't necessarily a bad thing. Generally, these conjurers don't waste their time trying to scare people without a good reason. She may wish to protect you in some way. Or, as Monique says, she may just be a disturbed woman. I'd ignore her. But, if she continues to annoy you, let me know."

A short time after lunch the doorbell rang and a young man came to collect Lola and take her to the Dew Drop Social and Benevolent Association.

Lola entered the club and caught Frenchie's eye while he was playing the trombone with his group. She leaned against the wall and enjoyed listening to the music.

After finishing the tune, Frenchie called out from the stage, "*Bienvenue*, Lola!" He pointed to a chair. "Have a seat. I'll be with you soon."

After the band had played several songs, Frenchie picked up sheets of music and took them to her. "Lola, these lyrics are written in English. Do you speak English? If not, I can help you with the lyrics."

Lola said in English, "I learned English and several other languages as a girl and, since I've been here, I've been brushing up on my skills. Let me see the lyrics. I will practice the words until I have a good idea of the song concept. I do not think it will take long, but putting the words to your music might take time."

"Don't be concerned. I'll sing and you listen. This should help you get the idea. All right?"

"Yes, I am eager to hear you sing."

Frenchie returned to the stage and signaled for the band to play. He sang a song called 'Careless Love' several times until Lola was ready to try it along with him. They moved to ragtime songs and popular musical tunes. They practiced until Frenchie was satisfied. "Lola, you're a natural. I think you'll do well."

Lola continued to practice by herself and knew she would be ready for her performance that evening. The audience began to arrive, slowly at first, until the room filled with people. Lola noticed the audience, mostly black, had many white people as well.

She said to Frenchie, "I had been told black people cannot congregate with white people—yet it does not seem to be a problem here."

He replied, "White people don't want to share the same restaurant or let their children attend the same school as we do. But when it comes down to it, white people know they have to join with us black folks to hear the best music!"

Lola said, "Now that makes sense!" She took her place with the band and when all was ready, she began to sing. After a while, she noticed Esther and Monique were in the crowd and waved to them from the stage.

The evening was a success and Lola continued to perform with Frenchie and the band. All was going well. Lola enjoyed New Orleans and living with Charlie's family.

But she missed Charlie. She missed his companionship and the comfort she felt when he put his arms around her. Most of all, she missed sleeping with him. Each day she asked Esther if a letter had arrived from Charlie, but was increasingly disappointed. Lola feared she would never hear from him again.

After two weeks of performing, Frenchie told Lola they would be moving on to a new venue outside of New Orleans. She enjoyed playing with the band, but she had to decide if she wanted to continue with Frenchie's band or stay and wait for Charlie's letter. The pay she received from Frenchie was not much. As a new member of the band, she did not feel it was right to ask Frenchie for more money. However, traveling with the band would mean she'd have to pay for her room and her meals. Lola would need to delve into her meager bank account. She would sleep on it and decide in the morning.

As usual, Lola tiptoed into the house trying not to rouse the sleeping family. But this night she felt something to be amiss. It was strange to see the lights were on. Fear gripped her when she heard loud wails coming from the kitchen. She rushed to see Esther sitting at the table with fat tears streaming down her face. Samuel stood behind her with a hand on her shoulder, his face contorted with anger. The agony on Esther's face made Lola's heart ache. She implored, "What's wrong? Why are you crying?"

Esther's sobs grew louder and more distraught.

"Please, tell me what's wrong."

Samuel commanded, "Esther, give Lola the letter!"

Esther's swollen face was covered in tears. Her chest heaved. Between sobs, she screamed at Lola, "My baby! They took my baby girl!"

"What? Who took her?" Lola saw a piece of paper on the table. She picked it up. It was a letter that resembled the one Charlie had shown her, except instead of a dagger through a heart, there was a drawing of a black girl hanging by a rope. Written in black ink, and with the same Black Hand signature, it said:

Sloan owes us $6,000. He ran away. Now you pay or the girl dies! On Tuesday noon put the money in a satchel and leave it in Jackson Square by the statue. Don't tell anyone. If you don't leave the money, the girl will be hanging from the statue by Tuesday night!

Ren'e Fedyna

Chapter 43

Lola dropped the note and murmured. "Oh Charlie, what have you done?" The anguish in Esther's face brought tears to Lola's eyes. Her sadness became a rage of furious heat. Lola slammed her fist on the table and shrieked, "We must go to the police!"

A thick vein pulsed in Samuel's temple, "We've already been to the police. They won't help us."

"What do you mean, they will not help?" Lola shouted, "They must help!"

A look of repugnance shot from his blind, opaque eyes, distorting his face into a twisted mask of hatred. He screamed, "No, they won't. The police said it was a joke. They said no one would waste their time expecting nigras to pay a ransom for their pickaninny. They said she probably got pregnant and ran off with her boyfriend. She must've written the note to cover it up."

"That is ridiculous! I am going to the police to tell them they better start looking for Monique right now!"

Samuel said, "You'll be wasting your time! We'll have to find another way!"

"There is no other way. They must find her!"

"If you insist on going to the police, it's best you wait until daylight. You'll never find a cab now."

"I do not care if I have to wait all night! I am going to the police station and find someone who will listen to me!" Lola grabbed the letter from the table and stormed from the kitchen. She exited the house and slammed the front door.

Lola's footfalls were heavy. Her anger grew with each step. She was angry with Charlie for causing this terrible situation and angry with him for leaving her. She was angry at her father for his cruelty towards her. If he had just been a caring father, she would never have left Paris and Monique would not have been kidnapped. But most of all, she was angry at herself.

How did I get so desperate? Why do I let Charlie get under my skin? What a fool I am. If I had the money, I would pay the kidnappers. It is my fault Charlie left town.

Determined to get to the police station as quickly as possible, Lola forced herself to focus on hailing a cab. She pulled her coat collar up and tried to ignore the chilly dampness of the misty night. Lola walked and walked but, not until the night's darkness gave way to morning light, was she able to get a ride to the station house.

Her fury had not dissipated. She marched up the police station steps and accosted the first policeman she saw. Lola waved the note at him. She demanded in French, "You must help!"

He was reed-thin, with small, unsympathetic deep-set eyes and no noticeable lips. "Lady, calm down. Not every person in New Orleans speaks French! If you want to tell me what's going on, you'll need someone to translate for you."

Lola continued to rant in French, and she showed him the note. She struggled to remember the English words she needed.

The policeman looked at the paper, and with furrowed brows, said, "You better come with me." He brought Lola to a portly grey-haired police officer who sat behind a high desk and said, "Hey Sergeant, this lady brought the same letter as those black folks brought in yesterday."

The sergeant took the note from the officer. From his perch he frowned at Lola. "What dis 'bout?" He glanced at the note and smirked, "I already dealt with dis. I told dem nigras dere's nothin' we can do. Dere girl musta' run owf."

Lola stammered as she grasped for the correct English words. "So...ah...you! You are the one...ah...the one who...re...refused to help?"

The sergeant narrowed his eyes, "Wat dis got to do wit chu, *cherie*?"

Lola put her hands on her hips and glared at the sergeant, "What does that matter? You must find Monique! Send your gendarmes to look for her immediately!"

"Hole on dawlin', you don go givin' orders aroun chere, I do! Now deres nothin' we can do 'bout it. If dis be from de Black Hand f'true, we ain't got no idea who's behind it. All we know is, dey's jus' a bunch of dago's from Italy who come here makin' trouble. But we don' know who dey is, so we cain't be no help!"

"What do you mean, you cannot help? It is your job, you must find her!"

"*Cherie*, you eva' hear a Enrico Caruso, dat famous opera singer? Well, even he was threatened by da Black Hand. He 'cided to pay up. So, if you really care about dis girl, I suggest you give dem the money, 'cause dey mean bidness!"

Lola stamped her foot, "*Toi idiot!* Do your job! I will not leave until you agree to help!"

Out of a nearby office came a man with chestnut brown hair, a bit of a paunch and a ruddy complexion, dressed in a vested suit. He appeared to be of a higher rank. "What's all this ruckus about, Sergeant?" He said as he gazed at Lola.

The Sergeant looked surprised to see the man. "Sorry Lieutenant, it's dis woman." He offered the note to the Lieutenant, "She showed us dis letter and claims a nigra girl bin kidnapped. I keep tellin' her dat dere's nothin' we can do 'bout it!"

He read the note and shook his head. He introduced himself. "I'm Lieutenant Grey, and you are?"

"My name is Lola Dupin."

"What is your relationship to this girl?"

"I am staying at the home of Charlie Sloan. Monique is the daughter of his caretakers."

"Oh, I see. And where is Charlie Sloan?"

"He went to Arizona."

"Arizona?"

"*Oui*, ah…yes. He said there was a gold strike there."

"Does Mr. Sloan owe this money?"

Lola hesitated. "Yes. But he left before this note arrived. He had no idea Monique would be in danger."

"Have you tried to contact Mr. Sloan and ask him for the money?"

"I have not heard from him since he left. It would do no good. He has no money."

The Lieutenant said, "That's too bad. I'm sorry. We've had cases like this before, but we haven't had any luck finding the perpetrators. We know there are a group of Italian immigrants who're behind this Black Hand ring. Everyone's afraid to offer any information about them. Unless someone comes forward and tells us who they are, we're powerless to arrest them."

"No! That cannot be. Are you saying you will let Monique die because you will not even try to help?"

"Do you plan on paying the money?"

"I would, but I do not have it."

"If you can get the money, we can try to catch them when they pick up the ransom. But that's the only way."

Lola wrung her hands. "*Mon Dieu!* What can I do?" She thought for a moment. "Wait, what if I leave the satchel where they said, but with no money. You catch them when they pick it up, *non*?"

"You don't understand." The lieutenant's voice was firm, "These are dangerous men. If they don't get the money, even if we arrest the men who attempt to take the satchel, their cohorts might still kill the girl. It's a tremendous risk and one I would rather not attempt."

Tears watered Lola's eyes. "Please! We cannot let Monique die. There must be something you can do?"

The lieutenant took a card from his wallet and said. "I'm sorry, Miss Dupin. Here's my card. If you can find a way to get the money, contact me. I'll arrange to have my men at the pickup site. If we catch them, we'll do our best to get them to tell us where Monique is. But keep in mind these men are treacherous and will stop at nothing to get what they want."

With a sunken heart, Lola took the card, thanked the Lieutenant, and left the police station. The bright sun stung her eyes as she found a nearby bench and slumped onto it. *There must be something I can do, but what? What!* Then she remembered the old woman. The one who said she and Monique would need her help. *What was it that she was supposed to do? She said to meet her, but where?* Lola put her head in her hands. *Think! Where? Where was it?* She envisioned the old woman in her white outfit and elaborately twisted turban. She remembered her large amber eyes and how uncomfortable the woman made her feel. Yet it came to her. She remembered the raspy voice say, *When the time comes, you will find me waiting for you at midnight at the grave of Marie Laveau.*

That's it! Tonight, I must go to the grave of Marie Laveau!

Chapter 44

Lola refused to return to Charlie's house. The thought of seeing the faces of Ester and Samuel, and telling them she failed to get help from the police, was more than she could bear. Instead, she decided to search for the hoodoo woman.

She thought back to her first encounter with Madame Charlot at the Decatur Street wharf. Lola headed there straight away. The wharf was more expansive than she remembered, with swarms of dockworkers loading and unloading heavy sacks of goods from trucks and seagoing vessels, and passengers meandering about. Although it was a daunting task, Lola questioned as many people as possible. She persevered until she realized no one was willing or able to help her.

Lola then rushed to the French Market where she worked her way through the dense crowd of shoppers. The muggy afternoon heat pressed upon her, making her hair cling to her as rivulets of perspiration trickled down her neck and back.

Undeterred, Lola stopped at each stall and asked each seller if they knew where to find Madame Charlot. Two had seen her occasionally but were unable to suggest where the woman might be found. Lola continued her search. Up and down the busy Charles Street Shopping District she went, questioning the staff in every store, to no avail. Exhausted and frustrated, she returned home.

The house was quiet when she entered. Only Alphonse was there to greet her. His face was troubled but hopeful. "*Bonjour*...Er...good day, Mademoiselle Dupin. Did you find her? Did you find Monique?"

Lola gazed at Alphonse with sad eyes. "No, I'm sorry."

His anxious words tumbled out, "Did you speak to the police? What did they say? Are they going to catch those terrible Black

Hand men?" Almost in tears, he blurted, "When will Monique come home?"

Lola had no answers for Alphonse. She put her hand on his shoulder, "Where are your *Mamá* and *Grand-père*?"

Alphonse sniffled, "*Mamá* is with her friend at the house across the street. *Grand-père* is asleep. He and I walked all over the Italian neighborhood searching for Monique, but we could not find her. What's going to happen to her? Are they going to kill her?"

Lola was relieved she didn't have to face Esther and Samuel with her disheartening news, but having no answer for Alphonse felt just as devastating. "I cannot imagine that will happen. I have a plan. I am going to meet Madame Charlot tonight at the grave of Madame Laveau. I believe she will help me find Monique."

Alphonse's face brightened. "You think so?" His eyes bulged with excitement. "May I accompany you?"

"Oh no. I am going by myself. I do not want anyone else to be in danger. But there are things you can do to help me."

"Of course! Anything!"

"First, please don't tell your mother or grandfather where I am going. Can you promise me that?"

Alphonse hesitated, "Why shouldn't they know?"

"I don't want to get their hopes up."

"All right, if you insist. What's the second thing?"

"I need to know how to find the grave of Madame Laveau."

He smiled and sat at an old desk placed against the side wall of the parlor. He removed a piece of paper and a pencil from the drawer. With lowered eyebrows and the tip of his tongue projecting between tightened lips, he drew a map. Alphonse held up the paper and scrutinized his work. "Here it is!" Beaming with pride, he brought it to Lola. "But I think it would be better if I came with you, so I can show you exactly where it is."

Lola reviewed the map and said, "Thank you. But no. I won't be able to meet with her until midnight and it is much better I go alone."

"But I want to help!"

She thought for a moment. "There is something you can do."

Lola fished in her purse and removed a calling card. "If I am not back by tomorrow morning, have your mother contact this detective. Tell her I went to meet Madame Charlot at midnight at the grave of Madame Laveau. Can you do that?"

"Oh, yes. Of course."

"But don't let anyone know where I am going tonight. Only tell them if I am not back by morning."

"I'm afraid you'll be in danger."

"Do not worry about me. I can take care of myself."

Lola headed towards the stairs to her room. She said, "I am going to rest now. This will be a busy night for me."

Too tired to remove her clothes, Lola dropped onto her bed and was asleep in an instant. Her sleep was not restful. Haunting visions of black hands and knives mixed with faces of the surly-looking men whom she remembered from L'antre Du Diable and the horrible façade of the Hell Cabaret, with its enormous hideous face, bulging eyes and huge fanged mouth caused her to toss and turn.

Lola woke with a start. A bright full moon peered through an open curtain. She took a moment to gather her thoughts. She panicked, fearing it might be too late to meet Madame Charlot. She turned up the lamp and searched for her timepiece. It was only ten o'clock. She exhaled a relieved breath then washed and change her clothes. Lola peeked into the hall. There was nothing but darkness and quiet, except for the muffled sobs emanating from Esther's bedroom. Lola stopped for a moment. Suppressing the urge to comfort Esther, she tiptoed down the steps and silently out the door. She managed to hail a cab soon after.

"St. Louis Cemetery Number One," she announced to the driver.

"Ya be sure Mamselle? Why ya wanna go dere at dis hour? It don be open now."

It had not occurred to Lola the cemetery might be closed. But there was no choice for her, she would have to get in. "Thank you for your concern, but that is where I want to go," she commanded.

"Oh, so ya be one a dem folk who want to see dem ghosts, eh?"

"Ghosts? No, I do not believe in ghosts."

"Not even da ghost of Marie Laveau? She be known ta wander through da cemetery. Ya know dis cemetery be scary at night. Unda da cemetary grounds dere be layers a bones. It be a hot night and ya best be hopin' it don rain none. Cause when dere be a flood, dem bodies a da poor dead folks, who ain't been buried in dem crypts, wash outta dere muddy graves, an f'true, dey come floatin' troo da streets a town."

Lola shouted, "Enough! I do believe you are trying to frighten me. Just keep quiet and get me to the cemetery quickly!"

"Aw right, Mamselle, you be da boss."

Soon the carriage slowed to a stop. The driver quipped, "Here we be, Da Cities a da Dead!"

Chapter 45

Lola swallowed hard, *Cities of the Dead, Mon Dieu!* She felt an icy shiver race up her spine as she paid the driver and stepped down. With only the light of the bright moon to guide her, she approached the gate, fearing it might be locked. A rusty chain was wrapped around the bars of the old iron gates, but the padlock hung open. Lola unwound the chain and pushed the gate. The loud creak of rusty hinges startled her. Once inside, she removed the map from her purse, grateful the full moon was bright enough to read by, as she did not think to bring any sort of torchlight.

Chills vibrated through her body as she wove her way through the labyrinth of narrow walkways amongst the aboveground crypts. The crypts reflected a variety of designs and sizes, topped with crosses or statues. Most were in the shape of tiny houses or chapels. This was truly a city of the dead!

The eerie quiet was disturbed only by the sound of her footsteps as she trod upon shattered shells and crumbling cobblestones. She shrieked and recoiled as a bat swooshed passed her face. Losing her balance, she grasped onto a moss-covered crypt but was unable to prevent her fall. "*Bordel de merde!*" she cursed aloud as she lay amongst the tombs. "*La vache!*" She shouted as she pulled herself up and dusted herself off.

Lola quickened her pace, yet it seemed like hours until she came across Marie Laveau's crypt. Lola didn't know what to expect. With all the fanfare about Madame Laveau's mysticism, she thought her crypt would have exotic adornment. But she saw only a whitewashed tomb with a plaque announcing the resting place of Madame Laveau and her family. Removing the pocket watch from her purse, in the moonlight she read eleven forty-five.

She checked her watch every few minutes. When the moon disappeared behind a cloud, the black night enveloped her like a shroud. She looked out into the darkness and hoped it wouldn't rain.

Lola tapped her foot and whispered under her breath, "Where are you, Madame Charlot?" Her pulse raced when she thought she heard someone roaming amongst the crypts. Lola shouted, "Madame Charlot, is that you?" When there was no response, she wrapped her arms tightly around herself and wondered, *Is there really such a thing as ghosts?* She began to hear sounds in more than one direction. Her breathing was shallow and quick. Her eyes searched the inky blackness. Lola shook her head as if to awaken from a bad dream. *Stop this! Do not let those ridiculous stories frighten you!*

She tried to relax, but when a rodent brushed across the tops of her shoes, she screeched. Waiting alone in the hot, muggy darkness with a sweating body and a pounding heart, she thought, *This is a foolish idea, but what else can I do? I will* wait *all damn night if that is what it takes!*

A tap on Lola's shoulder caused her scalp to tingle. Just as she turned, the moon peeked out from the clouds, making the amber eyes of Madame Charlot a glowing, sulfurous yellow.

Madame Charlot smiled with triumph. "So, ya see it be true! Ya do need me! Da young chile is gone an' I da only one who kin hep ya fine her!"

Lola felt suspicious of Madame Charlot. She did not like her smug attitude and feared she might even be part of the kidnap scheme. "How do I know you can help me find Monique?"

Madame Charlot gave a sardonic laugh. "Come wid me an' I'll show ya!" she commanded.

Following closely behind the woman, Lola asked, "Where are we going?" She received no response. Although she did not trust this woman, she felt she had no choice but to go with her. The two of them left the cemetery and walked hurriedly down the dark, deserted streets, passing shuttered shops and restaurants, warehouses, and homes in various stages of decay.

Lola had no way of knowing who might be lurking in the dark shadows. With each step, she became more concerned about her safety.

What fate did Madame Charlot have planned for her?

Chapter 46

Madame Charlot stopped before an old house and climbed a chipped marble step to the porch. She lit a lamp that hung on a rusted hook attached to an eave. The light allowed Lola to assess the ramshackle façade. The Franco-Spanish style house may once have been a proud beauty, with graceful gingerbread trim and a decorative iron fence. Now, peeling paint, a rotting wooden porch and a crooked front door made it appear tired and longing to rest in a collapsed heap.

She unhooked the lamp and pushed open the door, then beckoned Lola to follow her. It took every ounce of willpower for Lola not to run away, but she steeled herself and followed Madame Charlot inside. When the Madame closed and bolted the door, Lola feared she made a terrible mistake.

The woman proceeded to light their way through the shotgun-style house. The lamplight cast exaggerated shadows. Each narrow room was packed with shabby furniture. Sitting upon every flat surface was a chaotic mix of burnt candles, jars of various colored liquids and other strange paraphernalia. The air was thick with cloying scents of incense and sulfur. Heavy drapes covered the windows. Lola felt queasy from the overpowering smells and stifling heat.

In the next room, Lola stood beside her when she stopped before a tall cabinet cluttered with a variety of items. Lola realized they were standing before an altar of sorts. Atop a white cloth was a vase of flowers, a metal cross, a comb, a skull and candles. Madame Charlot mumbled to herself, seeming to be in prayer. The woman pointed to a chair and commanded, "Sit dere!"

Lola sat at a badly worn wooden table with two mismatched chairs. She asked Madame Charlot. "Why do you believe you can help me find Monique?"

The Madame sat across from Lola and responded with condescension. "My dawlin', I know ya be unfamiliar with da power of da hoodoo, so I'll 'xplain it. We, da livin' ain' alone in dis world. Our ancestors are da intermediaries 'tween da living and da divine. Although dey be dead, dere spirits continue ta dwell in da natral world. Dey have da power ta influence da fortune an' da fate of da living, an' dere strongest desire is ta protect dere fam'ly."

Lola could not believe she was asking this question. "How can the dead be of help to us?"

"You muz be patient if ya want ta understand! Do ya be willin' ta listen?"

"Uh….I am sorry. Please continue."

"Aw right den. I was born ta be a Conjure Doctor. I be chosen by ma ancestors ta assist dem in helpin' da livin'. Even as a chile, I was able ta help people by usin' various means, including divination reading, spell casting, anointing oils, an' many udder methods ta communicate with da helping spirits."

With strained patience Lola asked, "Madame Charlot, I appreciate what you are saying, but how does this help me to get Monique to safety?"

"I see dat you be a skeptic. No madder. My beloved *mamá* died in Paris many years ago, but she been born in Senegambia, Africa. Her spirit told me ya be arrivin' 'ere from France, and dat evil was awaitin' ya. My *mamá* sez I muz protect ya an' aid ya in ya destiny ta help da family of Louis Sinegal."

Lola's mouth dropped open. When she caught her voice she said, "Louis Sinegal? Is he the ancestor of ...?"

"Yeah, 'xactly! He da ancestor of Monique's fam'ly. He knows Monique is in danger and he gonna tell me how ta find dat chile. We don' have much time, so we godda begin." Madame

Charlot held out her hand. "Gimme dat letter. Da one wit da black hand."

Lola removed the letter from her purse and handed it to the woman.

Madame Charlot read the kidnap letter and said, "Yes, yes dis will do." She stood and walked to a cupboard, removed a bottle containing yellow liquid, and poured it into a glass. She brought it to Lola and said, "Drink dis."

Lola sniffed it and scowled. "What is this?" she demanded.

The woman chuckled, "F'true dawlin, I don' be goin' to meg ya no 'arm. It not be poison. It be a tea made from da Angelica Root powder an' some udda a nature's fine offerin's. It be for women, providin' strength an' da ability ta ward off de evil, an' to bring luck ta da family. Drink it. Ya gonna need it."

Lola took a sip of the foul-tasting liquid and was about to put the glass on the table.

"Drink it!" the woman demanded, "Alla it!"

Lola hesitated then swallowed it. She coughed hard and her eyes watered. But as the tea floated through her body, she felt a pleasant tranquility.

"Now, close ya eyes an' tink of Monique. Imagine dat chile safe in ya arms. Ya must be believin' she be in ya arms, feel her, smell her essence, hold her tight!"

Lola closed her eyes, trying hard to imagine Monique.

Madame Charlot began chanting the names Monique, Louis Senegal and St. Expeditus. "Do ya know 'bout St. Expeditus?" she asked.

Eyes closed, Lola shook her head.

"He da patron saint a all emergencies an' urgent madders. We got liddle time, so if we ta save Monique, we godda evoke hiz aid." Madame Charlot rose. When she returned to the table she said, "Lola, you kin open ya eyes now."

Lola saw that a candle had been placed on the table.

"Now we gonna pray!"

She watched the woman light the candle and thought, *This woman is a charlatan! I need to be caref—*

"Lizen ta me!" Madame Charlot shouted. "Ya must clear ya mind a doubt. If you want ta find Monique, you gotta pray wid me. Now repeat 'xactly wad I say!"

Lola felt foolish but repeated the prayer.

"Saint Expeditus,
Noble Roman youth, martyr,
Ya who quickly brings dings ta pass,
Ya who never delays, I come ta ya in need:
Help us ta find Monique safe and well.

"Do dis for me, Saint Expeditus, an' when it is accomplish,
I will rapidly reply with a' offerin' ta ya.
Be quick, Saint Expeditus!
Grant ma wish 'fore ya candle burns out, an' I will glorify ya name.
Amen."

With a wild look in her eyes, the woman loomed over her, "Is ya sincere in ya prayer?"

Lola thought this woman might be insane. "Madame Charlot, I can assure you I am sincere in my desire to find Monique."

"If St. Expeditus trusts ya be tellin' da truth, we gonna find dat chile. Watch da candle. If he believes ya, I gonna have da answer 'fore dat candle goes out."

Lola watched the flame sputter but remained unconvinced. Soon its hypnotic glow made her feel lightheaded. She felt transfixed by the colors of red, blue, orange and yellow when they transformed into a brilliant rainbow of pinks, purples and greens. The flame swirled and danced into various shapes. She felt giddy as her thoughts transported her back to her performances at The Moulin Rouge.

When the flame shuddered and changed to a dark angry red, a horrific dread engulfed Lola. She became one with Monique, experiencing her terror. When her fear reached a fever pitch, the cry, "Help Me!" exploded from Lola's lips. The flame roared bright and strong. Lola felt shaken as if she had awakened from a nightmare.

A broad smile crossed the old woman's face. "Yes! Yes!" exclaimed Madame Charlot. "Dank you, Saint Expeditus! I will glorify ya name! Lola, we need ta leave at once. First I muz protect ya. Ya need to wear a *mojo*."

"A *mojo?* What's that?"

Madame Charlot hurried to the counter and prepared a concoction and placed it into a red bag. She rushed back to Lola. "Now dawlin', you godda blow into it!"

Lola followed her instructions. "Now what?"

"Dis be ya mojo bag. Take da bag, keep it wid ya alla time. It's for ya protection. Now we muz hurry!" Madame Charlot grabbed Lola's hand and dragged her through the house. She unbolted the door and pushed Lola outside. Down many streets and alleyways, they went until Madame Charlot stopped short and looked around. She pointed to an old warehouse and said, "Dere! Monique is in dere!"

"Are you sure?"

"St. Expeditus believes you. He tole me ta come ta dis place. You muz go an' save dat chile!"

Lola could see the old woman's face in the glow of the lantern light that came from inside the warehouse. Her face appeared earnest and devout. The old woman may have been insane, but Lola was convinced she believed in what she said.

"Madame Charlot, let's get closer so we can see what's happening."

"No Lola, you muz do dis on ya own. Hold fast ta ya mojo, continue ta believe in St. Expeditus an' da good will a' Louis Sinegal, an' ya will succeed."

Madame Charlot disappeared into the night.

Chapter 47

Madame Charlot's hasty disappearance unnerved Lola. Standing alone in the misty moonlight she wondered, *Where am I?* She perused her surroundings but could see nothing but deserted streets lined with dilapidated buildings. The only other light came from the glow of a lantern from the old wooden warehouse. The warehouse sat on a lot surrounded by bushes and scraggly trees. Lola pulled back her shoulders, lifted her chin and took a deep breath. *It is all up to me now!*

Lola walked towards the warehouse. She crept through a thorny row of bushes to the window that had been covered with a few haphazardly fitted boards, allowing her a partial view inside.

She scanned the large interior space. The warehouse appeared to be abandoned, but several chairs, a table, ropes and various metal objects remained. *There she is! Dieu merci, she's alive!* Lola's heart bubbled with joy. She wanted to call out and let Monique know that she would rescue her. But Monique had been bound to a chair with a dirty gag tied around her mouth. Her eyes were swollen. She must have been crying for a long time. Lola realized rushing into the warehouse could be dangerous for them both. *What if the captor was lurking on the premises?*

She heard rustling in the bushes. *Someone's coming!* Lola remained motionless, but her breathing came fast and hard. The snap of a twig made her flinch. *A weapon! I need a weapon!* She saw only a nearby frail tree branch. Drenched in sweat, she felt certain he could hear each thump of her heart. Her nails dug into her palm as her fingers tightly clutched the branch. He was almost upon her. She was ready to pounce.

From the bushes, a voice called out in an undertone, "Mademoiselle Dupin, it's me, Alphonse!"

With mixed feelings of relief and concern, Lola began to shout, "Alph—!" and caught herself. "What are you doing here?" she whispered.

Alphonse ducked down beside her, "I'm here to save Monique!"

"How did you find me?"

"I followed you. Is Monique in there?"

"Yes."

Their heads touched when they peeked into the warehouse.

Alphonse said, "Let's go get her!"

He began to rise. Lola saw the surprise on his face when she pulled him back down. "Wait!"

"Why? Do you think I'm frightened? I'm not. I'm fourteen years old, almost a man!"

"I need your help, but in another way. Do you still have the detective's calling card?"

Alphonse reached into his pocket. "Yes."

"I'll keep watch. You go to the police station and bring them here. Do whatever you have to do to convince them of the danger Monique is in. Will you be able to find your way to the police station?"

"Of course, it's close by. But shouldn't I stay and help?"

"Alphonse, if you really want to save your sister, this is the best way. Go and be careful!"

"All right. I'll be back as fast as I can."

While she waited, thoughts swirled through her head. *Monique is only a few feet away. Why should she remain in fear, when it would be easy for me to rush inside the warehouse and rescue her? The police will be here soon. Why should I wait? No, it will be better to wait for the police. It is too dangerous.*

Time passed slowly and Lola's nerves were frazzled. *He said the police station was close by. What's taking so long? If the police do not come soon, I will get her.* She heard wood grate against wood as a sliding door scraped against the floor. On the other side of the warehouse, she saw a man slide open the large door.

He was short and thin. A hooked nose protruded from an unshaven face. His greasy black hair stuck out from under a peaked cap. When he approached Monique, Lola heard the man speak with an Italian accent, "Aaah, my nigra bambina. I hope you weren't lonely without-a me." His lips pulled into a smarmy smile. Monique cringed as she looked at her kidnapper.

He pulled a chair from the table and placed it under a horizontal beam. From the table, he took a rope and tied it into a noose. He said, "Nobody pays for you. Looks like ain' nobody cares iffa you die." He shrugged his shoulders with indifference. "So, now you gonna hang." He stood on the chair and attempted tossing the noose over the beam. It took him several tries.

Lola was frantic. She rushed around to the door. When she got close, she saw that the man's back was to her. Monique struggled while he tried to untie her. Lola grabbed an iron pipe and ran towards the man. Before she could hit him, he turned and blocked her arm, knocking the pipe away. He pulled a knife from his waistband and lunged. Lola jumped back, circled away from him.

He followed her and said, "You such a *bella signorina*, it's too bad I gotta kill you."

She kept moving backward, but he was getting closer. He tossed his knife from hand to hand. A diabolical smile stretched across his face.

Metal boxes and pipes of various shapes and sizes were everywhere. One by one, Lola hurled them at the kidnapper, but his reflexes were quick, and he dodged them.

"You no get-away from me!" he boasted. "But I have no time to play witta you." He sprang forward with the knife above his head and was about to plunge it into her.

Lola propelled her powerful dancer's leg into his groin. The kidnapper's face turned green and he doubled over. Lola ran to release Monique. She heard men's voices outside and muttered, "Please let that be the police!" She tried to untie Monique, but her trembling fingers wouldn't work fast enough.

The kidnapper grabbed Lola from behind. She screamed when she felt the pinch of the sharp blade at her throat. She smelled tobacco and garlic on his breath as he yelled to the police, "Stay away from me or I gonna kill her!" His arms were strong. He held Lola and forced her towards the door. From the corner of her eye, she could see the detective and four uniformed policemen with their guns pointed at the kidnapper.

The detective shouted, "It'll do you no good to hurt her. There's too many of us and you'll be shot dead for sure!"

He screamed, "You no shoot-a me. You gonna let me go, cause otterwise I gonna kill dis *bella signorina*. Get outta my way!"

Lola winced in pain when the knifepoint dug deeper into her neck and made her blood trickle. She knew he would kill her. She lifted her foot and stomped on his instep with all her might.

He screamed and released her. Lola dropped to the floor. Bullets exploded above her head. She heard a thud and realized it was the sound of the kidnapper's body hitting the floor.

One policeman helped Lola up, while the others rushed to the moaning Italian. They released Monique, who ran to hug Lola and her brother. The three huddled together crying tears of relief.

A policeman brought them home.

"Mama, we're home!" Monique shouted as she entered the house.

Esther and Samuel sat at the kitchen table. Esther looked at Samuel and asked, "Could that really be Monique?" Samuel joined Esther as they rushed to the parlor. When she saw Monique, she screamed and ran to her, "My baby! Thank the Lord! My baby's home!"

Hugs, kisses and tears of jubilation flowed throughout the day. But Lola was too overwrought from her ordeal to join the celebration. After giving and receiving a number of loving embraces, she headed for bed.

At breakfast the next morning Samuel asked Lola, "How did you know where to look for Monique?"

The family was fascinated as Lola relayed the events of her experience with Madame Charlot.

Esther asked, "So Lola, do you think there's something to this hoodoo after all?"

Lola shrugged, "I don't know if it was hoodoo or if Madame Charlot had another way to determine Monique's location." She smiled, "I am just so happy she is home safe." To Alphonse, she said, "I am grateful you followed me, but you could have been in terrible danger!"

"I wasn't scared," he said. "I just wanted to save my sister."

Lola smiled. "That was a brave thing to do, Alphonse. You saved our lives. You are quite the hero."

With a big smile, he rose from his chair and took a deep bow. They applauded Alphonse.

Monique ran over and hugged Alphonse. "I'm so proud of my little brother! And, of course, Mademoiselle Dupin, I can't thank you enough!" Returning to her seat Monique pulled an envelope from her dress pocket. "Oh, Mademoiselle Dupin, in all the excitement I forgot to give you this."

Lola accepted the envelope and stared at the return address.

Chapter 48

Lola endured an arduous journey to Rimrock Springs, Arizona, by rail, and now by stagecoach. Her back ached from bouncing over rough roads and bone-jarring potholes. She felt sweaty, grimy and uncomfortable in the overcrowded coach.

During her travels, thoughts of Monique and her family had churned through Lola's mind. The farewells had been so sad. She didn't want to leave but New Orleans would always be a bad memory. Her brain seemed to be stuck on the terrifying images of that night. *That monster would have killed Monique without a second thought!* Lola shivered as she brought her fingers to her throat. She could still feel the pain of the sharp blade as it penetrated her skin. *I could never forget what had happened if I remained in New Orleans. But is Rimrock Springs, Arizona the right place for me? Am I making a mistake coming here to see Charlie? Where else can I go? Besides, I want to see his face when I tell him we almost died because of him.*

As she had done so many times along the way, Lola removed Charlie's letter from her purse and re-read his words.

My Dearest Lola,

On my way to Rimrock Springs, many a chap tried to discourage me from coming here. They claimed there was no placer gold in Arizona and suggested I try my luck elsewhere. As it turns out, there's enough gold in Rimrock Springs to fill the coffers of anyone willing to work hard enough for it.

The town is more developed than I had expected. Although it's a rustic town, there are hotels, restaurants, and shops to purchase clothing and staples. The town is growing fast. More gold seekers are flooding into Rimrock Springs every day.

You may have guessed, panning for gold isn't my strong suit. There are other ways of making money here. In this town, gold flows like water. Those who have the most let it slip through their fingers without a care. Their philosophy is, "There's plenty more where this came from!" I'm having a great deal of luck taking advantage of the situation. Everything seems to be working in my favor, and I'm expecting a big windfall in a few days.

Lola, I'm telling you these things because I want you to join me here in Rimrock Springs. I miss seeing your beautiful face. I miss the taste of your sweet lips. I miss everything about you! By the time you arrive, I expect to have enough money to repay your loan and to take you anywhere you'd like to go. Imagine the fun we'll have traveling together.

Please come at once!
Yours forever,
Charlie

Lola's feelings for Charlie were a tangled mess. Repeatedly, she probed her mind for answers. She thought of Charlie's perfect face and his way of making her feel like she was the most special woman in the world. She missed his touch and the rapturous pleasure she experienced when they were in bed together. *Is that love? I do not know. Now we will have all the time in the world to find out if we love each other.*

She heard the driver shout, "Whoa." The wagon slowed to a stop. Relieved to finally arrive, Lola gathered her things while the other passengers made a hasty exit.

Lola saw three men pushing each other out of the way to be the first to greet her. Stepping down from the stagecoach, the largest of the three held her gloved hand.

Lola nodded and said. "*Merci, monsieur.*" She stifled a laugh when their mouths dropped open at the sight of her. With bright smiles, they removed their hats. The largest of the three men proudly announced, "Afternoon ma'am, we're the unofficial welcoming committee for the town of Rimrock Springs." He stared at her until his companion poked him. "Oh! Uh…mah name is Nappy Lanette." His shirt buttons strained to remain closed over his protruding belly. He had baggy eyes, unruly grey-brown hair and a bushy tobacco-stained beard. He hiked a thumb to the person beside him and said, "This here is Pee Wee Minikin."

The top of Pee Wee's head barely reached Lola's shoulder. At first, she thought he was a boy, but the wrinkles around his eyes and his wispy mustache made her realize he was a grown man. Pee Wee said, "It's a real pleasure ta meet ya." He pointed to the man beside him and said, "This here is Cross-Eyed Hank McGirk. He's cross-eyed, you know."

Except for his obvious disadvantage, Cross-Eyed Hank was the most average-looking of the three. He was about to speak when Nappy interrupted, "Pardon me for saying this ma'am, but you're the most beautiful woman I ever seen!" The other two nodded in fervent agreement.

Lola held out her hand expecting it to be kissed in the French tradition. The three men looked at each other in confusion. Pee Wee timidly took her fingertips and shook them awkwardly, as if it was a secret handshake. "Pleased ta meet ya ma'am."

She smiled, "You have unusual customs in Rimrock Springs, *non?*" Lola looked past the men to see if Charlie might be coming to meet her. But she saw no sign of him. Disappointed, she brought her attention back to the greeting committee. Lola found them staring at her body, but they quickly pulled their eyes to her face. She overlooked their typical male reaction and said, "My name is Lola Dupin and I am most happy to meet you all as well. Can you tell me, please, where can I find Charlie Sloan?"

"Charlie Sloan?" Nappy pulled at his beard as he repeated slowly, "Hmm, do I know Charlie Sloan?"

Cross-Eyed Hank, his face brightening at his apparent skill of recollection said, "Charlie Sloan? He was one of them fellers who played in that big card game."

Pee Wee nodded. "That's right!" He snapped his fingers and said, "That's who he is!" He looked at Nappy and asked, "Don't ya remember? From the card game." He looked at Lola and explained, "The miners have regular card games for big stakes. An' just last week they had the biggest game ever. There was a crowd of us folks watchin' it. They played all day and into the night until it got down to two players. Charlie was one of 'em."

"Yeah, yeah." Nappy agreed. "That was him awright! It was excitin' to watch. Charlie'd been so lucky winnin' at cards since he been here, we all thought Charlie would win for sure. Folks were even makin' side bets, expectin' Charlie'd win. He had a big pile of money in front a him, and he was real confident as he looked that other player dead in the eye. Both them fellers pushed everthin' they had into the middle of the table. You shoulda seen how big that pile a' money was. Everybody got real hushed while we waited to see what happened. When they laid their cards on the table, we was all shocked that Charlie lost. All them folks bettin' on Charlie groaned and was real unhappy with him. Charlie's face looked like someone punched him in the gut. But he didn't say nuthin'. He just got up and walked out. We watched him go to the hotel an' soon he come out with his bags. He got on his horse and left town. We ain't seen him since."

Lola was shocked. "Charlie left town? Is he coming back?"

Nappy looked at his companions. "Don't think so," they said in unison

"Did he say anything about me, Lola Dupin? Or where he was going?"

"Not to me, he didn't." Nappy looked at the other two men. "Did he say anything to you?" The others shook their heads.

Lola fumed. *He wrote that he had other ways of making money in Rimrock Springs. I am such a fool! I should have realized he was talking about gambling. I gave him all the money I had and he gambled it away. It is over! I am through with him!* Her heart sank. *Now I have nothing!*

Lola viewed her surroundings. Everywhere she looked, the dust-covered streets, the wood slat buildings, the wooden boardwalk. The entire town and everything in it were a dreary dull brown. *Mon Dieu, this place is ugly! There's nothing for me here. What will I do now?*

Chapter 49

Enough self-pity! It is time to depend upon yourself!

Lola stood tall and proud as she asked, "So, *monsieurs*, can you tell me please, where may I find the best cabaret in this town?"

Nappy scratched his head. "Caber-*whut?*"

"Cabaret." Lola wiggled her shoulders. "You know, for the singing and the dancing."

Cross-eyed Hank said, "Oh, yur talkin' 'bout a dance hall?"

"Oui, exactement!"

Nappy cautioned, "The place you want is The Golden Slipper Saloon. It's the fanciest place in Rimrock Springs. They got all kinds a' entertainment there, but most of it ain't the kind a lady should be seein'. This here is a pretty rough town, an' I don' think a lady like ya self will be safe here."

Safe! Lola laughed to herself. The words of Monsieur Salis echoed back to her. "You must be careful. It can be a very dangerous place." She remembered the night she had arrived at L'antre Du Diable. *The poorly lit streets, shabby buildings and menacing alleyways that had surrounded the old cabaret. I had been fearful of the pimps, thieves and local toughs who had been its patrons. I survived there. I will not be afraid here!*

Lola smiled, "Do not worry about me, *monsieurs*, I can take care of myself!"

Nappy looked at his companions. They shrugged. Nappy said, "Well if ya think y'ull be awright. It's just yonder, that big place on the corner." The welcoming committee pointed the way to The Golden Slipper Saloon.

The tap-dance of Lola's heels against the boardwalk had soon been drowned out by the plunking of a honky-tonk piano, the rattling of dice, the shuffle of cards and shouts of coarse men vying to hear each other over the din.

Lola propelled herself through the swinging batwing doors. Men ducked at the gunshot-like the sound of banging doors, but their attention swiftly turned to Lola. They watched goggle-eyed at the sway of her hips as she swept into the saloon. She cut through the swirling dense clouds of cigar smoke like a sleek battleship through a fog. In the center of the room, she stopped with her hands on her hips.

The immense Golden Slipper Saloon rose two levels high. The top floor had what appeared to be private rooms. On the main floor, there were a number of gambling tables, a brass-railed mahogany bar, an oversized bawdy oil painting of a well-rounded nude, and white-aproned handlebar-mustachioed waiters. Compared to the Moulin Rouge it was not much of a place, but it held many customers, it had a decent-sized stage and a great deal of potential.

Lola walked over to the bartender. "Young man, who is the owner of this establishment?"

The pimple-faced bartender ran his fingers through greasy hair. With a salacious grin, he asked, "Who wants to know?"

Lola knew that look and she did not like it. She insisted, "Bring the owner to me now!" The bartender hesitated. Lola demanded, "What are you waiting for?"

The busy room grew silent as the patrons stopped what they were doing to watch the bartender's reaction.

His pale blue eyes bored into Lola with an angry glare. She returned his stare with steely-eyed scorn. He sneered and disappeared into a back office. A few minutes later, the bartender returned accompanied by the owner. He pointed to Lola and said, "There she is, boss. Don't know what got her dander up, but that piece of calico seems ready to pitch a fit, so be careful."

The owner walked to Lola and boasted, "I'm Frank Walters, the owner of The Golden Slipper Saloon." Walters had long, neatly trimmed side-burns that met with his thin mustache. He appeared smartly dressed in a black-vested suit with a narrow-lapelled, unbuttoned jacket. His white shirt had a pointed stiff collar and he wore a blue silk tie. Burying his thumbs in his vest armholes he inquired, "What can I do for you, miss?"

"My name is Lola Dupin. I am here from Paris, France. I am *une chanteuse et danseuse extraordinaire.* You are the most fortunate of men, *Monsieur* Walters, because I have decided to entertain in your establishment."

"Entertain? Oh, so you're a dance hall girl?"

"Dance hall girl? Hah! I have entertained at Le Moulin Rouge, one of the best cabarets in Paris!"

"So, you think you're pretty good?"

"Good! Monsieur Walters, I am *the best!*"

Walters broke into a wry smile. "You seem pretty confident, young lady. Why should I give you a chance?"

"Because I will make your saloon famous!"

Walters looked Lola up and down. "Famous, eh? How do you plan to do that?"

"My performances will dazzle your audience in ways they could never have imagined!"

He cocked his head and said, "Well, I must admit you've got me curious, so I'll give you a chance. I tell you what. You bring a big crowd in here to watch you perform this Saturday night. If they like you, we'll talk about you becoming a regular performer. Agreed?"

Lola smiled. "*Monsieur* Walters, I am happy to agree! Now I will need time with your musicians to review my routine. I will also need a place to stay. I think, if you have an available room here, it would be the best thing. Do you have a room?"

Walters called out over his shoulder to the bartender. "Billy, show this lady to room two."

"But boss, do you think that's a good idea?"

"Just do it!"

Billy frowned as he approached Lola, "Uh. Okay, come this way, miss."

"Wait one moment." Lola looked towards the saloon exit. Nappy, Pee Wee and Cross-Eyed Hank, with their heads peeking over the barroom doors, had been watching Lola's interchange slack-jawed. She walked to them and asked, "My friends, would you please bring my baggage?"

"Be happy to," they said and scurried off.

Lola spent the week reviewing her routine with The Golden Slipper Saloon's small band. She also made sure the welcoming committee did a thorough job alerting the town about the date of her performance.

In a town as small as Rimrock Springs, the news spread quickly. Saturday night arrived and the air crackled with excitement. The audience entered to see the exotic creature they had heard so much about.

Peeking through the stage curtain, Lola was pleased to see the saloon had been packed with amusement-hungry men, yearning for the unbound naughtiness to come.

The announced time of Lola's performance came and went. However, she would not allow herself to be seen until the crowd started stomping, shouting and whistling, insisting she begin her performance. When the audience appeared ready to demolish the saloon, she entered into the glare of kerosene-lamp footlights. When Lola strutted out on stage looking as if she owned the world, all became silent.

Her gown was low cut, exposing her ample cleavage. Her tightly-cinched waist appeared small enough that a man could surround it with one hand. As she crossed the stage, dragging a long-feathered boa, her flowing diaphanous gown shimmered in the light. She could hear a collective gasp from the audience.

Lola slowly sauntered across the stage. She emphasized her physical attributes—hips and shoulders rolling and swaying with the look of nonchalance on her face. She tantalized and teased the spectators, captivating these female-starved men.

She came close to the edge of the stage, stopped, and jerked her posterior at one of the men sitting with his elbows perched on the stage. The imagined force made him fall out of his chair. Everyone laughed. She continued to circle the stage in the same silent, sultry strut until her back was to the audience. Unexpectedly, she stopped and did nothing. The audience murmured. With a stern expression, Lola whipped her head dramatically over her shoulder as if she were about to reprimand them. Instead, her lips curled into a slow, lazy smile. She purred, "*Bonsoir,* boys. My name is Lola and we are going to have fun tonight. If that is all right with you, say *oui!*"

The audience clapped and shouted, "*Oui! Oui!*"

Lola nodded to the bandleader and began to sing. She belted out a lively tune. Even though it was in French, she got the audience to join her in the chorus. After a variety of songs, she began to dance. The men gawked in amazement as she used her dress to make her appear like a butterfly floating and twirling in the air. She combined polka and ballet moves, style and grace, action and romance into her dancing. The crowd could not take their eyes off of her.

The evening climaxed with her special version of the can-can. She grabbed the folds of her skirt and waved and whirled the colorful fabric, revealing her long, curvaceous legs. When she grabbed her ankle and held her leg straight up in the air while leaping, the spectators cheered. For her finale, she leaped high into the air and came down in a split. The crowd stood, stomped, clapped and shouted, "*Lola! Lola! Lola!*"

Lola felt more fulfilled at this moment than she had ever been. The men in the audience may have been unsophisticated and rough-edged, but their admiration was genuine and overwhelming. The polite applause she experienced at the Moulin Rouge did not compare. The conditional love she received from her father did not compare. The disingenuous affection she received from Charlie did not compare.

She thought, *Maybe this little town is not so bad after all!*

The End. . . Of The Beginning. . .

Acknowledgements

I am grateful to everyone who helped me bring this long overdue book to life. To my friends Jackie and Dennis Kaperick, who, although I'd given up my dream to publish this book, encouraged me to persevere. To the Cuenca Writer's Collective led by Franny Hogg Lochow, whose critiques educated and inspired me to become a better writer. To my beta readers: Claire Middleton, Suzanne Ward, Brenda Schanzer, Pat Simmons, Laura Austin and fellow author Curt Locklear, who provided me with brilliant insights. To my mentor, editor and friend, Carolyn V. Hamilton, who took me by the hand and helped me through the maze of publishing and marketing. My thanks to each of you, for without your help, this novel would continue to collect dust in my bottom desk drawer.

Ren'e Fedyna, born in New York City, developed a love for historical fiction at an early age. After graduating magna cum laude from Mercy College, she worked for six years as a copywriter at an advertising agency in Los Angeles and later studied Interior Design at UCLA. After 25 years as a self-employed Interior Designer she retired and achieved her dream to become a writer of historical fiction.

Please visit my website at
www.renefedyna-author.com

A personal request:

If you enjoyed *Dance of the Restless Soul*, I would really appreciate it if you would go to Amazon, rate the book, and write a sentence or two about what you liked best.

If you have questions about *Dance of the Restless Soul* reach out me here::
Rene@renefedyna-author.com

If you'd like to be on my VIP list to be the first to learn about events and future books, please go here

Ren'e

www.ingramcontent.com/pod-product-compliance
Lightning Source LLC
Chambersburg PA
CBHW022147170626
46807CB00005B/2109